Bulldog appeared in the spotlight

GOLDEN PAVEMENTS

BY

PAMELA BROWN

Author of " The Swish of the Curtain "
and " Maddy Alone "

ILLUSTRATED BY

NEWTON WHITTAKER

THOMAS NELSON AND SONS LTD
LONDON EDINBURGH PARIS MELBOURNE
TORONTO AND NEW YORK

THOMAS NELSON AND SONS LTD
Parkside Works Edinburgh 9
3 Henrietta Street London WC2
312 Flinders Street Melbourne C1
91–93 Wellington Street West Toronto 1

THOMAS NELSON AND SONS
385 Madison Avenue New York 17

SOCIÉTÉ FRANÇAISE D'ÉDITIONS NELSON
25 Rue Denfert-Rochereau Paris Vᵉ

———

First published May 1947

FOR

LAUREL

WHO LISTENED SO PATIENTLY

CONTENTS

LIST OF ILLUSTRATIONS

GOLDEN PAVEMENTS

CHAPTER I

OVER THE THRESHOLD

"AND don't embarrass me by talking about the Blue Door Theatre all the time," said Nigel. They were sitting at breakfast in No. 37 Fitzherbert Street, W.1, on the first morning of the Spring Term. It was now nine o'clock. At nine-thirty they must set out for the British Actors' Guild Dramatic School. Nigel, who had already spent a year there, had assumed a somewhat superior manner and was giving them advice as to their behaviour.

"But why shouldn't we mention the Blue Door?" demanded Lynette. "I'm not ashamed of it—even if you are."

"My dear girl," said Nigel. "All the shows we used to do were amateur, decidedly amateur. Now that you're going to train for professional acting, you'll have to forget all that. Nobody's interested in it. It doesn't mean a thing."

There was silence except for Bulldog, who scrunched toast, regardless of his elder brother's sermon. Vicky, who was Bulldog's twin, and shared his red hair and freckles, looked round the table thoughtfully. Yes, it was rather obvious that Nigel had already begun his training for the stage. Whereas Bulldog and Jeremy were well-scrubbed and polished, with neatly cut hair and dark suits, ready for their first day at dramatic school, Nigel wore corduroy trousers, a green shirt, a yellow tie, and a sandy sports coat.

I

Occasionally as he talked a lock of dark hair fell over his brow and he shook it back with a careless gesture. The other five felt rather in awe of him these days. He seemed an actor already.

Sandra, practical as ever, glanced at the clock. " We'd better get a move on," she said ; " it would be awful to be late the first day. And whatever shall we do about the porridge ? " She indicated six bowls of grey lumpy mixture that stood untouched before them.

" Mrs. Bosham will be heartbroken if you don't eat it," said Nigel. " She takes it as a personal insult if you leave a crumb."

" Well, I'm leaving mine," announced Jeremy, wrinkling his nose fastidiously. " It's quite disgusting. What have you done with yours every day since you've been here, Nigel ? "

" This ! " said Nigel, as with expert aim he flung the revolting mass into the fire.

" But we can't *all* do that," objected Sandra. " It would put the fire out. And supposing Mrs. Whatnot comes in— oh, whatever shall we do ? " She looked helplessly round the ugly little boarding-house room, with its greying lace curtains, china animals, and photos of the Bosham family in every conceivable position, and many ornate little vases, presents from Bognor, Southend, or Margate.

" We could fill up some of the vases," suggested Vicky.

" But what would we do to-morrow ? " Sandra wanted to know. " And after a while it would begin to smell. No, we must do it all up in a parcel and dump it somewhere —in a litter basket." She snatched up the morning paper and began to scoop the glutinous messes into it.

" Who's going to carry it ? " Bulldog asked suspiciously.

" You ! " replied five voices determinedly.

2

" H'm ! Well, I will to-day, but someone else must do it to-morrow."

" We'll work out a rota," laughed Nigel. " Come on. Step on it. I'd like to get there early to-day to see if I've been moved up or not." They ran upstairs to their bedrooms to put on their hats and coats.

As Lyn arranged her furry Cossack hat in the mirror her heart was thumping with excitement. At last it was to begin—a real stage training. Her stomach turned over with a delicious mixture of joy and trepidation. Vicky was pirouetting across the landing.

" I do hope we have dancing to-day," she said.

" I hope we have singing," volunteered Sandra, brushing her fair hair until it gleamed.

" I don't," breathed Lyn, into the mirror. " I just want to act, and act, and act——"

" Come on, you hags ! " roared Nigel. " Stop titivating, for goodness' sake." They assembled in the hall, each clasping massive volumes of Shakespeare. Mrs. Bosham came out to wish them luck. She was a completely circular woman, round face, round body, eyes and mouth continually rounded with surprise at the world in general, and plump round hands that were always busy knitting some shapeless garment which she could never quite master.

" Well, well ! " she cried in wonderment. " So you're off now, are you ? (Two plain, two purl, slip one . . .) Well, I never did ! Did you enjoy your breakfast ? "

" Oh, yes, Mrs. Bosham ! " they chorused.

" I always think a nice spot of porridge is so warming of a cold morning." Bulldog clutched the sticky parcel closer to him. " I shall expect to see you come back to-night as famous actors—all of you ! (Knit two together.) "

3

They smirked feebly and Nigel opened the door with impatience.

Outside in the clear winter air they realized that No. 37 had a slight but permanent odour of cabbage. Fitzherbert Street was a dingy street, there was no denying it. On one side there were Victorian houses, like No. 37, that had come down in the world and were now cheap lodging-houses for students, artists, and workers of every nationality. The other side consisted mainly of restaurants—French, Italian, Greek, Hungarian, with stripy shades over the windows, and menus outside that read like poetry. It was a brisk winter morning, and the whole world seemed to be on its way to work.

" London ! " sighed Lyn contentedly.

" Is it far to the Academy ? " Sandra asked Nigel as they strode along.

" Five minutes."

They crossed Tottenham Court Road where the traffic roared and newsboys cried the names of morning papers, and entered a quiet square where plane trees braved the soot and dust. And there was a tall, grey stone house with lions at the doorposts. In simple lettering over the lintel were the words, " British Actors' Guild Academy," and underneath, " They have their exits and their entrances."

Instinctively their pace slowed, and they looked up at the many large windows, from which came the sound of laughter and tinkling pianos. A constant stream of students entered through the swing doors, all talking very loudly at the same time. Most of them had very long hair, wore gaily coloured clothes, and many of the girls wore slacks. Suddenly a tall girl with chestnut hair and a lot of lipstick put her head out of the door, saw Nigel, and launched herself at him.

4

"*Darling!*" she cried. "How are you? I've got simply *piles* to tell you! We've both been moved up, and *what* do you think?" Nigel was dragged inside the swing doors and out of their sight.

They turned and looked at each other in amazement. "Well, I do think that's rude!" exclaimed Lyn. "She didn't even speak to us. Now what do we do, I wonder?"

"Go in," said Sandra firmly, mounting the steps with an assurance she did not feel.

Inside was a large foyer that churned and swelled with a laughing, shouting, gesticulating crowd of young people. In one corner was a large, green-baize notice-board, which seemed to be the centre of attraction. Students would rush up to it with set countenance, elbow their way to the front of the crowd, and run their fingers down the lists. Then they would either crow with delight and embrace all within reach, or turn away with a wry smile saying, "Of course, I didn't really *expect* to move up."

The five of them stood in a timid group on the doormat, on which were the initials B.A.G.A. in large block letters. Only the violent entry of someone through the doors behind them propelled the five into the crowd. Lynette, being thin, was the first to reach the notice-board. There, at the bottom of the list, below fifteen other names, for Class One, she read, "Jeremy Darwin, Lynette Darwin, Sandra Fayne, Victoria Jane Halford, Percy Turnbull Halford." Vicky and Bulldog seethed with indignation.

"However did they get our middle names? I bet it was that Nigel's doing!"

At this moment there appeared on the broad marble staircase a smart, black-clad, grey-haired woman, who, smiling, rang a large bell to silence the din.

"If you wish to attend prayers, go down into the

theatre," she announced, when she could make herself heard.

"Prayers !" gasped Vicky. "Gosh ! Wouldn't our parents be surprised ? They were afraid we were coming to a den of iniquity."

The crowd began to surge down the stone stairs to the basement, still talking incessantly. The Blue Doors heard many intriguing scraps of conversation.

" . . . So I went round to the stage door and asked to see the producer—and *what* do you think ? " . . . " Are you going in for the fencing comp. this term ? " . . . " My dear, I've been in pantomime over Christmas. Yes, really— front row chorus—it was a scream " . . . " But she could *never* play Hedda Gabler " . . .

The theatre was small and cosy with red plush tip-up seats, and hanging round the wall a gallery of faces of famous ex-students.

"There's Felicity Warren !" Lynette pointed out. " And Roma Seymore ! Oh, how lovely to be here at last ! "

The hubbub silenced suddenly as Mr. Wainwright Whit-field, the principal, appeared in front of the curtains of the little stage. He was a tall, imposing, silver-haired man, with kind eyes and a furrowed brow.

" My mother told me he was a matinée idol when she was young," Vicky hissed in Sandra's ear. " Understandable, don't you think ? "

" Good-morning and welcome everybody," he began. " I trust that we shall all spend a very happy term together." He went on to explain some of the aims and rules of the Academy, and then stopped suddenly and said, " Let us pray." There was a shuffle and a squeaking of seats, and a hundred and fifty students stood with bowed heads.

Lyn was acutely conscious of the rise and fall of Wain-

wright Whitfield's velvet voice, the watching portraits on
the wall, and her own heart, thumping with a will to work
and succeed. The only phrase of the prayer that remained
with her was, " . . . and make us to be worthy citizens of
the London in which we live."

When everyone had trooped up into the foyer again, the
secretary with the bell appeared and rang it furiously for
silence.

"You will find a list of your classrooms on the notice-
board," she announced. "First-termers will please follow
me." There was a buzz of interest as the twenty beginners
detached themselves from the crowd and mounted the steps
in single file, running the gauntlet of stares from the senior
pupils. Nigel made a face at the Blue Doors, followed by a
cheering smile, and then resumed his deep conversation with
the chestnut-haired female. The first-termers were led into
a long light studio, surrounded with book-cases and portraits of Edmund Kean, Mrs. Siddons, and other famous
actors and actresses of the past. And there, behind a desk,
sat Roma Seymore. The Blue Doors knew her already, for
she had judged the amateur drama contest that they had won
at Fenchester, and it was very comforting to see a familiar
face amongst all these strangers.

"Good-morning," she said, smiling the famous smile
that had warmed the hearts of theatre-goers for the last forty
years. "Do sit down, everybody." They ranged themselves in chairs in a semi-circle around her. "Now some of
you I know, and others I don't," she continued, "so I'll start
the term properly by calling the register. Say ' Yes ' or
' Here ' or ' Adsum ' or whatever you please." Bulldog was
so busy taking stock of the other students that he missed his
name altogether, and it had to be called twice before he
came to with a start, and said " O.K.," which set the whole

class laughing. The other students appeared to be a great mixture. They varied from a mousey little girl of about fifteen, in pigtails and a gym slip, to an elderly foreign gentleman who seemed unable to speak or understand English. There was also a young Indian boy whom the Blue Doors recognized as having played several large roles in jungle films. In a group together sat three very beautifully dressed young girls of about seventeen, and two youths in stove-pipe trousers, wearing ties that Jeremy announced in a whisper were old Etonian.

When Roma Seymore had completed the register she said, " And now I want to get to know you, and to hear just how much acting you have all done previously." She turned to the Blue Doors. " You five, of course, I know your work. You've done a good lot of amateur, haven't you ? " The Blue Doors blushed scarlet and looked down as though it were a crime. " And a very good thing, too," she went on. "Don't look so ashamed of it. You'll probably have to unlearn a lot, but at least it's a start." She turned to the foreign gentleman. " Mr. Gottlieb, I know that you have made a fine reputation in Austria—I think we've all heard of Otto Gottlieb, haven't we ? " The class made vague noises of agreement, although nobody had. " And I hope we shall be able to help you considerably with your English ! "

" Thanks much, kind lady," was Mr. Gottlieb's appreciative reply, and although he was sitting down he bowed gallantly from the waist.

" And you too, Ali, must concentrate on your English, mustn't you ? " The Indian boy replied only with a shy flash of white teeth.

" I'm afraid I don't know anything about the rest of you, so I must inquire in turn what you have done." The three

8

society girls and the old Etonians replied " amateur " in rather bored voices, the little girl in the gym tunic said, " I've done some broadcasting," and two blondes, one fat and one thin, said they had done chorus work. A very ugly girl, in shabby slacks and a torn macintosh, replied, " Nothing," in a sulky tone.

" Then what has made you want to be an actress ? " asked Mrs. Seymore, quite kindly.

" Because I know I can," the girl replied almost fiercely.

A dark, statuesque girl with an elaborate hair style said she had done some film work, and a young man with numerous pimples on his face said he had been in the O.U.D.S. at Oxford. Of the remaining two, one was middle-aged and the other young. The woman was about forty with a heavily made-up face, and hair dyed an un-natural auburn. " Well, I've been in the profession for over twenty years," she began in a fruity voice.

" Twenty years ! " exclaimed Mrs. Seymore. " Then why have you come to the Academy ? " The woman laughed richly.

" A few months ago I found myself playing Wigan Empire for the tenth time, so I says to myself, ' Myrtle, my girl, if you're still playing Wigan Empire at forty there *must* be something wrong with you.' " After the laughter which followed this frank explanation, Roma said kindly, " Well, I think it's a very brave gesture on your part, and I hope we shall be able to help you."

The last member of the class to be questioned was a fat boy of about sixteen, who appeared to have an impediment in his speech.

" And have *you* been on the stage before ? " Roma inquired.

9

" Oh, yeth," he answered. " My Mummy and Daddy are in the profethion."

" Really ?   And what do they do ? "

" They have a theal act."

" A what ? "

" A theal act.   You know—with thealth ! "

" I'm sorry—I didn't quite——"

" *Performing* thealth," spluttered the boy, quite hurt by this time.

" Oh, I *see*. Performing seals. Oh, yes, that must have been interesting.   And what did *you* do ? "

" I uthed to throw the fish for them."   There were subdued giggles from various quarters, but Mrs. Seymore retained her gravity.

" Well, you'll be used to *appearing* on the stage, at least, won't you ? " she said hurriedly.

" Oh, no, I uthed to thtand in the wingth."

" What a collection of people ! " whispered Lynette to Sandra.

" P'raps we strike them as just as odd," she replied.

For the rest of the lesson Roma Seymore read to them the play in which she was to produce them during the term. It was Shaw's *Pygmalion*, and although Roma read all the parts, she seemed to change character visibly. One minute she was the little Cockney gamin, then the pedantic professor, and next minute the alcoholic dustman. They were in stitches of laughter by the end of the period.

" That was the most enjoyable lesson I've ever had in my life ! " said Vicky as they filed out. " I didn't dream that a school could be like this," and she wiped tears of hilarity from her eyes.

But the next lesson was more nerve-wracking. It was Shakespeare, taken by Mr. Whitfield, who went straight through the class, demanding a Shakesperian speech from every member.

The Blue Doors found themselves experiencing all the familiar symptoms of stage fright, a thumping heart, dry lips, a watery feeling in the knees. The first person to be called on was Otto Gottlieb. He did Hamlet's "To be or not to be" with great drama of expression and gesture. The only drawback being that not one word was intelligible. The next person to be called on was Bulldog. He walked to the centre of the room, which suddenly seemed very large. When he turned round to face the class he noticed the horrified expressions of the Blue Doors. What could be wrong ? Had he got a smut on his nose ? He smoothed down his ginger hair self-consciously and began.

"Friends—Romans—countrymen . . ." Suddenly he saw Vicky double up with laughter, and he stopped dead, with a horrible realization. He was still clutching the parcel of porridge ! Scarlet to the tips of his ears he stood rooted to the spot, looking at the disgusting soggy paper parcel. Then Sandra came to the rescue. She ran quickly across the floor, saying, "Give me the parcel, Bulldog." He floundered through the speech, completely unnerved, and received merely a cold, "Thank you. Sit down" from Mr. Whitfield. The only person who received any praise from him was the ugly girl in slacks, who did a speech of Lady Macbeth, and curdled the blood of her listeners.

"Very strong—sincere, but lacking in technique," was Wainwright Whitfield's verdict.

Lunch was the next item on the time-table. It was served in a long cafeteria, where, over coffee and liver sausage, more words per minute were exchanged than the Blue Doors had ever heard before. They sat at a table together, and just stared round them dumbly. "They're all so happy and self-assured," thought Lynette. " I shall never be able to behave like that."

Nigel was sitting at a long table with a lot of the senior pupils, and seemed to be in the middle of a heated argument. On the way out of the lunch-room he came over to their table with the chestnut girl. She was very tall and wore a scarlet jumper and emerald slacks. She stood with hands on hips and surveyed them, laughing.

" So these are the infant prodigies, are they ? "

" This is Auriole," announced Nigel. " She's heard a lot about you."

" Where's Maddy ? " she wanted to know. " I liked the sound of her best."

" We had to leave Maddy at home," explained Sandra. " She's too young to come to Dramatic School yet."

" What a shame ! You're her sister, aren't you ? And those are the twins, aren't they ? And that's Lynette and Jeremy. I say, come here ! " she cried to some of her friends.

" Come and look at Nigel's private repertory company." A crowd of seniors came and stared at them as if they were strange beasts. The Blue Doors glared back, and Auriole seemed to find their discomfort amusing. At last she took Nigel's hand and led him away, saying, " Come on, ducky. I want to know your hopes, your dreams, and your telephone number." When she had gone Lyn said, " She's just what our parents hoped we wouldn't turn into——"

" But rather attractive," added Sandra fairly. They were all somewhat upset at seeing Nigel so firmly under the sway of what they considered " an outsider."

The afternoon was taken up with a dancing class, in which Vicky outshone everyone. Very few had had any previous training except the two ex-chorus girls, and no-one as yet had the correct practice dresses or shoes. Bulldog, in his socks and shirt-sleeves, laboured away at the barre, puffing and blowing heavily, as the little dancing mistress prodded him in the back and knees with her ruler.

" Oh, dear ! Oh, dear ! All this to be an actor ! " he groaned.

When the day was over they felt completely exhausted, and when Nigel joined them on the stairs saying, " How about a cup of tea at Raddler's ? " it sounded like a very good idea.

Raddler's was a little baker's shop in Tottenham Court Road that smelt of fresh bread and coffee. Its windows were packed with gaily coloured cakes. The first floor was filled with respectable business men having their afternoon tea, but as one ascended the stairs a peculiar noise wafted down from the second floor—a sort of muffled roar. The low, smoky room was dim and filled to overflowing with B.A.G.A. students. Sprawled across the tables, they drank coffee, consumed enormous doughnuts, and reformed the theatre. Fanny, the harassed little waitress, shouted down the hatch unceasing and gargantuan orders.

" Ten white, three black, and sixteen éclairs, " or, " Three 'ash and baked."

Gradually the congenial atmosphere enveloped the Blue Doors and the constrained correctness that had hampered them all day fell away. Soon they were talking freely to all and sundry, telling of their past and planning for the future. The hours slipped by, and suddenly a completely strange boy came up to them and said, " There's a free pass for twenty B.A.G.A. students to-night at the Coronet Cinema in Tottenham Court Road. Coming ? "

" Rather ! " they chorused. As they trouped down the road a barrel organ played " Over the Sea to Skye," and the sadly sweet cadence filled Lynette with emotion. The cinema was tiny and uncomfortable, and showed foreign films that did not attract the public. But the Blue Doors sat enthralled at the acting of the French screen stars whom they had never seen before. " Gosh ! " exclaimed Jeremy afterwards, " and we think we can act."

Outside in the cold street they called good-night to the other students, and Nigel said, " Come on, I know a good place for supper."

In Fitzherbert Street they went into a Greek café opposite their digs and ate a delicious dish of meat balls speared on skewers, and spiced rice.

" Rather different from Mrs. Bosham's cooking," observed Nigel. " But we mustn't do this every night. It'll have to be the Corner House if you want your allowance to last the week."

They were too tired to talk much, but sat smiling contentedly at each other, listening to the jabber of the Greek waiters, unwilling to return to their cabbage-smelling digs.

" Well," said Nigel, with a proprietary air, " how do you think you'll like the Academy ? "

" *Like* it ! " cried Lyn. " I love it already. I'd not have missed it for the world. This has been the happiest day of my life." Nigel toasted her, raising his glass of water.

" And here's to many more ! "

CHAPTER II

SPRING TERM

" SO much to learn, and so little time to learn it in,"
sighed Lynette, stretching and yawning on her bed.
The five of them were gathered in the girls' bedroom as it
was the largest, doing their evening study. Although the
room was big, very little of it could be seen, for it was snowed
under with books and gramophone records. The ugly wall-
paper was nearly covered with ballet pictures by Dégas
belonging to Vicky and photos of film stars belonging to
Sandra, and the mantelpiece had been turned into what they
called " Lynette's Shrine." There were three photos, Henry
Irving, Ellen Terry, and Sarah Bernhardt, and two books,
a volume of Shakespeare and Stanislavsky's *An Actor Prepares*.
On each end of the shelf burned a twisty red candle in a
brass candlestick, throwing shadows on to the faces of the
Blue Doors as they bent over their books.

It was the fifth week of term, and all were endeavouring
to master their lines for the end of term shows. Not only
were they doing a complete production of *Pygmalion* with
two casts, but also some Shakesperian scenes produced by
Mr. Whitfield, and a Molière comedy in the French acting
class. Nearly every night there was a fresh speech to be
learned for the diction, voice-production, or verse-speaking
class next day. Bulldog interrupted the low murmur of
voices.

" Will you listen to my mime, for a minute ? "

" How can we *listen* to your mime ? " mocked Lynette.
" O.K. Go ahead."

Bulldog got up, made a gesture of opening a door, stepped in, stood still, bent his knees slightly, then straightened them, stood blank-faced, bent his knees once more, opened the imaginary door, and stepped out.

" What on earth . . ." they laughed.

" Bulldog, you are a fool ! Whatever is it ? "

" Going up in a lift," announced Bulldog proudly. " Now, what's this ? " He repeated exactly the same movements.

" Going up in a lift ! " they shouted.

" You're wrong," he grinned. " I was going down that time."

Lynette hurled a cushion at his head.

At this moment the clock struck nine and Mrs. Bosham shouted up the stairs, " Y'r supper's on." There was a stampede down for the rather watery macaroni cheese and college pudding that Mrs. Bosham served up regularly on Mondays, Wednesdays, and Fridays.

" Is Mr. Nigel in ? " she asked, as she entered the dining-room.

" Er—no," said Sandra, " I shouldn't bother to keep his hot. He probably won't appear."

" Well, I never ! " she cried, her eyes like saucers. " He *is* a one, isn't he ? (Would you mind kindly stepping off my ball of wool, Mr. Bulldog.) Never used to be like this, you know. First term he was here, he was up in his room every night, rantin' and shoutin' like one o'clock."

" The old ham," murmured Jeremy.

" Hasn't paid 'is rent this week, either," Mrs. Bosham replied, somewhat meaningly.

" Oh, dear ! " sighed Vicky. " I suppose I'll have to pay it again." She opened her handbag and took out the money.

16

" Well, thank you, Miss Vicky. Don't like to have it hanging over, y'know." After she had waddled out Vicky said, " Whatever does Nigel do with his money ? He gets a bigger allowance than we do, anyhow."

" What does he do with it ? I should think it's perfectly obvious what he does with it," Lyn said coldly. " He spends it all on that Auriole creature. He's out with her every night."

" But surely," objected Vicky, " she wouldn't let him *pay* for her when they go out ? I mean—no-one at the Academy ever does. It's always Dutch treat."

" H'm ! " growled Lynette. " Not with Auriole. She was boasting in the girls' dressing-room the other day that a Guards officer spent his month's pay in two evenings taking her out, so she must be going through Nigel's allowance like water."

" I tried to talk to him about it the other day," put in Jeremy, " but he wouldn't listen. Said he wasn't ' gadding about,' he was merely doing what old Whitfield is always advising—seeing as many plays as possible."

" But there are ways *and* ways of seeing plays," observed Sandra. " We've been to the theatre every Saturday this term, but we've stuck to the gallery, consequently we can pay our rent."

" And *our* theatre-going doesn't include an expensive meal afterwards, and dancing until all hours in some low dive," added Lynette acidly.

" Sometimes," Bulldog began timidly, " I wonder if we don't work a little *too* hard. It doesn't look as if it's getting us anywhere." They reflected for a minute. Certainly they had as yet made very little impression at the Academy. There seemed to be so many things to unlearn first.

" And they say that Nigel's student production is terrific," Bulldog went on.

The senior pupils were all allowed to do one act of a play every term, produced by one of themselves, and this time the honour had fallen to Nigel.

" He only chose *Macbeth* so that Auriole could play Lady Macbeth. I think she's rotten," stated Lynette.

" This is Friday night's college pudding warmed up," Bulldog suddenly announced.

" How do you know ? "

" Because it has the same funny taste."

" But it always tastes funny."

" Yes, but this is the same funny taste as on Friday—not a different one."

" Oh, let's fill up on bread and cheese."

" And pickled onions," said Bulldog, grabbing the bottle.

" What low tastes ! " sighed Jeremy, getting up from the table. " Oh, if only there were a piano ! " This was his one complaint. In order to practise he had to get up early and go round to the Academy.

" Who's coming out for a toddle before bed ? " inquired Bulldog. They all set out, muffled up to the ears against the biting February wind, and strode through Regent's Park, where frost and moonlight were silvering the trees.

" How different this life is from school ! " said Lyn, after an argument on voice production. " Can you imagine us going for a walk after we'd done our homework and arguing about long division or the rivers of Europe ? "

" No," laughed Sandra. " Our conversation was exactly the same in those days as it is now—theatre ! "

It was true. They talked, lived, and dreamed theatre.

They forgot to look at the newspaper, they had no hobbies, they met no-one who was outside the magic circle. At No. 37, over the lunch table at the Academy, in Raddler's Café at tea, over snacks in the Corner House, they spoke of nothing else. But their own particular problems depressed them at times.

" Why *isn't* sincerity enough ? " Lynette would demand. " Everyone talks about technique all the time—but what is it ? Nobody ever defines it properly."

" P'raps it's really experience, and that's why we haven't got it."

" And by the time we've gained experience and technique we shall be too old to play all the lovely young parts that there are."

" Oh, I know. Let's play the new game."

This game consisted of stating what part in what play at which theatre they would like to be performing that night. Vicky plumped for " Peter Pan " at the Winter Garden ; Sandra for " Candida " at the Phoenix ; Lynette for " Desdemona " in *Othello* at the New ; Bulldog for " Falstaff " in *The Merry Wives of Windsor* at the Haymarket, and Jeremy for " Hamlet " at the St. James. This game made them walk much farther than they had intended, and it was midnight when they returned. Nigel was still out. " He'll be late for the Academy again in the morning," sighed Sandra. " Can't you talk to him, Vicky ? He's your brother."

" ' Am I my brother's keeper ? ' " quoted Vicky. " I'll say he needs one."

They went to bed and their dreams were of diverse things, from learning how to control the diaphragm muscles, to the sound of an orchestra tuning up for the overture.

Next day at prayers Mr. Whitfield announced, " There

is to be a new competition this term. One of the governors has offered a prize for scenic design. The subject is James Elroy Flecker's *Hassan*. Only one set is wanted. It must be to scale, and must fit the model theatre in the workshop."
The Blue Doors looked at each other.

"Sounds like Nigel's cup of tea," whispered Sandra to Lyn.

"You're telling me ! He could win that with one hand tied behind his back."

"The work is to be done in spare time, not in Academy hours, but the workshop will be open in the evenings for this purpose. Will those who wish to enter give in their names to Miss Smith afterwards." Bulldog peered round the theatre for Nigel, but he was not present.

"Looks as if he's late again," he muttered. "We must make him give in his name."

"And *Hassan* too ! A wonderful subject," enthused Lyn. "We just can't go home these holidays with not one of us having won anything. And it's quite obvious that none of us five will."

Sometimes Lyn despaired of ever learning to act. There was so much to remember all the time. If she tried to think about her voice, she forgot her moves, and if she concentrated on her moves she forgot her lines.

"You don't know how to relax," she was told in Mime.

"Your voice is monotonous," she was told in Diction.

"You have no poise," she was told in Ballet. And as for Fencing—poor little Monsieur Desmoulins would twirl his moustache in anguish and cry, "Miss Darwin, please ! It is not a sword dance. From ze wrist, if you please."

In the production of *Pygmalion* that they were doing, Lynette and Vicky each had a scene of Eliza Doolittle, and

Jeremy was playing Professor Higgins, opposite Lyn. Sandra was playing Mrs. Higgins, a character part that she found very difficult, and Bulldog was playing Doolittle ; over-playing it, in fact. But Roma Seymore did not object to this at all.

" That's right," she would cry. " Go for it. I'd much rather have to tone it down than bolster it up."

Out of the six girls playing Eliza, the best was definitely Helen, the plain, mysterious girl who spoke to no-one and worked like a Trojan. She was never at Raddler's for tea, and always brought her own sandwiches and ate them alone in the classroom at lunch-time. Although she had had no experience, she was the only one who showed any spark of genius to warm Mrs. Seymore's heart. Lynette, perhaps, was the next hope, but at the moment her self-assurance was shaken by having all the new things to learn at once. At the end of the first term a scholarship was always given to the most promising beginner, and this was very often the subject of conversation for the Blue Doors on their way to the Academy.

" Wouldn't it shake our parents if one of us got it ? "

" Yes, but who could ? "

" Lyn might."

" No," growled Lyn. " Look at Helen—and Otto—and Ali—they're all better than I am."

" Your *Pygmalion* isn't as good as Helen's, but by the end of the term your *Shakespeare* will be."

" No, Bulldog must get it on his Mr. Doolittle."

" Don't be silly ! Old Whitfield will say I'm hamming. You know what a tartar he is for ' subtlety.' "

" The only one of us who can win anything this term is Nigel, for his scenic design. There's no-one half as inter-ested in it as he is," said Sandra.

21

" And even he doesn't seem madly enthusiastic, you must admit," added Jeremy.

" Oh, I don't know," said Lyn. " He's been going down to the workshop every night this week." There was a rather meaning silence. Lynette looked up sharply.

" Or has he ? Do you mean he's been going out with that Auriole atrocity instead ? " The others nodded dumbly. " Well, I'm blowed ! What a fool the boy is ! He could win the prize with so little effort, if he'd only *make* the effort."

" He hasn't even started," said Vicky. " I went down into the workshop and had a snoop round. There are about four sets by different people lying about half finished, but nothing of Nigel's at all."

" I think," Lyn said determinedly, " that I shall have a word with Miss Auriole."

" But you daren't ! " cried Vicky.

" Why not ? "

" Well—I mean—she's a senior."

" She's only a girl, the same as me. If she's a few years older and smokes Turkish cigarettes in a silly great holder, I can't help it. I shall speak to her after lunch."

Auriole was holding court on a sofa that stood in an alcove in the foyer when Lyn found her, Nigel at her side mending a fencing foil for her. Ignored by Nigel, Lynette broke through the little group of students who were hanging on every word spoken by the chestnut-haired beauty. " Could I have a word with you, please, Auriole ? "

" Oh, look, darling," said Auriole to Nigel, " here's your protégée. What do you want, my child ? "

" I want to speak to you—privately."

Auriole looked surprised.

" Good gracious ! If you're wanting good advice don't

come to Aunty Auriole. She's sure to lead you astray ! "
She rose languidly and followed Lynette up the stairs.

" Well, what is it ? "

Lyn swung round sharply, her dark eyes flashing. " I
want to ask you to leave Nigel alone. At least until the end
of the term."

Auriole looked at her closely for a moment, then
laughed loudly.

" What a child you are ! Why should I leave him
alone ? "

" Because you're interfering with his work."

" Work ? What's that ? " laughed Auriole.

Lyn lost her temper. " No, I don't believe you *do* know
what work is ! I've never seen you do anything except
lounge about flirting with people. Before Nigel met you
he was keen and hard-working, but now he's getting to be
as idle as you are. And you're spending all his money. Do
you know he hasn't paid his rent for three weeks ? "

" Hasn't paid his rent ? " Auriole sounded astonished.
" But I thought . . ."

" What did you think ? "

" Well, he always seemed so free with his money. I
thought he was very well off. I thought you all were—the
whole gang of you. You always look it."

" Nigel and all of us have a very small weekly allowance
from our parents, which just about pays our rent and leaves
a few shillings over for pocket-money—certainly not enough
to cater for expensive tastes like yours. Anyhow, it will *have*
to stop soon, because Nigel is absolutely broke."

" Well thanks, dear, for telling me. Saves me from
wasting my time, doesn't it ? " And Auriole sailed down
the stairs to lavish her attentions on one of the old Etonians
from the beginners' class.

From then on Nigel returned to the fold. He spent his evenings either working on the model theatre at the Academy or at No. 37 with the Blue Doors, studying and talking. On Saturday he accompanied them out to the theatre queues, where they sat outside on hard little stools for several hours, reading, eating chocolate, and doing crossword puzzles, until the doors opened and they scrambled in to get the best seats in the front row of the gallery. Entranced, they sat through Shakespeare, ballet, American comedies— all that the theatres offered them, and returned to Fitzherbert Street drunk with excitement and ambition.

On Sundays they had a system of going to a different famous church each time. In this way they visited St. Paul's, Westminster Abbey, St. Martin in the Fields, Westminster Cathedral, and Brompton Oratory. Sunday afternoons usually found them walking over Hampstead Heath, and having tea at one of the little old inns that held the ghosts of so many poets and great men of the past.

As the end of the term drew near the whole Academy was in a turmoil. Each day in the little theatre there were performances by one class or another, and the rest of the students turned up in full force to applaud, laugh, or boo with twice the vigour of an ordinary audience. There was always a smattering of friends and relations of the performers at these shows. Lynette had an unfortunate experience of this. She was watching a particularly agonizing performance of *Dear Brutus*, in which a very fat girl was playing the " dream child," and, turning to Sandra in the interval, Lynette remarked, " Some *dream* child—more like a nightmare. She ought never to be allowed on the stage."

" I agree," said a voice on the other side of Lyn, " and I'm her mother." For the rest of the show Lynette was so covered with shame she could hardly look up at the stage.

24

" And to think," she said to Sandra afterwards, " that before long it will be us up there on the stage with everyone in the audience being catty about us. Oh, how awful ! "

Their first show was the Molière comedy, but as the French class included students out of all the classes in the Academy, the Blue Doors had very small walking-on parts.

As the day approached for the performance of *Pygmalion*, the rivalry between Helen and Lynette became more and more keen. One day Helen remarked to her bitterly, " Of course you'll get the scholarship. You're bound to. Our performances are about equal, but you *look* all right on the stage." This made Lynette feel guilty somehow.

Helen seemed to be growing very strange and nervy. One day in class Roma Seymore asked her suddenly, " Do you come from a theatrical family, Helen ? " Helen looked at the floor, flushed brick red, then burst into tears and ran out of the room.

" What an odd thing ! " said Mrs. Seymore. " Lynette, dear, go and see if she's all right."

Lynette found her crouching outside on the stairs, racked with sobs.

" Whatever's wrong, Helen ? "

" Go away. Don't touch me. How dare she pry into my affairs."

" But she wasn't prying. It was meant as a compliment, really it was ! " Helen rose unsteadily, her pale face blotched with tears.

" Well, I don't want compliments. They're no good to me. All I want is that scholarship—and I know I shan't get it." She hurried off down the stairs before Lyn could stop her. But it was not long before Lyn saw her again.

That evening Lyn could not settle down. There was

nothing to be learnt. She had polished her Eliza Doolittle scene and her Constance in *King John* until any more work on them would probably only make them worse. Sandra was sewing some of their costumes that needed alterations. Vicky was mending ballet shoes. The boys were spread out on the floor discussing some of the technical details of Nigel's model stage set.

" I'm going out," said Lyn. " Shan't be long."

She walked as far as Trafalgar Square, down Whitehall, and on to Westminster Bridge. The air was salt, as if it were the seaside, and the Houses of Parliament towered grey and delicate. All along the riverside the lights glittered and were reflected in the water. She leaned on the bridge for a long time. Suddenly she felt hungry, and decided that a cup of coffee was necessary before she attempted the long walk home. On the other side of the river she found a little café called the Riverside Dining Rooms and went in. While she waited to be served she drew out her pocket volume of Shakespeare's sonnets and was deeply immersed when the waitress asked, " What can I get you ? "

Lyn looked up quickly and her mouth fell open. It was Helen in a shabby cap and apron, with a tray in one hand, looking down at her viciously.

" I feared someone from the Academy would come here one day," she hissed. " Why did it have to be you ? "

" But do you—do you *have* to do this ? " Lyn asked timidly.

" Yes, I do ! I haven't got any parents to send me a nice little weekly allowance. I had to do this for a year first, to save enough to pay my fees for this term. And now if I don't get the scholarship I'll have to leave until I can save enough to pay my fees for another term. It's going to take rather a long time, isn't it ? " she snarled.

26

" How dare she pry into my affairs ? "

" But how long do you work here ? "

" From six in the evening until one in the morning."

" You must get tired."

" I'm used to it now. Look, I'd better serve you or the old dragon will be nattering."

The " old dragon " was a skinny old woman who sat behind the cash desk in a dirty black dress. When Helen brought her coffee Lynette said, " Won't you tell me why you were so upset when Roma Seymore asked if you came from a theatrical family ? "

Helen looked sullen for a moment, then said, " My mother was Deirdre Anderson. I expect you've heard of her. She was a wonderful actress in her day—but extravagant. She died three years ago when I was fifteen. She didn't leave anything—except debts. All her friends had deserted her by that time, so I started to work, but I knew—just knew that I had to act. So even if it takes me years to save enough money, I'm going to get my training."

" But why don't you find a job in a nicer place ? "

Helen laughed cynically. " That's the joke. I can't work anywhere where I'd be likely to meet any theatre people. I thought this place was as safe as any, until you walked in."

" But why should you be ashamed of it ? " cried Lyn. " I should be proud—terribly proud."

"Waitress ! " came a vexed shout from another table, and Helen hurried off. Lyn paid her bill and went out. On the way home she was deep in thought.

Next day neither Helen nor Lyn spoke to each other, and Lyn did not tell the rest of the Blue Doors about their meeting.

The performance of *Pygmalion* went off quite well, with Lynette and Helen both acclaimed as excellent " Elizas."

Bulldog's " Doolittle " was much appreciated by the students, who laughed every time he opened his mouth, but Mr. Whitfield was not particularly amused. Their Shakespeare scenes were performed on the day before the last day of the term. Helen had a scene from *Cleopatra* which brought the house down. Lynette's " Constance " was equally good. When the show was over and Lynette had removed her grease-paint she ran down the stairs to Mr. Whitfield's office, knocked, and walked in.

" Please, Mr. Whitfield," she said, " I'm going to be terribly presumptious. But everyone says you don't know whether to give the scholarship to me or to Helen. Even Mrs. Seymore said that. So please don't think I'm being impertinent when I ask you not to give me the scholarship. I can do without it, but Helen can't. I've got a small allow-ance, and though a scholarship would help, it's not terribly necessary. But Helen will have to leave to-morrow unless you give her the scholarship. Oh, please do."

Mr. Whitfield smiled quietly. " But how do you know that I am not intending to give the scholarship to Bulldog —or our Indian friend ? "

" Well, you might be for all I know. But if you're thinking of giving it to me, please give it to Helen instead.'

He looked thoughtfully at her for a few seconds, then said, " How much does the stage mean to you, Lynette ? "

" Everything."

" You can go now."

Next day, at the end-of-term prize-giving Lyn clapped loudly as Nigel received the prize for scenic design, which was a beautifully equipped model theatre, like the one belonging to the Academy. " Alone I did it ! " she whispered to Sandra.

And when Mr. Whitfield announced that the beginners' scholarship had gone to Helen, Lyn clapped until her hands nearly came off.

"You ought to have had it ! " all her friends told her. " It's a shame ! "

" No, it's not. I'm quite happy about it," she told them. And to herself :

" Happy about it ? I'm positively smug ! "

CHAPTER III

" FIT UP "

A FEW days before the end of the spring term a notice
was pinned on the green-baize notice-board which read:
" Any students interested in taking part in an Easter play
to tour the rural schools during the holidays, please attend
a meeting at ten-thirty in Room Four, the day after the
end of term." The Blue Doors argued about it at length.

" Our parents are expecting us to go home."

" But it's a chance to get some experience."

" What about poor little Maddy, though ? She's looking
forward so much to seeing us again."

" But we'd probably get quite good parts, because I
don't suppose many people would want to work in the
holidays." Finally they decided to go along to the meeting
and see what it was all about.

Only thirty pupils from the whole Academy had turned
up. Nobody knew anyone else, and there was silence except
for the chattering Blue Doors, until Mr. Whitfield appeared
with a pile of books in his hand.

" Good-morning," he said. " Now, I expect you're
wondering what exactly this show is to be. We are planning to take out this rather beautiful Easter play to schools
all over the country, in remote parts where they get very
little theatrical entertainment. You will have two weeks'
rehearsal and six weeks' tour. The Academy will pay your
expenses and a small sum for pocket money. Now, the cast
only calls for twenty, I'm afraid, so some of you will be
disappointed. I shall not pay any attention to seniority in

giving out the parts, but I will audition you as if it were a normal professional engagement."

The light of battle shone in all eyes, and when the scripts were handed out the students glanced hastily through to see which parts they hoped to get. Lyn immediately pinned her hopes on the part of Mary Magdalene, who had some wonderful speeches. The play was very simple but beautifully written, with a child in the main part. It was obvious that this part would fall to Wendy, the little girl in the beginners' class, for a term at the Academy had done nothing to sophisticate her. She still wore plaits and kilts and jumpers. It was rather nerve-wracking to read an entirely strange script as an audition, but the Blue Doors put up quite a good show. The reading lasted the whole morning, and by the end of it everyone had read every possible part.

" Now run along and have your lunch," Mr. Whitfield told them, " and I'll think over the casting and let you know this afternoon at two-thirty."

Lyn remarked over lunch at Raddler's, " We kidded ourselves we were only going to the meeting this morning to see what it was all about, but of course it's quite obvious that we're all dying to go on the tour."

" I wonder where it's going ? Wouldn't it be funny if it went to Fenchester ? " said Vicky. " To our old schools. Gosh, I'd love to see their faces—if we were in it."

The atmosphere was tense when they returned to the Academy and Mr. Whitfield read out the cast. Bulldog was the first of the Blue Doors to be mentioned.

" P. Halford—Roman centurion." Bulldog blushed with pleasure under his freckles. And then, on top of that came Nigel and Vicky's names.

" V. Halford, an angel. N. Halford, Judas." Nigel tried to look as if he'd been expecting a good part all the time.

33

"Your family are in favour," Lynette whispered to Vicky, not without envy. But the Darwin family were luckier still, for next minute Lyn and Jeremy heard their names read out for the parts of Mary Magdalene and Pontious Pilate. Lyn was so thrilled that she broke into an enormous grin that would not be controlled. It seemed to be spreading itself right round to her ears, and nothing she could do would stop it. She tried to appear nonchalant, like Nigel, but without success. And then, as the cast list was finished she realized suddenly that Sandra was the only one of them not included.

"Oh, Sandra!" she said. "I *am* sorry!"

"Doesn't matter," replied Sandra quietly. "I must admit I'm disappointed, but it's all to the good that one of us should go home. And Maddy will be pleased." But inside she was very miserable. Mr. Whitfield told them that rehearsals would start the following day, and all the fortunate ones gathered together to discuss the tour excitedly —what they should take with them, and where they were likely to go.

Rehearsals in the empty Academy were rather exciting. It seemed a very different place from the noisy hive of activity of term time. Now that the days were getting warmer they often took their own lunch and ate it on the flat roof, from which there was a magnificent view over London. One could see as far as the dumpy trees of Hampstead Heath. Bulldog delighted in climbing the tall flagpole, from which vantage point he would terrify passers-by in the street below by pretending to lose his balance.

For this production their lines and moves had to be learned much more quickly than the Blue Doors had ever before found necessary.

"Do you remember," said Vicky, "when we used to

34

rehearse for about six months, and then never be word perfect on the night ? "

" That was because we used to make up the plays as we went along, almost," laughed Lyn. " Oh, what fun those days were. But how long ago they seem ! "

" I suppose one has to work harder than this in rep.," said Nigel. " Gosh, what a strain ! "

" Won't it be fun," said Bulldog, " when we turn the Blue Door Theatre into a professional rep. ! "

" Do you think we ever shall ? " asked Lyn. They all turned on her in surprise.

" But of course ! Why, we've promised our parents and the Bishop. It's what we've come to the Academy for."

" Yes, of course," said Lyn slowly. " I was forgetting."

" But don't you *want* to ? "

" Oh, yes," said Lynette vaguely. " Yes, of course."

" Everybody on stage, please," interrupted the stage manager, and they ran down the stairs to the theatre, hastily munching the remains of their sandwiches.

Gradually the play, which was called *Within Three Days*, began to take a hold on them. At first the Blue Doors had been a little awed at having to work with seniors who were much older and more experienced than themselves, but Mr. Whitfield treated everybody equally, and was either encouraging or sarcastic, according to the effort that was being made.

" Your voices are not doing their work properly," he told them. " Don't you realize that you are speaking some of the most lovely lines ever written ? So give them full value. Don't hold your voices back."

During the second week of rehearsals they had to go into the wardrobe to have their costumes fitted. Mrs. Bertram, the motherly old wardrobe mistress, who had worked there for years, welcomed them with pins in her mouth, then

35

said firmly, " Girls, I'm telling you now once and for all
—you will *not* be allowed to have any hair showing. With
Biblical plays we always have trouble over curls and rolls
appearing on people's foreheads. It's to be a plain wimple
or nothing."

"It's all right for you, Lyn," Vicky grumbled. "You
can take it."

"What are you, duck ? " Mrs. Bertram turned to
Vicky. "Oh, you're the angel, aren't you ? Oh, well
you can have some hair if you like. I should think Mr.
Whitfield would allow it."

The colour scheme of the whole show was almost entirely
in varying shades of blue, white, and gold, which gave the
effect of a medieval illumination. Bulldog surveyed his
short centurion's tunic with disgust.

"Why do I *always* have to wear skirts on the stage ?
And with *my* knees."

"And I seem fated to wear crêpe hair," joined in Nigel.
"Face fungus all the time—whatever the show."

Vicky made a lovely angel in gilt robes and enormous
feathery wings made of cotton wool stuck on to a wire-and-
paper frame. And Jeremy in his toga and laurel wreath
looked an extremely patrician Roman.

All the staff of the Academy and a few friends came to
the dress rehearsal, and in spite of many hitches enjoyed it
tremendously. Bulldog, as usual, struck several people as
being rather funny. "But never mind," said Nigel comfort-
ingly. "A year ago if you'd appeared in that kilt arrangement you'd have stopped the show."

That night they had to pack away their costumes and
properties into large hampers, called skeps, ready for their
journey next day. They were starting off the tour in the
Lake District, and were to travel in their own bus.

The two girls had bought their first pairs of slacks especially for the tour, and felt very daring as they put them on next day. The boys, of course, expressed conventional disgust.

"What would you say if *we* turned up in skirts ? "

"Well, Bulldog, *you* can hardly talk, can you ? "

"But I don't wear mine for fun."

"Nor do we—we wear them for comfort and warmth while travelling."

Mrs. Bosham greeted the slacks with her usual amazement.

"Well, I'm blessed ! Natty, eh ! Bye-bye, dears. (Knit two together, slip one.) See you next term."

It was a bright spring morning as they carried their cases to the Academy. Outside the lion gateway stood a shiny red omnibus.

"Oh, what a beauty ! " cried Bulldog. "Gosh, I'd like a chance to drive that——"

"Let's get in quickly and bag good seats."

They had parked themselves in front seats, and Bulldog was examining the brake and gear levers, when Mr. Whitfield appeared in the doorway of the Academy.

"Come on, you slackers ! " he cried. "There's a lot of loading to be done."

Gaily they carried out the heavy skeps and scenery. Even their own footlights were taken along, as they would be playing on very rough stages.

At last they were all aboard, and the luggage had been checked. Roma Seymore appeared on the steps and waved her handkerchief.

"*Bon voyage !* " she cried. "Give my love to the Lake District."

The driver, a fat little man called Sam, started up the

engine, and they were off. London slipped by them, streets and streets of shops and houses and cinemas. Soon all this fell behind and they seemed to smell the country air.

Everyone had brought enormous supplies of food, and as they munched apples and cake they came to the conclusion that touring was good fun.

" I'm glad I'm on the stage ! " announced Bulldog. " How awful it would be to be a plumber—or a—an undertaker."

" You wouldn't be much of a success as either," mocked Nigel. " The stage is always the last resort of someone who has slight artistic tendencies, but can't sing, dance, paint, or write."

" Look who's talking ! And how dare you say I can't dance ? I'm a riot in the ballet class, aren't I, girls ? "

" Riot is the correct word, especially when you kicked poor old Madame in the tummy when she was showing you how to lift."

At midday they stretched their cramped limbs, and had lunch at a country pub called " The Deerstalkers " with a crowd of villagers watching their every movement.

" Must be some o' they circus folk," Jeremy was amused to overhear. Bulldog greeted this with delight, and immediately ran out to the bus and chalked " Whitfield's Circus " in large letters across the side. Mr. Whitfield unbent considerably over lunch and told them stories of his early days in the theatre, and of all the famous actors and actresses with whom he had worked.

" Oh, dear," sighed Lynette. " Why aren't there any great personalities like that in the theatre to-day ? "

" Well, if there aren't," laughed Mr. Whitfield, " it leaves all the more scope for your generation to create them, doesn't it ? "

Back in the bus they sang choruses as the green country-side sped by. Sam, the driver, taught them a lugubrious little ditty, the chorus of which went :

> Boom-boom, boom-boom,
> Boom-boom, boom-boom,
> Y-es, you're going to die.

And they yelled it joyfully.

" Where are we staying to-night, Mr. Whitfield ? " Lyn inquired.

" At a Youth Hostel near Windermere. I believe it's a very lovely old house. You'll stay sometimes in Youth Hostels, sometimes in hotels, sometimes in digs. The local education people are arranging all that."

The country became gradually more wild and beautiful, and they were soon " ooh-ing " and " ah-ing " out of the windows at torrential waterfalls, looming hills, and stretches of clear, silvery lake.

" And to think," said Vicky, " that we're being paid to do this ! "

" You wait ! " laughed Mr. Whitfield. " You'll be playing twice daily after to-morrow, and only one night stands, so it won't be quite such a picnic as to-day has been."

" But it'll be fun to be doing the show," said Lyn, almost indignantly. Mr. Whitfield laughed at their enthusiasm.

By the time they reached Windermere, dusk was creeping on and they were tired and silent.

" I didn't know sitting still all day could be so tiring," sighed Vicky. " I feel as if I'd done hours and hours of ballet practice."

" This looks like the place ! " cried Mr. Whitfield, as they neared a large grey stone house among some dark trees, with a Youth Hostel sign on the gate-post.

(606)

After an enormous meal in an airy, white-washed room, they sat round the wood fire and made an effort at a word rehearsal, and then retired to bed.

"Now no midnight feasts or anything," warned Mr. Whitfield. "I know you're in dormitories, but please don't go all fifth form about it." But in spite of this, on the landing at some minutes past midnight there was a violent battle with pillows, girls versus boys. And if the Matron of the hostel heard the muffled yelps and laughter and thud of pillows she turned a deaf and kindly ear.

Next day dawned clear and warm, and over breakfast they made the discovery that they could see the lake at the bottom of the garden.

"Dear Mr. Whitfield, please may we go on the lake this morning ? "

"By all means, but don't (a) fall in, (b) be late for lunch, or (c) catch colds."

Soon an armada of little boats set out across the smooth surface of the lake.

"Yo-o-heave-ho ! " sang Bulldog, very flat, catching crabs with both oars at the same time.

"Thank goodness Maddy isn't here ! She'd be sure to fall in," said Jeremy, stretched out in the stern.

"Oh, isn't it heavenly ! " Lyn cried, posing in the bows, knowing that she made a good picture in a red jumper, with the wind streaming her dark hair out behind her. Bulldog caught a particularly large crab, and it was Lynette who nearly went overboard. They had boat races, they towed each other, and drank fizzy lemonade, purchased at the boat-house. By lunch-time they were at the opposite side of the lake.

"Heavens ! " cried Vicky, " and the call is at two."

Everybody took an oar, and they skimmed back across

the lake, panting with the effort, only to find that Mr. Whitfield was still on the lake with the Matron. When he arrived he said, " Let's start prompt at two. It's not a very long journey, but I should like to have a little run-through before the show. We go up at five, and afterwards there's a long journey to where we stay the night."

The bus stopped at a tiny village hall right among the hills.

" But wherever will the audience come from ? " they asked, dismayed. " There aren't any houses."

" They'll be the pupils from the school over there—children who live on farms scattered all round here."

It was a tiny stage with holes in the floor-boards, and it needed all the initiative of the stage management, plus assistance from Nigel and Bulldog, to get it into shape for the show. Everyone was so busy fetching and carrying, ironing dresses, and making-up that all forgot to be nervous. The hall began to fill up with children whose shouting and screaming penetrated to the tiny dressing-rooms where the students were struggling into their Biblical costumes.

" Hark at the lions roaring for their prey," remarked Lynette.

" They're only excited," Vicky said in her best motherly voice.

" Little dears ! " said Lyn sarcastically, smoothing on an olive foundation.

" Five minutes, please," shouted the assistant stage manager, diving hastily into her costume.

When the curtain went up there were loud cries of " Sh ! " from the teachers, but the children, who seemed never to have seen a play before, still chattered quite audibly. Soon, however, they became immersed in the adventures of the centurion's little daughter, at the first Easter time. They were completely natural in their reactions and booed the entrances of Judas and Pontius Pilate, as if they were at the cinema. It all reminded Lyn of the old days in the little Blue Door Theatre, when they had sometimes given shows for the Sunday School children, and she completely forgot the anxieties of technique that had troubled her all the term. She let herself go and thoroughly enjoyed the performance, stimulated as she entered by the loud whisper from a little girl in the front row, " Don't she look lovely, eh ? " Afterwards, when the children had cheered their heads off, Lyn turned to Vicky.

" Wasn't that fun ! " she said. " For the first time in months I couldn't have cared less what my diaphragm was doing, and I'm sure it was working properly."

" Mr. Whitfield says I look too much like a pantomime fairy," said Vicky. " I'll have to cut out the gold dust on my hair."

" Hurry up and get your make-up off, and come across to the schoolroom. There's a meal for us," Mr. Whitfield shouted. " We'll pack up afterwards."

They suddenly realized they were hungry, and slammed on the removing cream. As they went to the schoolroom they were waylaid in the streets by nearly all the audience, clamouring for autographs. It gave them a wonderful illusion of being professionals as they signed their names with appropriate flourishes.

" Never seed a play before," one adenoidal child said to Lynette. " Enjoyed it ever so. Think I'll be a nactress."

It was on the tip of Lynette's tongue to say, " I should get those adenoids seen to first," but remembering how kindly she had been treated by Felicity Warren, the actress, when begging an autograph, she smiled and said, " Well, dear, I wish you luck."

The meal in the schoolroom was delicious. It consisted of jugged hare and home-made apple pie with clotted cream. The teachers all expressed their joy at seeing a play in this out-of-the-way corner of the Lake District, and it was after nine before " Whitfield's Circus " could drag themselves away to load up the bus and depart. At eleven o'clock they were still speeding through the dark country lanes.

" This," said Bulldog, " is going to become a little wearing after five weeks, don't you think ? "

" It's a very good thing for you," said Mr. Whitfield, over-hearing. " Your first tour being rough and ready—a ' fit-up ' as we call it in the theatre—will make you appreciate the moderate comfort of an ordinary commercial tour playing the provincial theatres. Some of the best actors have started their careers in ' fit-ups ' doing one-night stands. It will teach you that acting isn't all long psychological discussions on what Ibsen really meant, and chocolate cakes at Raddler's."

They laughed at this description of Academy life, and Lyn said quietly to Vicky, " I'm going to enjoy every minute of it ! "

And so she did—for the first three weeks. The country through which they travelled was delightful in these early days of spring, and they stayed in pleasant old inns with oak beams and no hot water. But the late hours, night after night, two shows at different places during the day, and the loading and unloading began to tell on their inexperience. Gradually the days seemed to merge into one another. On waking in the mornings they could not remember in which town or village they were. Their mail from home seemed to have lost touch with them, and all contact with the outside world was gone. There was only the show, the same nineteen other students, and, every day, two different halls filled with children who all seemed to have the same faces and to make the same noises as on the previous day. At the meals they were given after the performances they tired of the same polite conversation of school teachers and local education committees.

"I shall pin a label on me," sighed Lyn wearily, "saying 'Yes, I'm enjoying the tour. No, I don't know where we're playing next. Yes, I think the country is lovely.'"

"I shall put on mine, 'Tea—strong, plenty of sugar, plenty to eat, and leave me alone, please,'" growled Bull-dog. "What do you think that hearty old dame asked me just now? Didn't I think that country dancing was jolly good fun!"

"What did you reply?" laughed Nigel. "'Madam, I am dedicated to the ballet'?"

Windermere, Ullswater, Keswick, and on up to the Border—halls where the stoves smoked, halls where they wouldn't light at all. Halls where the curtains stuck, halls where there were no curtains. Audiences of twenty or thirty, audiences where the auditorium seemed jammed to the ceiling. Sumptuous spreads of country fare or watery tea and digestive biscuits. Hard, narrow hostel beds, voluminous feathery mattresses in country pubs. Digs where they could not understand the dialect of the cottagers, hospitality in the mayor's house, where their host dressed for dinner. There was constant change, and yet a sameness. The students all became so well acquainted that before it was made, they knew each other's every remark and gesture. There were little feuds, and days when some people were 'not speaking,' but usually the need to do the show well bound them together. Once or twice there were accounts of the show in the little country papers, and Lynette was always praised enthusiastically.

" The *Much-Stooging-in-the-Mud Courier* approves of you, my child," laughed Nigel, " so what more can you want ? Next stop—the West End."

The days got warmer and they ran about in slacks and jumpers, and paddled in streams wherever they got the chance. The Academy seemed far away and forgotten, so that it came as a surprise one day to see Mr. Whitfield making out the form lists for the following term. Lyn, peering discreetly over his shoulder, noted that she and the other five had all moved up one class.

" How lovely not to be a beginner ! " she thought.

" Only another week," Mr. Whitfield reminded them, " so make the most of this vagabond life."

But by this time they were too tired to rise early in the mornings to explore each new neighbourhood. The Blue Doors worked out a rota for taking up the others' breakfasts in bed in the morning, so that only one need get up for it. Mr. Whitfield tried to keep the journeys short, but Sam often lost his way in the unfamiliar lanes, and they rarely reached home before midnight.

At the last performance it seemed hard to realize that they would never again say the words that had become so familiar to them. To combat the feeling of slight dismay that this caused they were inclined to clown somewhat. Bulldog appeared wearing Nigel's beard, which dissolved Lynette into helpless giggles, and the school children were quite convinced that the centurion was meant to be a comic character.

When the curtain fell the Director of Education made a speech. Mr. Whitfield replied, and there was a little bunch of violets for each of the girls, and bars of chocolate for the boys.

" I shall press these," said Lynette, sniffing the fragrant little bunch. " My first bouquet ! "

" I shan't keep mine !" said Bulldog, scoffing his chocolate at one go.

That night they sat over cups of cocoa in a youth hostel.

" You've all done very good work," Mr. Whitfield told them. " You've had a tough time and stuck it very well. I hope to take you all out on tour again before you leave me."

" Thank you, Mr. Whitfield," said the stage manager, " for looking after us so nicely."

On the long journey back next day thoughts had already turned to the coming term.

" I wonder if I've moved up ? "

" I wonder what show we'll do ? "

" I wonder if old So-and-so is coming back ? "

Soon the greenery disappeared. They saw the first tube station, the first red omnibus, the first dumpy taxi, and London engulfed them once more.

CHAPTER IV

DANCING IN THE SQUARE

No sooner had they stepped inside the murky hall of No. 37 than the telephone shrilled. It was fixed on the wall between a large photo of the late Mr. Bosham and the head of a melancholy-looking horned animal that the late Mr. Bosham claimed to have shot. When the phone was answered they both seemed to peer down in a wistful manner, as if wondering why nobody ever rang for *them*. The Blue Doors all leaped to answer this ring, and Nigel got there first. Sandra's voice came from a long way off.

" Don't say you've come back at last ! I've been ringing you for days. Have you got my letters ? "

" No. All our post seems to have gone astray."

" Then—you haven't heard ? "

" Heard what ? "

" About Maddy ? "

" Maddy ? No. What has she done now ? "

" She's a film star."

" A what ? "

" A film star ! "

" What *are* you talking about ? " Nigel's tone made the rest of the Blue Doors gather round, straining their ears to hear the squeaky little voice that came through the receiver.

" Maddy has been given the leading part in a film about Fenchester. It's called *Forsaken Crown*, and she plays a little girl of Tudor days.* It all happened because she met one of the film men on the bumper cars at Browcliffe, and he

* See *Maddy Alone*.

47

took her down to see the filming, and *who* do you think was playing the lead ? "

" I thought you said Maddy was——"

" Oh, this was before she went down. It was Felicity Warren ! You see, she didn't know that Elizabeth was only a little girl, and——"

" I don't know what you're talking about," said Nigel, crushingly. " It all sounds quite impossible. You'd better wait till we see you. Are you coming up to-morrow ? "

" Yes. But don't you understand ? Maddy is a film star ! They've got on quite a bit already, and I've been in the crowd. Oh, it *has* been fun ! "

" Your time is up," said the operator, and the pips pipped. Sandra was still chattering away excitedly as Nigel rang off.

" The girl's quite crazy," he said. " Nattering away about Maddy being a film star or something. Couldn't make head or tail of it."

" Y'r supper's on," said Mrs. Bosham, who had been registering surprise in the background ever since they arrived.

In the dining-room. " Why, it's macaroni cheese and college pudding ! What a *lovely* surprise ! " cried Bulldog with heavy sarcasm.

Sandra arrived next day bubbling over with news about her little sister's lucky chance, and the Blue Doors listened, open-mouthed, to accounts of film life.

" And sometimes," said Sandra, " we'd spend the whole day shooting over and over again a little scene that will only take up one whole minute on the screen."

They plied her with questions.

" What was Felicity Warren like ? "

" Is film make-up different from stage ? "

48

" How much is Maddy being paid ? "

And far into the night Sandra regaled them with fresh tit-bits as they came to mind. It struck them as funny that, while they had been pitying Sandra for missing the tour, she had actually come in for more excitement than they had.

" Well—Maddy has certainly stolen a march on us, hasn't she ? " said Vicky. " The little monkey ! I suppose she won't want to come to the Academy now ? "

" Oh, yes, she will ! " Sandra contradicted. " She is awfully condescending about film work. It's rather funny. She says it's not real acting at all, and she's still awfully envious of our being here."

" But she won't need to come to the Academy if she's a full-blown film star—she'll probably be kept filming for years," Nigel objected.

" Oh, I don't think so," said Sandra. " The theatre is still her first love."

" Well, I never did ! To think of our little Maddy ! "

Next day at the Academy some of the other pupils, having read in the film magazines about Maddy's piece of luck, crowded round the Blue Doors asking questions. No-one thought to inquire about the holiday tour.

It was certainly pleasant not to be a beginner any more, to inspect the term's new-comers and say casually, " They don't look too bright, do they ? " to greet class-mates with cries of joy and long accounts of the holidays.

The days seemed to fly by as spring turned into summer. All the windows of the Academy were kept open, and passers-by could hear the rise and fall of chorusing voices, the rhythmic beat of the dancing-class piano, and the clash of fencing foils from the flat roof.

When lessons were over the Blue Doors and gangs of

friends would clamber on a bus for Hyde Park, and swim and sunbathe by the Serpentine, eating cherries, learning lines, and pushing each other into the crowded water. Somehow, they did not seem to get so much work done this term. There was always a film or a play to be seen, or an expedition to be made to Richmond, Roehampton, or Kew. The long summer evenings tempted them out of the gloom of No. 37 into the sunshine. And yet their progress did not seem to suffer. Vicky was the one and only star pupil of the ballet class. Lynette still tied with Helen for a first place in all-acting classes. Nigel made wonderful plans for immense and spectacular Shakesperian productions, and Sandra and Bulldog jogged along in a mediocre manner, neither shining nor lagging behind at anything. Sandra was most popular in the wardrobe, where she would turn up on Saturday mornings to give Mrs. Bertram a hand at sewing on sequins and turning up hems.

Throughout the term there was much talk of the Public Show to be given in July. This was for the benefit of the pupils in their final term, and gave them a chance to be seen by agents and producers. One day after prayers Mr. Whitfield announced that the show would take place in four weeks' time, and, as an innovation, would not be held in the theatre but in the square outside.

"Weather permitting," he added with a wry smile. "And there will also be a chance for pupils other than the Finals to take part, as there will be a student production competition for a one-act play open to everyone. The best will be performed at the Public Show. Student producers should bear in mind the fact that it will be staged out-of-doors."

The Blue Doors sat in conclave on the grass in Regent's Park that evening, eating cherries.

" Of course everyone will do scenes from *A Midsummer Night's Dream*."

" Or *Twelfth Night*."

" Or *As You Like It*."

" Or even *The Tempest*."

" But they're all the obvious things," continued Nigel. " We must think of something original."

" What about Maeterlinck's *Blue Bird*?" suggested Vicky.

" A bit airy-fairy for us," objected Nigel. " I don't think I could produce it." They discussed this for some time, between competitions in cherry-stone spitting. At supper, over corned beef and a few tired lettuce leaves, Bulldog suggested a scene from *Treasure Island* and was immediately squashed. They retired to bed, still saying, " What do you think about such-and-such a play ? "

In the middle of the night Nigel leapt out of his bed with a glad cry, switched on the light, and shouted, " I've got it ! "

" What's the matter ? " growled Bulldog. " Don't you feel well ? "

" I'm fine ! " cried Nigel. " What do you think about *Tobias and the Angel* ? "

" Oh, not more angels ! " said Jeremy, blinking as he awoke. " Didn't we have enough of them at Easter ? "

" Yes—there's that to consider." Nigel's enthusiasm began to abate. He was about to switch off the light when there was a patter of feet along the passage and an urgent knock on the door. Lynette's excited face appeared round it saying, " What about the garden scene from *The Importance of Being Earnest* ? We've got the cast exactly."

Nigel reflected aloud, " You and Vicky for the two girls, Jeremy and I for Algernon and Jack. Sandra, Miss Prism, Bulldog—Chasuble. It's an idea."

"I'd love to play Algernon," came Jeremy's muffled voice from the depths of his bed.

"I'd *adore* to play Chasuble." Bulldog's imagination fired, he leaped out of bed and did what he thought was a Chasuble walk round the room. Two tousle-headed figures appeared at the door to inquire what was happening.

"And you could play Cecily, Vicky, and Sandra could play Miss Prism."

"Another character part," sighed Sandra. "Doomed to senility. Fifty if I'm a day!"

"But it's a gift of a part!" expostulated Lynette.

"Oh, yes," agreed Sandra. "A jewel."

"Wait a minute. I've got a copy of it!" and now Jeremy was out of bed and ferreting through the pile of books stacked up in the corner. "Yes! Here it is." Soon they were squatting round the gas fire that popped and flared, reading the scene delightedly, passing the one book from hand to hand, peering at it over each other's shoulders, and occasionally breaking out into hastily suppressed giggles.

"Lovely!" sighed Lynette. "Yes, I think we shall do it well."

"And the costumes will be fun," said Sandra.

"Nigel must produce, of course."

"And we must get some stray male in to play the butler." They were still discussing it excitedly when Mrs. Bosham's alarm went off at six o'clock, and they realized that they had only a couple of hours in which to sleep before the day's work.

They went to the Academy heavy-eyed, yet still infused with excitement at their idea. Nigel went straight to the office of Miss Smith, the secretary, and gave in their names for the contest. When she heard what they were doing she said, "Thank Heaven you're not doing *The Dream*!"

" Why, Miss Smith ? "

" Because everyone else is. There are five other casts, besides yours, entering, and four of them are doing *The Dream*. Yours will be a nice change."

Sandra went straight to the wardrobe to Mrs. Bertram, and told her of their decision.

" I thought I'd let you know well beforehand, Mrs. Bertram, because I know how busy you are."

" Busy, ducks ? I'm half crazy. Well, have you any line of costume you particularly fancy ? "

" Bright colours, I think," said Sandra, " as it's out of doors. And quite a lot of white."

" I'll see what I can do, deary, and I'll hold back anything I think may be useful."

" Don't bother about any alterations for us," continued Sandra. " I'll manage them. We've got four weeks."

For the next few weeks there were no more swimming expeditions or lazy Sundays on Hampstead Heath, for, as well as the normal amount of term's work, they were rehearsing their scene for the contest night and day.

" It must be subtle—slick—polished," Nigel would insist.

" And graceful," added Lyn, who never could help butting in on the production side. It had always been her job in the Blue Door Theatre, but now, somehow, Nigel's seniority seemed to make it his job.

" Yes, and graceful. Sandra, you must play more for comedy, and Bulldog—er—just a little less."

One evening Sandra came running up into the bedroom where they were rehearsing, her face pallid.

" Something awful has happened," she gasped.

" What's up ? "

" Mrs. Bosham wants to come to the Public Show ! "

" Oh, gosh, no ! "

53

"She said that she'd heard us 'practising' so hard that she'd love to come to the concert and see our 'little piece.'"

They looked at each other despairingly.

"We can't possibly tell her she can't."

"But everyone else will have their parents there—and there are going to be some awfully important people too," objected Lyn, "and she might wear that terrible feather boa arrangement."

"Oh, aren't we snobs!" sighed Sandra. "But it will be awful not to have any of our parents there—only one moth-eaten landlady."

"Hey! Wait a minute!" Bulldog cried suddenly. "We're talking as if we were in the show already. It's got to be chosen as the best, first of all."

"True, O King. But I think there's a pretty good chance of it, as we're doing something slightly different from the others."

"Oh, well, let's cross the Mrs. Bosham bridge when we come to it."

A few weeks later a notice appeared on the board saying, "After the Public Show there will be a Students' Dance in the Square. Tickets for students and visitors on sale in the Canteen."

"What fun!" cried Lyn. "I've never been to a real dance. Oh, we must be in the Public Show."

The heats for the student productions were held in the theatre a week before the Public Show. The Blue Doors had rehearsed and rehearsed until they were as near perfection as they could be under their own direction. Mrs. Bertram had come up to scratch and provided them with some gems of costumes. Vicky wore white and green, Lyn white and red, and Sandra a hideous creation of mauve velvet. The boys were very smart in stove-pipe trousers, and Bulldog's clerical black had a faintly green tinge of age. They had borrowed Billy, the little boy from the "theal act," to play the part of Merriman, the butler, in a very unsuccessful grey wig.

The four *Midsummer Night's Dream* scenes were performed first, with a galaxy of fairies in various coloured chiffons. The audience consisted only of the other entrants and the staff who were judging, but when their turn came the Blue Doors managed to extract quite a lot in the way of laughter from them. There was one awkward moment when Jeremy choked over his muffin, and they had to wait for about a minute while he gasped and spluttered and tears ran down his cheeks making little streaks on his "five and nine" grease paint. At the end the applause was considerable.

"But there's one more cast to play yet," Sandra reminded them. The last effort was by some of the Finals, and was a stark Irish drama in which everyone eventually got drowned. As it was performed by five Irish members of the Senior class it was convincing and extremely moving. Lyn and Sandra were soon both in tears, partly of emotion at the morbid drama, partly at disappointment in finding that their scene was not the best.

"They're so good!" sniffed Sandra, as the five Irish corpses resurrected to take the curtain. In the judges' box at the back of the hall Mrs. Seymore said, "Of course the Blue Door gang are quite good enough to be put on show."

"Yes, but there's not time for more than one student production. I'm afraid it must be the Finals' group. A pity —I wanted to give some of the juniors a chance—but one must be fair," said Mr. Whitfield firmly.

The Blue Doors took it with very good grace, as there was obviously no question as to which scene had been most effective. On the way home Sandra said, " Oh, well, we must just resign ourselves to enjoying the Public Show from the point of view of lookers-on."

" And then there's the dance," put in Vicky. " I know what ! It's Saturday to-morrow. Let's go out in the morning and be very daring and each buy a new dress."

" Ai shall choose a powder blue bombazine," minced Bulldog. " Just my shade, my dear ! "

Next morning they set out along Oxford Street, and tried every shop in their efforts to find something that would not make too much of a hole in their allowances. The assistants nearly had epileptic fits when, after trying on every dress in the shop, and parading in front of the boys, under a stream of caustic comment, the girls would smile sweetly and say, " Well, perhaps we'll leave it for to-day . . ."

At last they had all found what they wanted. Lynette had an emerald green short-sleeved suit, Vicky a little black silk creation, and Sandra a peasant skirt and chiffon blouse.

" And now for goodness sake let's have lunch ! I'm a nervous wreck," complained Jeremy. " Thank heavens I can wear my cords, same as usual ! "

They had lunch at a vegetarian restaurant just for a change, and between shredded carrot and sips of orange juice stole peeps at their new purchases. As consolation for not being in the show, Mr. Whitfield had asked the Blue Doors to sell programmes.

" So we shall be able to have a good look at everyone," remarked Lyn.

" And there'll be no Mrs. Bosham, plus feather boa," added Bulldog. " That's one good thing."

The day of the Public Show dawned bright and cloudless.

" Thank heavens ! " cried the Blue Doors, as they drew back their curtains. The morning was spent in slacks and

The Blue Doors in " The Importance of Being Earnest."

57

dungarees, helping to cart chairs into the square, and to decorate it with flags and fairy lights. There was no stage, only a terraced bank at the far end, and convenient bushes, behind which were erected little canvas tents to act as dressing-rooms. All the Finals were in a terrific state of tension. On this performance their futures depended. One student would win the Gold Medal, there were several other awards, but, above all, they would be seen by theatrical people and anything could happen.

"This time next year—it will be us taking part," said Sandra.

"I wish it were this year," grumbled Lyn, sweeping leaves off the lawn. "It's just the right sort of day for our *Importance* scene."

"Still, it'll be fun selling programmes," said Sandra.

"Gosh, look at the time!" shouted Vicky, who had been doing a few surreptitious acrobatics in a corner. "We must dash home and change."

Helter-skelter down Fitzherbert Street they ran, and bathed and changed and did each other's hair, and showed their new frocks to Mrs. Bosham, whose eyes nearly popped out of her head with sympathetic excitement. The boys merely damped down their hair with a little water and ran a brush carelessly over their shoes. They were back in the square, which was gay and spruce, before the first visitors arrived.

"It's like Sports Day at school," said Bulldog, "only even more exciting."

And then the guests arrived. Parents and friends, agents and producers, film stars and stage stars. Between handing out programmes the Blue Doors would whisper to each other, "Look! There's So-and-so."

Felicity Warren arrived, very smart in a summery dress

and a tiny hat. She spoke to Sandra for several minutes, telling her how the film was going, and how lively Maddy was.

" That was Felicity Warren ! " Sandra told Lyn, not without pride.

" So we saw. How lovely she is ! "

At last all were settled in their seats, the people who preferred the shade had changed places with those who liked the sun, and the Prologue was spoken. From their perch in one of the tall trees the Blue Doors were enjoying the show, but not without a touch of disappointment at not being in it. The Finals all acquitted themselves nobly, and the square echoed to the laughter, applause, and music.

Before the student production, which was the last item, there seemed to be a hitch. The interval music was played over and over again. Mr. Whitfield, with an harassed expression, kept popping back and forwards between the canvas dressing-tents. Finally, one of the first-termers came running up to the Blue Doors' tree.

" Mr. Whitfield wants you back-stage," she gasped.

" All of us ? What on earth for ? "

They trooped across the grass stage under the curious eyes of the audience. Mr. Whitfield greeted them wryly.

" You'll have to go on after all," he told them. " Three of our Irish friends had lobster for lunch, and are being very ill in the shrubbery."

" Oh, dear ! " said Sandra. " It must have been off."

" Very," agreed Mr. Whitfield. " But there's no time for dietetic details. Run over to the Academy and get your costumes from Mrs. Bertram, and get back here as soon as you can. Don't bother about make-up. You don't need it in daylight. I'll see about setting the stage, and the muffins, and such like. Off you go ! "

Single file, at a canter, they set off again, breaking through the bushes to get to the Academy. Mrs. Bertram received them imperturbably.

" What a life it is, eh ? " she said, and pinned them into their costumes with deft fingers. The girls held their skirts high above their ankles, and ran full pelt back to the square, followed by the boys, still tying their cravats. There was no time to check their props, no time to be nervous, no time even to powder their noses. They were on, and the cream of the London theatre was in the audience.

Sandra and Vicky, the first to appear, hardly became conscious during the first five minutes, and their voices were rather uncertain through breathlessness. With the entrance of Bulldog as " Chasuble " the scene woke up, and there were several good laughs. Although they had not rehearsed for a week their previous hard work was rewarded, and they were as slick as Nigel could wish. When Lyn swept in, complete with parasol and beflowered hat, several members of the audience sat up saying, " Who's that ? " and looked in vain for her name on the programme. The muffin business went down very well, and at the end, when they took their bows and disappeared through the bushes, the applause roused the sleepy square. Some of the students even cheered.

In the stuffy canvas dressing-room the girls fell on each other's necks almost weeping with relief.

" Oh, my knees are trembling so ! " Lyn fell into a deck chair and mopped her brow. Mr. Whitfield came up and pumped their hands.

" Good show ! " was all he could say. " Good show ! You really saved the situation."

Felicity Warren appeared in the door of the tent.

" May I come in ? Congratulations, Blue Doors ! " she

61

said. " I'm going back to Fenchester and the film to-morrow, and I shall tell Maddy what clever friends she's got."

Then the rest of the students overflowed into the tent, and the Blue Doors were drowned in a sea of " Darlings ! How brave ! " " But however *could* you ? "

Even the grey-faced Irish invalids turned up to thank them. And, incredibly, there was Mrs. Bosham, flaunting her mangy boa, and somehow it didn't seem to matter.

" Just 'appened to be passing. And, well I never. You could've knocked me over with a feather ! "

Their friends plied them with lemonade, ices, and strawberries, and they soon felt restored enough to go over to the Academy wardrobe and remove their Edwardian finery.

In the square the radiogram was playing dance tunes, and, soft-footed on the grass, the students danced. Most of the celebrities had departed, and the fairy lights were lit as dusk fell. All the windows in the square were alight, and dark figures leaned out, watching the dancers. The Blue Doors were the heroes of the hour, and were danced off their feet, until the square and the plane trees and the tall grey houses reeled round them, and the evening breeze blew through their hair.

At last the radiogram played " Good-night, Sweetheart." The fairy lights were extinguished, and it was time to wander home through the darkening streets, tired, yet unwilling to end a golden day.

CHAPTER V

BEGINNERS, PLEASE !

AFTER the excitement of the Public Show the usual end-of-term performances in the theatre seemed rather an anti-climax, and the Blue Doors were inclined to rest on their laurels. The holidays came ever nearer, and Sandra got excited about returning to her filming.

"And what are *we* going to do in the holidays ? " demanded Bulldog.

"Work ! " came a chorus of voices.

"But where ? "

"We really ought to try to get into reps," said Nigel, " to see how a professional company is run."

"But who'd have us ? "

"We can but try." That evening they sat round the large dining-table at No. 37, armed with pens and ink and imposing notepaper, and photos of themselves.

"I wish we had a typewriter ! " sighed Bulldog, after he had written his first three letters. "From my writing it looks as if it's a slightly rheumatic spider who's applying for the job."

"It's awful to apply for a job and have to say that you've not had any professional experience at all," grumbled Lynette. "I almost wish I'd been like Billy—part of a ' theal act ' ever since I could walk."

During the next week Mrs. Bosham would appear at breakfast clutching several large envelopes and say, " Well, I never did ! What a lot of post for you again ! " And although the Blue Doors opened each letter with trembling hands, they knew that they would only find their own some-what battered photos and a brief note from the secretary of a repertory company saying that they would be " put in the files " and " borne in mind."

" It's quite obvious that with our lack of experience we shall never get a job," growled Lynette.

" But how *do* people get their first jobs ? " asked Vicky. " One must start somewhere."

Then one morning Lynette and Vicky received identical envelopes with red crests on the outside, and inside the most beautiful letters they had ever seen :

" If you are willing to assistant stage manage a ten-week season with this company at a nominal salary of two pounds ten shillings a week, and a chance of playing small parts, we should be glad to see you about 29th July. Please let us know as soon as possible."

Vicky and Lynette looked at each other.

" Is yours the same ? "

" Yes. A rep. at Tutworth Wells." They giggled inanely with excitement, and handed the letters round to the others.

" A *very* nominal salary ! " remarked Nigel, not with-out envy.

" But why did they pick on you two ? " Bulldog queried. " We all wrote."

" Liked our photos, I suppose," said Lynette smugly.

" More likely they thought they'd choose two rather silly-looking young females so that they could offer them a ridiculously low salary," suggested Jeremy.

" I do think you're beastly ! " flared Lynette. " It's a wonderful piece of luck, even if the pay is bad."

" Yes, we're only envious," Bulldog admitted.

" Oh, well, you'll just have to tell them that you've got

three no-good brothers on the dole to keep, so they must raise your salary."

But next day the boys were invited by Mr. Whitfield to go on a schools tour of *Julius Cæsar*.

"We're only playing odd citizens and messengers," said Bulldog. "But it will be something to do."

The night before Sandra went home and the two girls departed for Tutworth Wells, in the depths of the Midlands, they had a little celebration at a Chinese restaurant in Soho. Choosing at random from the mysterious menu they found that they had ordered a meal large enough for ten, but somehow it all disappeared.

"I never wish to see another noodle," gasped Bulldog, leaning back heavily. The little almond-eyed waiter brought them pale China tea in tiny dolls' cups, which they pronounced delicious, although secretly it struck them all as rather resembling dish-water. There was a tinny, four-piece band, consisting of a negro drummer, a Chinese pianist, an Indian trombonist, and a Cockney trumpeter who occasionally crooned through a rather crackly microphone. There was a pocket handkerchief space in which to dance, and this was crowded with young people of every nationality.

"I suppose we've got to dance," remarked Jeremy unenthusiastically.

"Yes," said Sandra firmly. "But no jitterbugging, Vicky and Bulldog. There isn't room."

"I could no more jitterbug in my present condition than I could fly." They stayed until the restaurant closed, just to be sure of getting their money's worth, and then split the bill scrupulously between the six of them.

"I hate leaving London," remarked Lynette on the way home. "Even though it's only for ten weeks and I'm very keen to go."

" Think what it will be like in about a year's time, when we leave for good," reminded Jeremy.

" Oh, don't ! I shan't be able to bear it."

" Even Mrs. Bosham's seems lovable when one's about to leave it."

But next day the excitement of packing and catching the train obliterated any sorrow at leaving London. First they all saw Sandra off at Victoria.

" Don't break the camera ! " they shouted rudely as the train steamed out. Then the boys saw Lyn and Vicky off at Paddington.

" Good ' Cæsar-ing ' ! " Lynette wished them.

" H'm ! We'll never make our names by shouting ' Hail, Cæsar ! ' "

" And mind you insist on playing small parts," Nigel said paternally. " Don't slave away A.S.M.-ing all the summer for nothing."

" And don't be rash with your wages ! " Bulldog teased.

" Well, at least we shall be *working* for ours ! "

As the train drew out of the station they waved from the window, then sank back into their corners and looked at each other.

" Funny not to see them again for ten whole weeks. Just you and I. We've never been away for so long before, since we met." They watched the rows of grey little houses slipping by, then the factories, and on out into the country-side, and bound for Tutworth Wells.

" I wonder what sort of place it is," Vicky speculated.

" I should imagine it's very respectable if it's a spa," said Lynette. " Dowagers in bath chairs and all that sort of thing." Vicky wriggled in her seat.

" Oh, I'm so excited ! How long do you think this slow train will take ? "

" I wish we knew more about real stage-management," said Lynette. " We've never done any at the Academy, and at the Blue Door Theatre it was all rather hit-or-miss."

" And we usually left it to the boys."

Throughout the journey they tried to read, but their eyes kept wandering from the pages and meeting, which made them giggle excitedly.

"I wonder if there will be anyone to meet us ?" said Vicky.

" I don't expect so. A.S.M.'s are such a low form of life I don't suppose they'll bother. Anyway, we didn't let them know what train we were coming by."

The station at Tutworth Wells was remarkably neat and clean for a station. But there was no-one to meet them. They lugged their cases out and decided to leave them in the left luggage office for the time being until they had found digs.

" But first let's find the theatre. That's the most important." They set off through the wide airy streets with little flowering gardens on either side. There were many elderly people in bath chairs as Lyn had prophesied, but also quite a large percentage of younger holiday-makers. There seemed to be hundreds of hotels and boarding-houses, and the shops were attractive.

" I think," said Lyn, " I like it here."

" Let's ask the way to the theatre," suggested Vicky, and stopped at the next policeman.

" Ah—you'd be wanting the rep. Good show there this week," he remarked as he directed them.

" Seems popular," observed Lyn.

The theatre was small and rather ugly, fronted with red brick. It was called the Pavilion and the play billed was *George and Margaret.* They studied the photos outside with interest.

"I don't know the names of any of them," said Lyn, "or the faces."

"Ought we to go in through the front of the theatre or through the stage door ? " puzzled Vicky. Lyn thought they should go through the stage door. Vicky thought the front entrance would be better. Finally, they could not find the stage door, so they had to enter past the box office and through the door marked " Stalls." Inside, the theatre was dim, with only a working light on the stage where a rehearsal was in progress. A pale-faced young man and a rather pretty girl were going through a love scene somewhat half-heartedly. Every few minutes they dried up and either stopped despairingly and said " Sorry," or threw a brusque "Yes ? " to someone in the wings who gave them the line in a muffled voice.

Lyn and Vicky slipped into seats at the back of the auditorium and drank it in. Just as all seemed to be going well for a few minutes, both the people dried up and shouted " Yes " and " Please " in vexed tones, but no reply came from the prompter. Someone sitting in the front row of the stalls jumped up angrily.

"*Where* is the prompter ? " she cried. " Is there no-one on the book ? " There was still dead silence.

"Well, I mean—we can't go on like this," the pale youth muttered sulkily. " And whoever's that at the back ? " The three members of the company all turned and stared accusingly at Lynette and Vicky. Lyn plucked up her courage and stepped into the gangway. Her voice quavered slightly as she said, " Please, we're the new assistant stage managers."

"Thank heavens ! For goodness' sake get into the wings and prompt, will you, dear ? " Lyn was handed a tattered script and she mounted the wooden steps on to the stage.

"How lovely to see an assistant stage manager!" said the pretty girl. "And *two* of them—amazing!" The tall woman, who appeared to be producing, called back to Vicky, "Would you like to go round into the yard and help Terry with some painting?"

"Yes," said Vicky helplessly.

"Well, go by that little door and you'll find him." She pointed vaguely and returned to the rehearsal.

For the next three hours Lynette prompted until her eyes swam so that the print danced about uncontrollably, and she thought she would faint with hunger. Out in the yard Vicky found a lanky youth with a fringe like a Shetland pony's over his eyes, slamming brown paint on to a piece of scenery.

"Er—hullo. I'm one of the new A.S.M.'s. I've been sent to help you." Immediately he handed her the brush and said, "Oh, then you might as well be getting on with that. I've got some designs to do." And for the rest of the afternoon he sat comfortably on a packing-case, with a cigarette hanging out of his mouth, drawing vague sketches on a block, and directing Vicky's painting efforts. Her best suit, which she had worn to travel in, became more and more spattered with paint, until she was almost in tears of vexation and hunger.

When the rehearsal broke up, the producer fetched Vicky in and said to her and Lyn, "Well, we're very glad to see you. We've only had one person on the stage-management side for the past few weeks and it's been pretty ghastly." She was tall and swarthy, about thirty-five, and wore her dark hair in braids round her head. She had about her an air that was always abstract, as if she were trying to think about several things at once, as indeed she was.

"You both look very young. How old are you?"

69

" Seventeen," they chorused indignantly.

" You've not done any A.S.M.-ing before, have you ? "

" No," they admitted, shamefaced.

" Oh, well, Jean will soon break you in. She's the stage manager. You'll see her to-night. She seems to have disappeared at the moment. The curtain goes up at eight. So be here by seven, as there are sure to be lots of odd jobs to be done, as it's only the second night of this week's show. Where are you staying ? "

" We're not staying anywhere yet."

" Well, you'll have a bit of a job, I warn you. The town is packed. You might try at the Parade Private Hotel. It's a bit grim, but quite clean." When they got outside they saw that it was five-thirty.

" So our time is our own until seven," said Lyn.

" I'm *so* hungry," groaned Vicky. " Let's eat first. I cannot dig-hunt on an empty stomach."

" Yes," agreed Lyn. " Mine is absolutely concave."

All the cafés looked very arty-crafty, and advertised " dainty teas."

" I'm not in the mood for lavender and old lace," said Lyn. " Let's find somewhere where we can let ourselves go."

In a slightly less respectable quarter of the town they found a fish-and-chip shop, and in the greasy dining-room they consumed a large quantity, washed down with plenty of strong, sweet tea in thick cups.

" Oh, I feel better ! " sighed Vicky. " Gosh. I've worked hard this afternoon ! I ache all over."

" And now to find somewhere to rest our heads."

This seemed an impossibility. Everywhere was filled with visitors and invalids. One of the large hotels would have put them up at eight guineas a week each, but they had to refuse and walk ignominiously out of the gilt and stuccoed building. At last, weary and footsore, they reached the Parade Private Hotel. "Family and Commercial" it said outside ; but seated in the lounge window was a collection of old ladies who looked too good to be true.

" I'm sure they're stuffed ! " whispered Lynette, as they rang the bell. The door was opened by an old lady in a white starched uniform that made her look like a hospital matron. When they asked if there were any vacant accommodation she said disapprovingly, " I shouldn't think so, but I'll just ask Miss Blackman."

She disappeared into the gloom, and Lyn and Vicky fidgeted on the doorstep under a battery of lorgnetted stares from the window.

" We're fifty years too young for this place," remarked Vicky. At last Miss Blackman appeared, wearing a velvet band round her throat, and looking as if she had swallowed a poker.

" Well ? "

" We're from the theatre," Lynette began, proudly, but it was quite the wrong approach.

" Oh, dear ! " said Miss Blackman. " I do dislike having you people. Such late hours—I like to lock the doors at ten o'clock."

" Oh, I see ! " Lynette said forlornly, and leaned against the doorpost. Vicky felt like sitting on the step and taking her shoes off.

" Come on, Lyn ! " she said. " It's almost seven. We shall quite obviously have to sleep in the gutter."

The idea of this seemed to trouble Miss Blackman. She thought again.

" Well, if you wouldn't mind sharing, I might be able to put you up in an attic."

"Anywhere," breathed Lynette. "The coal-hole will do."

They followed her up many flights of stairs lined with heavy oil paintings of ugly ancestors, to a small attic at the top of the house. It contained two rather hard-looking little beds and a wash-basin.

"Three guineas all in," she announced. It seemed a lot, but "all in" sounded comforting.

"Thank you," said Lyn. "Our luggage is at the station. Could it be fetched?" Miss Blackman looked aghast.

"Oh, no! We haven't the staff! This is the Season, you see." She spoke of it in capital letters. When she had gone they looked wistfully at the beds.

"No. It's nearly seven o'clock," said Lynette firmly.

There was only time to wash their faces and dry them on the counterpane, as there were no towels provided, before they set off for the theatre once more. As they entered by the stage door they were greeted by a lumpy female wearing a turban and dirty dungarees. She surveyed them without enthusiasm.

"New A.S.M.'s?" she inquired brusquely.

"Yes."

"I'm the stage manager. My name is Jean. What are yours?" They told her their names shyly.

"Academy?" They nodded.

"Hm! I was at the Crosby-Wade School. Well, you'd better get cracking. I want the stage swept and dusted first. There are some old overalls behind the door in that dressing-room. You'd better put them on."

"What we go through for our art!" murmured Lyn, brushing away at the torn carpet that seemed to stretch for miles.

" So many times I've told my mother I wanted to go on the stage, even if only to sweep it, and now I'm doing it ! "

When it was finished Jean set them to polishing silver, which had obviously not been done for some time.

" Now I'll show you how to check the props." She handed them a typed list under the headings, " Off right," " Off Left," " On Stage," " Plant for Act Two," " Strike for Act Three," that completely bewildered them, and went round with them seeing that everything was in its correct place. There seemed to be hundreds of meals in the play, entailing trays of imitation foodstuffs that all had to be carefully checked, as one missing plate could ruin a piece of " business."

" Run and call the half-hour, Lynette," the stage manager ordered. " Knock on all the doors, or they'll say they didn't hear." Timidly Lynette tapped on each dressing-room door and said, " Half an hour, please." The usual reply was, " Oh, bother ! " or " Not already." Hurrying figures in wrappers with half-made-up faces flitted from one dressing-room to another, and stared at the new members of the company with interest. The quarter of an hour was called, then the five minutes. " It's time to start the panatrope." Jean showed them how it worked, and put on a record of a dance tune that soon blared out over the audience, who sat talking and eating chocolates and rustling programmes.

" Watch for the buzz," Vicky was told as she stood in the prompt corner.

" Watch for the buzz ? What buzz ? Where ? " she thought frantically.

" Beginners, please ! " Jean shouted in stentorian tones. And a little buzzer buzzed in the prompt corner.

" It buzzed ! It buzzed ! " cried Vicky wildly.

73

" Take the curtain up, then.—Here ! Press that button."

Vicky pressed it with all her might. And miraculously the heavy curtain rose. It was not for some minutes that she realized that the button-pressing had caused a little red light to go on on the other side of the stage, which was the signal for a stage hand to wind away at an enormous handle. Vicky felt a terrific surge of power as she stood in the prompt corner with Jean showing her how to control the house lights, while Lynette sat with her eyes glued to the prompt book, trembling lest anyone on the stage should falter. In between each act there was sheer chaos. Terry, the boy who had been painting scenery, and two decrepit stage hands, appeared to help change the set, but Lyn and Vicky carried " flats " and hammered in " braces " with the enthusiasm of novelty. There was no time to notice the other members of the company, nor what the show was like. It was " Lynette, run and wash these cups up." " Vicky, take the book for a minute." " One of you pop round to the front of the house with this message, please."

The play seemed to be going well, for the audience were laughing considerably, and Lynette did just notice that the players were well dressed. There was one hitch when the leading man opened his cigarette case and found no cigarette there. He made his exit smiling gaily, but once in the wings he turned on Jean in a fury. " Why did you let me go on without a cigarette ? "

" If you're not capable of taking a cigarette out of the prop box and putting it in your case, I'm sorry for you ! " she replied tartly. He snorted, muttered something about " These women stage managers," and strode off. Jean grimaced. " That's the sort of thing you have to put up with," she remarked. " All the kicks and *no* halfpence. Not even thanks when everything goes all right."

74

" What a horrible man ! Who is he ? "

" Mark Gregory, our *dear* leading man, bless his little silk socks ! "

Vicky and Lynette changed records on the panatrope, brought the curtains up and down, and even helped the leading lady in a quick change. At last it was time for the final curtain to be brought down, and there was a jumble of lighting to be changed, the time to be noted down in the time book, and the whole set to be moved, ready for to-morrow's matinée. It was about eleven o'clock when Jean finally said, " You'd better run round to the stalls bar while there are still some sandwiches left."

In the saloon the whole company were assembled, eating sandwiches. When they entered, the producer, whose name they had discovered to be Diana, said, " Oh, here are our two new ewe lambs, Lynette and Vicky. Be nice to them. They're so hard to get." Everyone laughed, and the two girls covered their confusion by purchasing orangeade and sausage rolls from the bar.

The youngish girl whom they had seen rehearsing that afternoon came up to them and said, " I hear you're at the Academy. I was there two years ago. How is everyone ? Old Whitfield, Roma, etc. ? "

They told her all the latest Academy news, which seemed to interest her.

" These Academy folk ! Always hang together, don't they ? " laughed the character woman, a plump, pleasant person of fifty or more. " I was there—about thirty years ago—so that dates me, I'm afraid."

" Are you going to play any parts ? " Chloe, the girl, wanted to know.

" We hope so."

" Well, we're doing *The Constant Nymph* in a few weeks'

75

time, so I hear. There are enough young parts in that. You're bound to get something."

" *The Constant Nymph* ! " breathed Lynette. " Oh, how simply wonderful ! "

" I suppose you've always longed to play " Tessa " in it ? Haven't we all ? " laughed Chloe.

" I'm the only woman in the company who won't be envious of it," laughed the character woman.

At this moment a grey-haired man wearing pince-nez came into the bar, and was saluted with respect.

" That's the boss," Chloe enlightened them. " He's Diana's father. Handles the business side." After a while he came up and spoke to them, more kindly than anyone had done throughout the whole day.

" I'm very glad to see you both. I hope you will be happy with us and learn a lot."

" Thank you, sir," they said.

" How long have you been on the stage ? " he inquired.

" Well, this is our first professional engagement," Lyn explained. " We're still at Dramatic School, you see."

" Ah, of course. I forgot. So you're only with us for ten weeks ? A pity."

Before the last lights in the theatre were switched off and the doors locked Jean said to them, " Rehearsal is at ten to-morrow, but be here by 9.30. There are a hundred and one things to do."

On their way back to the hotel Lyn said suddenly, " You know what ? "

" What ? "

" Our cases are at the station."

" Oh, gosh ! Don't let's bother——"

" But our washing things ! Even our tooth-brushes, and our slacks for to-morrow——"

"And hair-brushes," agreed Vicky. "Oh, how awful ! And our cases are so heavy !"

"I wish the boys were here. We could send them. They'd grumble—but they'd go."

They trailed down the long road to the station, almost numb with tiredness, only to find the left luggage office shut. It meant a long argument with a half-witted porter before the key could be found and their cases extracted. They stumbled back to the hotel, with frequent intervals of sitting on their cases, looking at the moon, saying, "Oh, why do we do it !"

"Why didn't we decide to be school teachers ?"

"Or clerks ?"

"Or merely to sit at home and wait for 'Mr. Right' to come along." But although they said these things, beyond their fatigue there was a feeling that something very exciting was starting, and that Tutworth Wells held out opportunities of work and experience and Life with a capital L.

On the hall table of the Parade Hotel (Family and Commercial) there was a note saying, "Please lock doors and see lights out.—Emily Blackman."

They toiled up the stairs with their cases, but then were too tired to make much use of the tooth-brushes, sponges, and hair-brushes which they had rescued. Lyn's last words before she fell into a deep sleep were, "Rehearsal to-morrow at 9.30. Oh, gosh !"

CHAPTER VI

THE ENVIOUS NYMPHS

IN Tutworth Wells it was high summer. The streets flocked with holiday-makers, and there were queues to book at the box-office of the Pavilion Theatre. Even the Wednesday matinées were packed out to the doors. And while the young people on holiday in the town swam in the river, played tennis, listened to the music round the bandstand, and went to the theatre in the cool of the evenings, Vicky and Lynette worked harder than they had ever worked before.

Inevitably, every morning, they over-slept. The decrepit chamber-maid seemed incapable of calling them at the correct hour. They would leap out of bed, fling on the workman's blue dungarees they had invested in for comfort and coolness, and dash down to the dining-room, where the waitress would infuriate them by serving watery haddock and cold toast at a snail's pace. Consequently they had to run down the hill to the theatre in time to set the stage ready for the morning's rehearsal. While one of them held the prompt book, the other would be despatched round the town to collect properties. Vicky and Lyn were soon known in the town as being "from the theatre" and were welcomed by the shopkeepers in varying manners. From their ingratiating smiles and remarks about the weather, it was always obvious that they were "on the scrounge."

"Well—what is it *this* time?" the ironmonger would inquire, assuming a fierce air.

" I *wonder*, Mr. Cardew, *could* you, *would* it be possible—to lend us a wheelbarrow ? "

Mr. Cardew would wooffle into his moustache, and disappear into the jumble at the back of his shop, and soon Lyn or Vicky would be wheeling a barrow proudly through the streets of Tutworth Wells. But in some shops the welcome was very different.

" Ah—yes. We've lent things to the theatre before now —and never seen them back."

" But we're different people. We'd be sure to bring them back. "

" Ah ! That's what they all say." And it would need a lot of reassuring, and perhaps a complimentary seat for the show, before the wireless set, or the tin bath, or the rolling pin would be lent.

Terry, the vague young scenic artist, was always needing a hand with the painting of the set. There were last week's costumes to be packed up and despatched to the costumier's in London, and next week's furniture to be sorted, and re-covered and disguised. Occasionally the girls had an hour to spare between tea and the evening show, and they would fling themselves on the grass of one of the parks, and doze over next week's prop list. Saturday nights were the worst, for after the evening show the set had to be taken to pieces, the furniture lugged to the store-room, and the properties returned to the prop-room. They were lucky if they reached the Parade Hotel before midnight. Sunday mornings were occasionally free from rehearsal, and they slept until lunch-time, did odd jobs at the theatre in the afternoon, and went on the river in the evening. They would try to get to bed early, but Sunday was a favourite night for members of the company to throw parties, and Lyn and Vicky were invited to several of these. After an extremely noisy and late night, it was awful to have to rise early on Monday morning, with the nightmare prospect of a dress rehearsal that would last all day, and the first night of a new play in the evening. And, then, on Tuesday, rehearsals of the next play would begin.

"Oh, it's a vicious circle!" cried Lynette, as on a Tuesday night she vainly studied two different prop lists, and carried three different play scripts around with her.

But in spite of the hard work they were happy. Here was the enthusiasm and team spirit of the Blue Door Theatre and the Academy, but on a larger and grown-up scale. Granted, the company all adopted a rather *blasé* air towards their profession, and often spoke of it as merely a money-making concern, or discussed taking up other careers, but on a Monday night there was the same atmosphere of striving and achievement that exists from Tutworth Wells to Drury Lane.

Although Jean ranted at them when things went wrong, she soon became attached to Lyn and Vicky and did her best to teach them all there was to learn. But when Vicky messed up a lighting cue by turning all the lights *off* when someone in the play remarked, "I'll just turn the lights *on*," or when Lynette forgot to put a wedge in the folding legs of the table and it folded up as the hero leaned amorously across it to the heroine, these things made Jean come out with a stream of unkind epithets that reduced Vicky to tears and made Lynette seethe with anger at her own stupidity. But it was soon forgotten after the first flare-up, and Jean would buy them corned-beef sandwiches after the show as a peace-offering.

Week followed week, and still there was no sign of the "small parts" mentioned in the letter. Diana, the producer, and her father had a system whereby the taste of the Tutworth holiday-makers and their own slightly more intellectual tastes were both satisfied. One week was a " dope " week, in which they performed a light modern comedy, likely to please the audience, and during the next week they did some more original play that the company would enjoy.

One Saturday night, after an interesting week of rehearsing Ibsen's *The Wild Duck*, Lyn said, " I believe next week's cast list is up. Let's go and look."

" Oh, it's only a dope week," said Vicky, but followed Lyn to the notice-board.

" Cast for *The Constant Nymph*," it read. All the parts were cast except Tessa, Antonia, Paulina, and Kate, the four girls.

" There will be a reading for these parts on Sunday afternoon at two-thirty. Will Chloe Pettinger, Lynette Darwin, Vicky Halford, and Ingrid Ringman please attend." They gazed spellbound at this notice and read and re-read it.

" There are four parts," Lyn began, wonderstruck.

" And only four names," finished Vicky.

" That means we've *got* to play something."

" Oh, Lyn, how wonderful ! How wonderful ! "

" Chloe is sure to play Tessa," said Lyn. " She plays all the *ingénues*."

" But even to play Kate—or Paulina."

" You're sure to play Paulina, Vicky, you look so young."

" I wish we'd got some scripts. D'you think they've arrived yet ? "

" Let's go and see." They ran down to Diana's office, and she handed them much dog-eared copies of the play.

" D'you think you'll be able to play parts next week as well as stage-manage ? " she asked.

" Oh, yes ! " they cried, fearing lest this opportunity should be snatched away.

" Good. Well, we'll sort you out to-morrow afternoon."

All the next morning they lay in bed reading the four girls' parts aloud, but always returning to the part of Tessa, the ill-fated little schoolgirl. The ancient chambermaid kept appearing in the doorway, anxious to " do " their room.

" We'll make our beds," they reassured her loudly on account of her deafness.

" Got bad heads ? " she misunderstood them. " Well they'll be better when you get out in the air."

" It's no good," said Vicky despairingly. " We'll have to get up." They went outside into the park and sprawled near the bandstand, where the Tutworth Wells Civic Band was playing military music with a lot of very brassy instruments. Lyn buried her face in the grass and repeated some of Tessa's lines that she had already learned by heart, and the band pounded away at the *Marche Militaire.*

They could hardly eat the cold mutton and rice and prunes of which lunch consisted.

By this time they were quite friendly with several of the old ladies in the hotel, who would engage them in long conversations at the slightest provocation. They were sure that one of them, whom they had christened Hepzibah, had been stage-struck in her youth, for she would pump them for the minutest details about their work and sigh wistfully as they described it. To-day she opened up and became quite informative.

" You know, I had a brother who was very interested in theatricals and all that sort of thing, and one day he had an offer from Mr. Hayden Coffin, of whom you have probably heard. But my mother was very strict and she said, ' No, Walter. Rather than see you with Mr. Coffin, I'd see you *in* your coffin ! ' And within six months he was ! *Wasn't* that a funny thing ? " Lyn and Vicky, with their mouths full of prunes, tried not to laugh, and agreed that it was. "Hepzibah" was full of morbid stories of the deaths of her relations.

"I saw you sitting out on the grass this morning. You know that's not at all a wise thing to do. Oh, no ! Now a second cousin of mine who lived at Chiswick once sat on the damp grass on a Sunday, and the following Sunday we went to her funeral." Lyn and Vicky registered interest, and hastily excused themselves to get down to the theatre for the reading.

Diana was there with her father and Mark, the leading man, looking handsome in flannels that were just too light and a tie that was just too bright. The other two girls, Chloe and Ingrid, both appearing very confident, read Tessa first. Chloe had played so many *ingénues* in her months at Tutworth that she made Tessa sound just like all the rest. Ingrid read it well, but appeared rather tall for the part.

"We can do it better than that ! " Lyn kept whispering to Vicky, who was feeling sick with nerves. Lyn read next, and put all she knew into it. When she had finished, Diana's father said, " Very nice." Vicky was terribly nervous and stumbled and fluffed all over the place. She knew that she had lost all chance of playing Tessa.

"Thank you, everyone," said Diana. " Pop and I will have a little confab about it, and we'll put the complete cast up to-morrow morning."

Going out of the stage door Lyn and Vicky heard Chloe say to Ingrid, " I've got a scream of a gym tunic to wear if I play Tessa, and if you play it, you can borrow it, if you like."

"It'll shake them if one of us plays it," Vicky remarked softly. That evening it was hard to settle to anything, and they wandered aimlessly about the hotel and the park.

83

"Our one free evening—and we just squander it."

It was quite a relief when they saw Terry puffing up the road towards them, his hair almost completely hiding his vague eyes.

"For goodness' sake come down to the theatre and help me!" he implored. "The set will never be ready for dress rehearsal to-morrow."

"My goodness," Lyn told him. "I could paint ten sets in the time you take to do one."

But somehow, as they splashed paint about in the court-yard behind the theatre, they were happier and thought less of to-morrow's cast list.

Next day they were up before the ancient chambermaid had mumbled outside their door. They gulped down the watery coffee and toast, and could not stay to dissect the herrings. But when they arrived, panting, at the theatre, the cast list was still as it had been on Saturday, with the four vacant spaces.

"Let's tidy the prop-room," sighed Vicky. "It will pass the time."

"There's certainly plenty of scope for tidying!"

The prop-room, which was approached by a wooden ladder, was in a little attic built over the stage. One could look down through the cracks in the floor into the wings. Lyn and Vicky were soon covered in dust and cobwebs as they piled up old books and pictures of all descriptions. There were a few old hats, which they tried on each other, giggling and making silly faces. Lyn found a piece of paper on which was scrawled in a large, childish hand, "Progress on the stage is often crab-like, and little parts, big parts, and no parts at all must be accepted as 'all in the day's work.'— Ellen Terry in her memoirs."

"Listen to this!" she cried, and read it. "I wonder

who copied that out? Some previous little A.S.M., I suppose."

"It's a jolly good motto," said Vicky. "I've been madly crab-like so far."

They had momentarily forgotten *The Constant Nymph*, when Chloe's voice floated up through the floor boards.

"Well, I'll be blowed! Ingrid, come here! The cast list has gone up, and—that Lynette is playing Tessa."

"Lynette!" Ingrid's voice chimed in. "Why, it's crazy! That kid has never played a really long role in her life. She'll never do it."

"Oh, won't I, Miss Pettinger!" Lyn breathed softly.

"And the other one is playing Paulina. Oh, it's too awful!"

"What am I playing?" demanded Ingrid from her dressing-room.

"Kate."

"Oh, bother! She's an awful drear! And you're playing Antonia?"

"Yes. It's a nice little part, even if it is short."

"But you ought to be playing Tessa."

"I know. I was engaged to play *ingénues*—and if Tessa isn't an *ingénue*—what is?" Their voices merged into discontented mumblings.

"So it's like that, is it?" said Vicky, turning to Lyn with a pale face. "Oh, whatever shall we do, Lyn?"

"Do? Our best, of course. We can't do any more. I suppose we should feel the same if someone younger and less experienced than us took our opportunities."

It was hard to concentrate on the dress rehearsal of *The Wild Duck*, and Lyn and Vicky missed "noises off" and lighting cues.

"If it's bad this week, it will be worse next week, when

we're all three playing," seethed Jean, and ranted on about the inefficiency of A.S.M.'s, the bad policy of the theatre, and the poor salaries. But the first performance that evening went off with as much ease as was possible, after the brief week's rehearsal.

" And this time next week," Lyn whispered to Vicky, " we shall have made our first professional appearance."

" Oh, gosh, I shall never learn Tessa in a week, and all the stage management, too."

" Don't worry," Vicky said valiantly. " I've got piles less to learn than you, so you needn't bother about the stage management. I'll cope all right."

" Thanks, ducky. Oh, how I wish I'd got a whole term to study it in ! And to think that at the Academy, with all the time in the world, we usually only have one scene of a play each ! "

" I'm dreading the first rehearsal to-morrow, aren't you ? " said Vicky. " Though *you* read all right. My tongue never seems to do what I want it to."

Next day at the reading everything seemed to go at a terrific speed, and very often they had not enough time to write in their moves in pencil on the battered scripts. Mark was playing Lewis Dodd, and seemed affronted at having to play opposite a mere A.S.M. He sighed heavily whenever she stopped to make sure of any certain point with Diana, and tapped his cigarette testily on his elegant gold cigarette case. Chloe and Ingrid didn't seem to take the rehearsal at all seriously, and clowned about until everyone got the giggles, including Diana. But Lyn and Vicky were too harassed and anxious to join in.

" Don't worry, dear," Diana said kindly to Lyn afterwards. " You're going to be quite all right. I'll try to get in some extra rehearsal for you and Mark."

" And won't Mark *love* that ! " thought Lynette.

After the evening performance Lyn and Vicky took their sandwiches home and ate them in bed as they learned their first-act lines ready for rehearsal next day. It was past two by the time they could reel them off.

" Like parrots ! " said Lynette bitterly. " Oh, it's a wicked system ! I take my hat off to all the poor wretches who've been playing big parts in rep. week in and week out."

There was hardly time to write to the Blue Doors to tell them of her piece of luck. By Friday Lynette felt that she had her lines, but knew that she was going through her part like a puppet. By this time Chloe and Ingrid, and even the character woman, appeared to be thoroughly bored by the play, and were constantly chatting in corners, and missing entrances. Vicky was always being sent off on errands concerning the stage-management, and missing rehearsal of her scenes. On Saturday night, after taking down the set, they returned home almost demented.

" I've not even *thought* about clothes for Monday night," wailed Lynette. " Oh, thank heavens it's Sunday tomorrow ! "

" I should sleep late if I were you," advised Vicky. " You're not rehearsing until the afternoon."

The question of sleep had now become of the utmost importance, and they found themselves snatching snoozes in odd corners of the theatre whenever they had the chance.

As Lynette entered the theatre on Sunday she heard Diana saying sharply to Mark, " So I *do* think you might be a bit more charitable towards the child. She may be inexperienced, but I can tell you this—she's a harder worker than you'll ever be in a thousand years ! " Lyn crept out and came in again a few minutes later, singing loudly to warn them of her approach.

" You sound happy ! " Diana laughed. " Come on, let's get cracking." Diana's little lecture must have done Mark some good, for he was quite helpful and pleasant, and in the absence of the rest of the company Diana had more time to go into the psychology of the play. Lynette began gradually to feel the exalting " larger than life " feeling that she recognized from the unself-conscious days of the Blue Door Theatre. But Mark was all wrong for Lewis Dodd. He played it as a matinée idol, instead of a dream-ridden, aesthetic musician. " But still," thought Lynette, " all the women in the audience will be crazy about him. They won't know that he plucks his eyebrows, and that when Vicky and I are nearly killing ourselves sweeping the stage he complains of the dust ! "

That evening Lynette, Vicky, Terry, and the character woman went out on the river. It was a warm, still evening, and they lazed back on the cushions, just drifting, pretending to go over their lines, and the elderly actress gave Lynette some last-minute tips from her considerable store of theatrical wisdom, that had only taken her as far as the Pavilion, Tutworth Wells.

" Pick your cues up more quickly, dear. In what is supposed to be normal conversation, it's always the sign of an amateur when there's even a split second's pause before someone speaks. And you could play Tessa as a little bit younger. I know you're about the right age to begin with, but the important thing about Tessa is her youth, so you can afford to accentuate it."

That night Lynette slept badly. For a long time she tossed and turned in the heat of the low-ceilinged attic, going over and over her lines. And even when she finally fell asleep it was only to dream that on the first night of *The Constant Nymph* she found that she had learned the wrong play altogether. Then she and Mark were in a little rowing boat trying to row up Tutworth Wells High Street to the Pavilion in time for the show, but all the old ladies from the hotel kept crossing the road in front of them so that they had to slow down.

She woke with a sense of foreboding. At breakfast " Hepzibah " came up to her and said, " I'm coming to your first night to-night. I hear it's a very nice little play."

" Er—I hope you'll like it," Lyn said doubtfully.

" I wonder," the old dame pursued, " whether you would accept this little trinket to bring you good luck." She handed Lynette a tiny silver charm representing a Cornish pisky. " It belonged to a very dear aunt of mine, who died of food poisoning some twenty years ago."

" Thank you *so* much. It's sweet of you. We must fly."

" I hope it brings you better luck than it brought her very dear aunt," giggled Vicky, as, loaded with their clothes for the show and shiny tin grease-paint boxes, they made their way to the theatre.

The dress rehearsal could not have been worse. As it was such a large cast they had had to call in several amateurs to play tiny roles, and they seemed to be under everybody's feet all the time. No-one seemed to know any lines, and the set was still having last minute touches added, so that people got paint all over their costumes.

" I wish," Mark said sourly to Lynette, " that you would not cling round my neck quite so tightly. I can't get my lines out."

" But she would—she would," cried Lynette. " Don't you *see* she would ? "

" I only know that my face is completely screened from the audience, and that you have wiped your grease-paint all over my clean shirt. Don't they teach you anything at that Academy ? " This was the cruellest taunt of all, and Lynette shed a few tears in the toilet. Vicky called her excitedly when the rehearsal was over.

" There are *tons* of telegrams for you." There were six : two quite normal ones that said, "Best of luck for to-night—Love, Mummy and Daddy," and " Trembling for you, but know you'll be terrific—Love, Maddy and Sandra," and four crazy ones, one saying, " Up, Guards, and at them," signed " D. Wellington," another, " Madly envious, darling," which was signed " G. Garbo," and one supposedly from Pojo, Maddy's little dog, saying, "Thinking of you with sympathetic growls," and one which terrified Lynette, that said, " Coming to see your show, dear girly—Mrs. Potter-Smith."

" Oh, Vicky," gasped Lynette. " That awful Fenchester hag."

" It's only one of the boys being clever," Vicky pointed out. " Look ! It's been sent from Nottingham. That's where their tour is this week."

" Oh, gosh ! It gave me quite a shock."

" Come on. We must dash back to the hotel if we want to eat."

" Eat ! " cried Lyn. " I couldn't ! "

" But you must ! " insisted Vicky, and dragged her back to the hotel, where in the deserted dining-room a sort of high tea was always provided for them at six o'clock.

" If only I'd had more rehearsal ! " mourned Lynette. " I'm going on when I've only reached the state one should be in about a week *before* the first night. Oh, thank goodness, no-one from the Academy will see me ! "

On the way back to the theatre Lynette wished with all her heart that she was merely to stage-manage that night's

" *I wish this charade were over !* "

show. As they approached the Pavilion some children of a family who were walking along behind them whispered loudly, " I wonder if those two are in it this week ? " and their parents replied, " Well, you'll soon see to-night, won't you ? " And it was with a certain sense of pride that Lyn and Vicky entered through the shabby stage door of the Pavilion.

Lyn insisted on helping with the dusting and sweeping of the stage and the last-minute oddments. Diana, entering the theatre, remarked, " Well, I'm glad to see that you haven't gone all ' leading lady ' on us. But you'd better get your make-up on—not much, remember. You want to look rather pale."

Lyn and Vicky were in the same dressing-room as Chloe and Ingrid.

" I wish this charade were over ! " Chloe grumbled.

" Oh, so do I ! " Lyn was the first to agree.

She looked at her terrified reflection in the mirror—two enormous eyes, and very little else. She had pinned up her telegrams, and the Cornish pisky sat in the tray of her make-up box. Vicky kept dashing off to call the time, but would not let Lyn take her turn.

" Save your voice," she said. " You're going to need it."

Diana looked in to tell them that the theatre was packed, and the " house full " board up already.

" Let's tell them the plot and give them their money back," suggested Lyn.

" You'll be all right," Diana told her. " I have perfect confidence in you." Terry slipped round to wish her luck, and Chloe and Ingrid did the same, but the naked envy in their eyes embarrassed her.

When Vicky called the five minutes, Lyn tried to start

93

" thinking herself into the part " but could not concentrate, so she went on to the stage and listened to the overture on the panatrope, and the mumble of the audience on the other side of the curtain, as she wandered round the stage re-arranging cushions and ornaments. Then Jean yelled, " Be-ginners, please ! "

She went and stood in the wings—shivering in her simple gingham dress, although the evening was warm. She and Vicky had to enter together after the first five minutes or so of the play. They stood hand in hand, great shivers shaking them from head to foot.

" We've got to be gay ! " Lynette whispered sepulchrally.

" And young," added Vicky shakily.

" And care-free—*care-free*, of all things." Their cue approached ever nearer. There was no escaping it.

" I can't ! " whispered Vicky.

Then it came, and they ran, laughing, on to the stage.

CHAPTER VII

INDIAN SUMMER

THE first act was a trifle wobbly, there was no denying it. It contained so many entrances and exits and meals and even some operetta singing. All the week Lyn had been terrified of the little song that she had to sing, but to-night it came out without a false note. For the first time since they had started rehearsing the story felt real, and her discovery of the death of her father brought down the curtain of the first scene to loud applause, the audience having completely forgotten that there had been two rather loud prompts, and that Mark's spectacles had fallen off and been trodden on. During the interval Vicky, in her little short dress and hair in pigtails, scurried about like a mad thing, refusing to let Lyn help. By this time Lynette was as happy as a sandboy. She knew she was doing well, and realized that she was at last playing a part that had been on her little list for a long time.

The second act went off without a hitch with an inspiring hush of attention from the audience. Even Mark seemed to be enjoying himself, and actually deigned to offer Lyn a cigarette between the second and third acts. The third act contained some difficult scene changes, and for these it was " all hands on deck " to get it done quickly. Jean was playing the part of the lodging-house keeper in the last scene, and this she did so well that Lyn wondered why she ever bothered to slave away as a stage manager when she was such a competent actress. By this time Lynette was exhausted by the mental strain and physical effort of the part, and was pale as death without the help of make-up. She wore a white petticoat during most of the scene, and this had a curiously shroud-like effect. At the end of the scene, as she died upon the ugly iron bedstead, there was a flutter of handkerchiefs among the audience and a clearing of throats.

" Tessa's got away. She's safe. She's dead ! " Mark cried in an effectively strangled voice, and then the curtain fell.

" Are you all right ? " Mark asked anxiously. Lyn sat up and blinked.

" Er—yes, I think so."

" You *look* so awful. You quite worried me."

As she slipped her coat on to take the curtain everyone crowded round and whispered, " Jolly fine " before lining up to bow to the enthusiastic audience. Lyn was too tired to think consciously that this was her first professional appearance safely over, but Vicky was simply glowing with achievement. In the bottom of her mind had been the faint fear that the audience might boo or hiss her, but no-one had seemed to notice anything odd in her performance of the small part of Paulina. She had even got a few laughs. Diana hurried round to the dressing-room with some notes she had made during the performance, and a lot of praise.

" Lovely, dear ! You made *me* cry as well as all the old ladies. But you must speak up more in the last scene, and you could be a bit more gay in the gay scenes at the beginning. Vicky, dear, you did very nicely. Pick your cues up a bit more quickly, though, and try not to stand with your feet in ballet positions. Quite nice, Chloe and Ingrid, but you could both put a little more life into it. Rehearsal not until eleven to-morrow. You all need a bit of sleep."

" A bit . . ." sighed Lyn, as Diana went, " I need æons and æons."

" Now you see the trials of a leading lady," said Chloe.

" An A.S.M. has a much quieter time, don't you think ? But of course—to be both at once . . ." But Lyn was too tired to retaliate.

In the sandwich bar some of the regular patrons of the theatre had stayed behind to chat to the artistes. An elderly and slightly military-looking gentleman came up to Lyn and said, " Congratulations, Miss Darwin. You made me cry like a child.'

" Oh, I'm glad—I mean, I'm sorry," stuttered Lyn, feeling very embarrassed and not carrying it off at all in the way she had always imagined an actress should receive flattery from a " fan."

On the way home Vicky danced along the starlit streets. " Oh, isn't it fun ! " she cried. " I could stay here for ever. It's worth all the hard work. Lyn, we're real actresses now—before any of the others, too."

" Except Maddy," Lyn reminded her, laughing. " And I expect she's being paid fifty times as much as we are for her film work."

" Lyn ! That's not like you ! Why you sound—you sound dissatisfied."

" I'm not dissatisfied," contradicted Lyn, " just—ambitious. I'm glad to have this opportunity at Tutworth, but I couldn't stay in Tutworth all my life."

" Oh, nor could I ! But we're going back to Fenchester, aren't we ? And that will be fun. And as for money—well, we don't have time to spend much of our wealth, do we ? "

" Oh, it's not really money I'm talking about—it's—— Oh, skip it. At the moment I'd give my week's wages, all fifty shillings of it, in exchange for bed. And to-morrow we start thinking about the prop list for *You Never Can Tell*— I shall write to the R.S.P.C.A."

" Whatever for ? " queried Vicky.

" I mean the Royal Society for the Prevention of Cruelty to Actresses."

To Lyn and Vicky it seemed that they had been at Tutworth Wells all their lives. For now that they were appearing in a show they were known in the town. Complete strangers would say good-morning to them in the street, and perhaps stop to say how much they enjoyed the play. They found the shopkeepers more lenient towards them when they were on scrounging expeditions. And they seemed to belong to the company more. Terry became their constant companion, and talked his head off as they painted scenery late into the night in the deserted theatre. He was an odd boy, temperamental and taciturn until his affection was won, but then a devoted friend. They told him all about the Blue Doors, and promised that when they returned to Fenchester to form a professional company they would try to include him as scenic designer.

" Nigel is keen on it, but I expect he'll want to stick to acting and producing," said Lyn.

On the last night of *The Constant Nymph*, Lynette was touched to receive a bouquet of large yellow roses.

" Who on earth is this ? " she said, peering at the card on which was written, " All good wishes, Letitia Bixby."

" Letitia Bixby—Bixby ? "

" Why, it must be Hepzibah," suggested Vicky. " I think I've heard the waitress call her Miss Bixby."

" How sweet of her to send these ! I'll take them back to the hotel to brighten up the attic."

The next week it was rather dull to have to return to stage-management, with all its trials and tribulations, and not to put on grease-paint every night. Jean took them aside one day and said :

" Listen, you two. Will you do me a favour ? "

" Yes, of course."

" Well, I've not had a rest for ten months. I've stage-managed over forty plays without a break, and I certainly need a holiday. So I wondered if I could ask Diana to let me have a week off, if you would be able to cope with the stage-management for a week by yourselves."

" Oh, gosh ! " The prospect alarmed them. It was all very well doing the hundred and one chores of an A.S.M. when Jean was behind them to chivvy them, but without her reminders of " Have you called the half yet ? " and " Don't forget the panatrope " where would they be ?

Lynette gulped. " Yes, Jean, I think we can manage. Which week will you be going ? "

" I thought of making it the *Private Lives* week. There's nothing very difficult there." But there was the anxiety of knowing that the full responsibility was theirs, that if the curtain were late in rising it was no-one's fault but their own, that if they forgot a prop there was no Jean to rush on with it just in time and return to blow them sky high.

On the first night the scene-shifters did not turn up, and the two girls and Terry struggled manfully with the heavy " flats," while Mark lounged in an armchair on the stage, saying, " This is a very long interval, isn't it ? "

Although nothing went radically wrong, they were in a fever of anxiety every night, and almost held their breaths until they brought down the final curtain. The preparations for the following week's show were rather more fun, for they could decide for themselves what furniture and curtains and properties to use, without waiting to be told.

" Jean will probably alter everything when she comes back," said Lyn, " but *I* think we've planned the set very nicely."

And so did Diana.

" You know, you two," she told them one day, " you don't *have* to go at the end of your ten weeks. We'd be very pleased to keep you, if you'll stay. Father would probably raise your salary to three pounds ! "

They were quite shocked at the idea.

" But we *must* go back to the Academy——"

" Why ? You're learning as much here, if not more, and being paid for it."

" Oh, no. We must finish our course. Thank you very much for suggesting it, though."

" I couldn't bear not to go back, could you ? " Lyn asked Vicky afterwards.

" No, it would be quite out of the question. I'm longing to see everyone again—the Blue Doors, and Roma, and Mr. Whitfield—even Mrs. Bosham. We seem to have been away for years."

" But we have learned a lot," admitted Lyn. " I shall feel frightfully superior to everyone at the Academy who has never been in rep. I wonder if we shall have any more parts before we leave ? "

They did, but none so exciting as the first. In one play they appeared as guests at a dinner party and had about one line each, and in *Pride and Prejudice* Vicky was given the part of Lydia. By this time she was so tired after all the weeks of hard work that she could not learn her lines, and on the first night she disgraced herself by having three " dries."

" I think it's a good job we're going back to the Academy," she told Lynette, " if only for a rest cure."

As the weeks went by and the time for their departure drew near they became more and more attached to Tutworth Wells. Most of the visitors had gone and the audiences were smaller, but somehow the town seemed more friendly. Snatching a cup of coffee in " Ye Olde Oake Tea Rooms," walking through the woods where the beech trees were already showing brown, or dancing in turn with Terry at the Town Hall tea dances, they felt that they were lords of all they surveyed, and pitied the shopgirls and typists and undergraduettes whom they saw around them.

At the end of September it turned cold, and the gas fire in their attic had to be fed with valuable shillings from their meagre salaries. They wore heavy coats over their slacks in the prompt corner, and Jean told them dour stories of winter in Tutworth Wells. But this only lasted a fortnight, and October came in with soft summery winds and mellow sunshine.

As they would not be present for the following week's show they were told it would not be necessary for them to attend the rehearsals for it during the daytime, so they took this opportunity to explore the surrounding countryside, accompanied sometimes by Terry.

" I wish you weren't going back," he would say. " You won't forget about having me as scenic artist when you open the Blue Door Theatre again, will you ? "

" No," said Lyn, " but frankly you'll have to work a jolly sight harder than you do here, because *we* shall be too busy to help you."

" You don't think the others will object to me, do you ? " Terry asked anxiously. " They won't think I'm butting in ? "

" Oh, no," Lyn assured him. " We realize that we shall have to add to the company when we make it professional, and we've been on the lookout for people for a long time. It's nice to meet a scenic artist who at heart doesn't want to be an actor."

"Me—an actor ? " He wrinkled up his funny face. "Can you imagine that ? But listen, what are we going to do to celebrate your going ? I mean, as a parting fling."

"There's nothing we can do——"

"Let's think of something really unusual that we shall remember."

"We could have a midnight feast," said Vicky, harking back to the Fourth Form.

"Where ? "

"In our attic. Very select. Just the three of us."

"But whatever would Miss Blackman say ? "

"It would be rather fun. We've got a gas ring. We could cook things on it . . ."

On the Sunday night before they left they stayed late at the theatre painting scenery, and at midnight three stealthy figures ascended the stairs of the Parade Hotel loaded with food. First they cooked corn cobs over the gas ring, in an ornamental vase of a particularly ugly lime green, and ate them in their fingers, soaked with butter. Then they made cocoa in tooth glasses and toasted welsh rarebits by holding them on forks over the gas ring. They were inclined to fall off into the flames, but tasted good all the same. They finished up with walnuts and chocolate, and felt very full and very tired, and it seemed as if the party were over. Suddenly Terry said, "I know what. Let's go for a swim——"

"At *this* hour of the night ? "

"Yes, it'll be wonderful by moonlight."

"But cold——"

"Refreshing. Do us good. Come on. I dare you to."

That was enough for the girls. They rolled up their bathing costumes and crept down the stairs, which by this time vibrated with the noise of all the old ladies' snores.

Outside it was a crystal-clear night with a silver moon, and the streets as light as day. A policeman on his beat looked at them suspiciously as they ran, laughing, down the street to Terry's digs, where he collected his costume. They pranced down to the river, singing and shouting, almost drunk with the exhilaration of the night air. The river was very high and rushing swiftly over the rocks.

" I'm frightened," said Vicky. " It looks so cold."

" Come on. We've been dared."

In a few seconds Lyn was into her costume and wading through the icy waters. It was impossible to swim as the current was too strong. Terry and she clung on to rocks and splashed each other, shivering audibly. After a few minutes Lynette shouted, " Come on, Vicky, you old funk." But there was no reply. The bank was deserted.

" Vicky ! " they yelled in unison, and from farther down the river came a feeble " Help ! " Lyn's knees felt weak with fear, and the night suddenly seemed cruel and terrible. But Terry took charge of the situation.

" You run along that bank," he ordered brusquely, " and I'll run along this one."

He clambered on to the left bank, and Lyn plunged across to the right one. She ran as though wild horses were after her, the stones cutting her feet, and the cold wind piercing her wet body. A good quarter of a mile down the river Vicky was clutching desperately at rocks as she was swept by in the black swirling current. Her red hair was flattened out by the water, and she seemed like a mermaid in distress. Lyn looked round wildly for some means of rescue. It was no use for her or Terry to go into the water as well. Terry flung himself on to a bush that grew near the edge of the river, pulled off several long branches, and threw them to Vicky, who clutched them, gasping and choking. As the stream bore Vicky past her Lyn, lying full length on the bank, grasped some of the green foliage, then a few twigs, and finally the thick branch, and pulled Vicky ashore, where she lay stretched out half laughing and half crying.

" Oh gosh ! " she gasped, " Oh gosh ! "

" Are you all right ? " yelled Terry. " I'm not risking coming across. I'll run back to the bridge. Will you bring my clothes ? "

Frozen to the skin and shaken by Vicky's narrow escape, they ran all the way back to the Parade to try to get warm, and consumed more cocoa, huddled over the gas fire.

" Thank you, one and all," said Vicky, " for rescuing me."

" Only did it because I want that job as scenic artist," Terry said gruffly.

" Only did it because I thought Bulldog and Nigel might be a bit hurt if I went back to-morrow and said I'd mislaid their sister," teased Lyn.

" That's what comes of saying we wanted a binge we would always remember," remarked Vicky.

It was about three o'clock by this time, and with a view to catching their train they decided that the binge was over.

" And if I bump into Miss Blackman on the stairs," said Terry, as he departed, " I shall ask her to come for a swim."

" What a night ! " sighed Vicky, as they prepared to sleep. " Oh, Lyn, we're leaving to-morrow. I can't bear the idea."

Next morning even the cool haddock at breakfast aroused a nostalgia of its own. They dressed more soberly than they had for weeks. " Don't skirts seem funny after slacks," remarked Vicky, before the mirror. And as for their packing. . . . They seemed to have collected twice as many belongings during their stay, and their battered cases needed much bouncing on before they would shut.

" Do you remember carrying these up from the station on the first night, when we were so tired ? Doesn't it seem ages ago ? "

They put off going down to the theatre to say good-bye for as long as possible by going round the town first. They saw their friend the ironmonger, and Hepzibah wheeling a friend in a bath chair, and several regular patrons of the theatre, who all expressed their sorrow that Lyn and Vicky were going.

" Tutworth won't seem the same without you two popping round the town in your little blue overalls," they were told.

" Come on," said Lyn. " We'd better go down to the theatre or they'll have broken rehearsal for lunch." They crept into the back of the stalls as they had done on the first day, and watched the rehearsal. It was funny to think how well they knew all these people who had been strangers to them then.

" It's a very sweet little theatre, you know," said Vicky. " I wonder if it will ever be famous because we made our first appearances here ? "

" Of course it will," Lyn said sarcastically. " Pilgrims will travel here from miles away so that there's a deep groove worn right down the middle of the High Street."

Hearing them laugh, Diana looked up and said, " Hullo. You've come to say good-bye, I suppose. Hold on just a second."

" How scared we were of her at first ! " reflected Lyn.

They went up on to the stage when the rehearsal was over and shook hands with everyone. The character woman gave them a little embroidered handkerchief each, and kissed them on both cheeks. Mark said, " Oh, you're leaving to-day, are you ? " as if he couldn't have cared less, and Chloe and

Ingrid were very gushing, although Lyn and Vicky could not help feeling that it was mainly relief at seeing the back of them. Jean said, " Well, I hope we haven't worked you too hard. You've certainly done your share," which was praise coming from Jean. The business manager, Diana's father, shook hands with them with much old-world courtesy, and told them that while Tutworth Rep. was open they need never be out of a job.

" Which is quite something in this profession," said Lynette to Vicky.

The faithful Terry was waiting to take their cases to the station.

" Good heavens ! " he cried. " What on earth have you got in here ? Miss Blackman's flat-irons ? "

Miss Blackman, looking quite human for once, wished them good luck as they settled the bill in her aspidistra-filled office, and a bevy of old ladies bowed and smiled from the windows as they set off down the street. Hepzibah wiped a tear away with a cambric handkerchief, and the Tutworth Wells Civic Band seemed to be playing the *Marche Militaire* with greater abandon than usual. On the way to the station Terry was silent and depressed.

" I shall never get the sets done in time without you two," he grumbled. " Will you come again next vacation ? "

" No, I don't expect to," said Lyn. " Sad, isn't it ? We shall probably go home for Christmas."

At the station they leaned out of the window engaging in rather embarrassed conversation. The engine kept making false starts, so that they would say " famous last words " and start waving, only to find that they were still standing at the platform. When this had happened a few times Terry said, " I know what—I'll go and get you some lemonade from the refreshment room. Shan't be a tick." He loped off.

And while he was battling with the crowd in the refreshment room the train slid slyly out of the station.

" Oh, Terry . . ." cried Lyn and Vicky, leaping to the window. Just as the train rounded the bend they caught a glimpse of Terry, balancing three glasses of lemonade, emerging in a dishevelled condition on to the platform. They laughed shakily.

" How like him."

" Oh, Lyn ! " sighed Vicky, " I wish I didn't get so attached to places. It's so awful leaving them."

" Yes, I know. And Tutworth had a very special atmosphere of its own."

They watched the fields speed by, feeling very lost and empty inside.

" *Are* we silly to be going back to the Academy when we were getting professional experience ? " mused Vicky.

" No. Not really. We're only half-trained, aren't we ? There are so many things we've still got to learn."

" And it will have been wonderful experience when it comes to starting up the Blue Door, won't it ? "

"Yes. The boys and Sandra ought to get into rep. first, oughtn't they ? And however we're going to manage the business side, I don't know."

" Lyn," said Vicky slowly, " do you realize something ? "

" What ? "

" All these years we've been talking about starting the Blue Door professionally, yet we've never thought of the most important thing."

" What do you mean ? "

" Well, I heard Diana telling someone that it was impossible to start a decent rep. without a capital of several thousand pounds."

" Gosh ! " Lynette, electrified, shot up in her seat,

awakening an elderly farmer who was dozing next to her. "I never thought of that ! And I'm sure the boys haven't. Of course—there's advertising and scenery and salaries. What idiots we are ! We'll never do it."

The rest of the journey was taken up with schemes and ways and means of making some money. Now that they had experienced how a professional company was run, the old Blue Door system seemed very meagre and amateur.

"We'll have to have a confab with the others when we see them," said Lyn. Soon the carriage became stuffy and they dozed fitfully, tired after their midnight adventures. Tutworth seemed to have vanished as if it had never existed. It was hard to imagine Terry still painting scenery, the shows going on, and the band still playing in their absence.

They woke in time to see a red tube train emerge from its burrow into daylight, and realized that they were in London again. They breathed deeply.

"Lovely to be back."

"But a few hours ago we were nearly in tears at leaving Tutworth."

The factories, the little houses, and then the gloom of Paddington. They tidied themselves and lifted their cases down from the rack. With much snorting and hissing the engine bumped on the buffers and recoiled.

At the barrier were the three boys and Sandra, all looking very brown and healthy. They started waving excitedly from yards away, and fell on Lyn and Vicky's necks as soon as they had given up their tickets.

"You two look awful," they were told. "What *have* you been doing ? "

"Working," said Lyn and Vicky proudly.

CHAPTER VIII

MAINLY CRAB-LIKE

ONE evening early in the Autumn term the Blue Doors had a council of war. It all started because Nigel had not paid his rent again, and neither of the twins could help him out.

" And we're *not* writing home for any more," said Vicky firmly.

" Well, what are we going to do ? It's quite obvious we can't live on our allowances."

" But we can't possibly ask for any more. It was bad enough to come to Dramatic School when our parents didn't want us to, but then to keep on asking for money . . ."

" Why is it we can't manage this term ? " asked Sandra. " We did it perfectly for the first two terms."

" It's because our expenses have gone up," explained Nigel. " Do you realize that half our pocket-money this week has gone on play scripts that we simply *must* have ? And then there's food and shoe repairs. We're in a jam, if you ask me. We should have saved during our holiday jobs."

" We weren't making enough to save."

" Let's sing in the street," suggested Bulldog flippantly.

" We'll have to get jobs to do in the evenings," said Lyn firmly, remembering Helen.

" On the stage, you mean ? "

" Of course—if we can. Vicky could easily get a chorus job. And we could—walk on or something."

"It's an idea," said Nigel. "But we're not really supposed to do it during term-time."

"Lots of people do, though. There are two girls in our class who are in the Hippodrome chorus at the moment."

"And what about matinées ? "

"Oh, we'll just have to miss classes on those days."

"Come on," said Lyn, putting on her coat, "let's go down to the Leicester Square reading-room and look at to-day's copy of *The Stage*."

In the reading-room of the Leicester Square Library there was a queue of out-of-work actors in faded teddy bear coats, waiting to look at their last hope—the "Artistes Wanted" column of *The Stage*. While they waited the girls looked at old numbers of *Vogue* with rapturous sighs. At last the six of them were huddled round the theatrical newspaper, breathing down each other's necks and running their fingers down the column which was already grey with much fingering.

"Refined chorus ladies wanted. Able to dance. Tap and ballet. For West End production. Audition Abbey Theatre, Saturday morning, eleven o'clock. Practice dresses." Vicky read it out excitedly.

"Am I refined ? " she asked anxiously.

"You'll just pass," Jeremy told her.

"I think I'll try."

"Hey ! " cried Bulldog, so loudly that the librarian nearly turned them out. "What about this ? "

"Ladies and gentlemen required to walk on in spectacular musical production. Must be tall."

"Oh, dear ! Must be tall," sighed Bulldog. "I don't think I'm slender enough to look tall."

"*We* could try it," said Lyn. "Sandra, you're not short, neither is Jeremy nor Nigel." They took down the address and departed, chattering at the tops of their voices, having completely disturbed the breathless hush of the reading-room.

Luckily both the auditions were on the following Saturday, so they did not have to take any time off from the Academy. Vicky, carrying her toe and tap shoes and blue-spotted practice dress, approached the stage door of the Abbey Theatre with a fast-beating heart. It seemed so impudent to enter a London theatre for an audition. There was a stream of girls and women of all shapes and sizes being directed by the stage door-keeper down on to the stage. The audition had already begun, and a piano was beating out a jazz rhythm, while on the stage a girl in a bathing suit was dancing excellently. Vicky gave her name in to the stage director and was sent up to the chorus dressing-room to change. There she almost decided to turn round and go home. The other girls looked so grown-up and glamorous and well-poised. They all seemed to know each other and discussed previous auditions that they had attended. In the wings Vicky was about twentieth in the queue to perform. At last her name was read out, and she went on to the enormous stage on which so many spectacular revues had been performed. Now it was empty and lit only by a cold rehearsal light. In the front row of the stalls sat three men with spectacles and bald heads, talking to each other, completely absorbed. Vicky handed her music to the pianist, saying, " Not too quickly, please," and consequently the tempo was more like a funeral march.

" Yes, we'll see her ballet," came a bored voice from the stalls. This was cheering, for some of the girls were sent home after their tap dance. As she changed her shoes, Vicky vowed to make the silly old men look up at least. As she handed the music to the pianist, she whispered, " Stop after the first eight bars, and give me eight silent bars, please."

It did the trick. The sudden silence made the three men look up in time to see Vicky do a very showy series of pirouettes.

" That's enough," one of them shouted. Vicky prepared to retire defeated.

" Give your name to the stage director," she was told, and when she did so he said, " Rehearsal, Monday at eleven."

" You mean—you've engaged me ? "

" Yes. Next, please."

On airy wings Vicky floated up Charing Cross Road, and it was not until she was nearly back at No. 37 that she realized that she had not asked what the salary was to be, nor even what the show was called. At No. 37 she found a message from the Blue Doors, " Meet us at the Acropolis for lunch."

" That means they've got their jobs," she guessed, and ran across to the little Greek restaurant at which they ate when in funds. The Blue Doors were immersed in platefuls of mousaka and their faces were smug.

" What luck ? "

" I got it," said Vicky airily. " Rehearsal Monday."

" So did we. Also rehearse Monday. But not Bulldog. He wasn't tall enough." Bulldog stuffed rice into his mouth.

" I'll get something," he vowed. " Never you fear."

" What do you have to do ? " Vicky asked them.

" We're courtiers in Queen Elizabeth's court," explained Lyn. " We just wear lovely clothes and drift about, evidently. It'll be rather boring, because it's a silly spectacular sort of thing—from what I can gather—but the pay is wonderful. What's yours like ? "

" I forgot to ask," confessed Vicky.

" You goop ! That's the whole point of getting jobs."

The other girls looked so grown-up.

113

" But what on earth are they going to say at the Academy when we're missing for rehearsals next week."

" I'll have to say you've all got 'flu," said Bulldog. " It'll be rather fun. I'll describe your symptoms in great detail to everyone." He carried this out so well that the following week he was continually bringing home gifts of books and grapes and chocolate from their sympathetic companions at the Academy.

" It was all I could do to dissuade Myrtle from coming round to see you," Bulldog told them with glee. " She said she was sure I wasn't looking after you properly, and you needed a mother's care."

They ate the grapes with relish and guilt.

" It's a good job we're only rehearsing a fortnight," said Lyn. " Think what a lot we shall miss."

" It's all for the good of the cause," Sandra reminded her.

" I don't think we'll tell our parents, shall we ? " asked Vicky.

" Oh, no. They probably wouldn't like you to do chorus work," said Nigel.

" I wish there were some circuses in London," complained Bulldog. " Then I'd try to get a job as a clown." But next day he returned late in the evening glowing with achievement.

" I've got a job ! " he shouted, pink to the ears. " And it's not in the chorus, and it's not walking on."

" What is it, then ? "

" In the zoo ? " suggested Jeremy.

" A sandwich man ? " said Nigel.

" I'm doing a cabaret act in that most select of night haunts, ' The Hotch Potch.' "

" ' *The Hotch Potch* ' ! Don't be silly, Bulldog."

" It's true. The brother of a boy in the Juniors plays in the dance band there in the evenings. I was talking to him to-day, and he said that they wanted a comedy act for the cabaret, so I went along and saw the manager, a funny little Frenchman, and I did a few impressions and sang 'Don't put your daughter on the stage, Mrs. Worthington,' and—the job was mine."

"You—you sang?"

"Yes. And they seemed to think it was jolly funny, too."

"I don't wonder."

"Bulldog, you're a dark horse! When do you start?"

"Next Sunday. I do ten minutes at nine and again at eleven o'clock, and oh, boy, the cash! It's only for four weeks, though, which is a shame."

As their shows were not opening until the following week they decided that they must go to "The Hotch Potch" for Bulldog's first night.

"But we haven't got evening dress," objected Jeremy.

"You must hire it—like Bulldog is doing."

"I hope ours will look a bit better than his does."

Bulldog certainly presented a rather odd spectacle in his hired evening dress. The trousers were too tight, the jacket too loose, and his tie would not stay in the right place.

"Oh, well, I'm meant to be funny," he sighed, trying to see himself sideways in the fly-blown long mirror. Jeremy and Nigel went along to a theatrical costumier's in Lisle Street, and for a very reasonable charge hired evening clothes that were slightly more presentable than Bulldog's.

The girls got round Mrs. Bertram in the Academy wardrobe to lend them evening cloaks to go over their old evening dresses, and there was much altering and trying on and ironing for days beforehand.

Bulldog rang up and reserved a table for them, and then said, "I wish you weren't coming."

"Why?"

" Well, if they don't think I'm funny it will be so much worse if you're there."

" But we'll laugh at you so infectiously that everyone else will join in," Lyn promised.

Then came the question of transport.

" We *must* have a taxi," Vicky insisted.

" We just *can't* afford it."

" Well, we'll have to sell something—or pawn it. We can redeem it the next week out of our wages."

They looked round the room. There seemed to be nothing but books, and they knew that, valuable as these were to themselves, they would not raise much.

" I'll pawn my wristwatch," offered Bulldog. " That should about pay the taxi, and also the dinner bill. Mine will be free, as I'm performing, but your bill will be pretty heavy."

" No ! no ! " they argued. " Why should it be you ? "

" Well, it's on my account you're coming, isn't it ? And I can get it back next week. I shall be a millionaire on Friday when I get my pay."

So they sallied out to a murky little pawnbroker's on the corner of Fitzherbert Street and haggled with the little man behind the counter until he gave them almost the amount they had asked for.

" Phew ! " said Sandra as they came out. " That's the first time I've ever been in a pawnbroker's ! What *would* our parents say ? "

Lyn walked along the street grimly for a few minutes and then expostulated, " Oh, it's horrible——"

" What's horrible ? "

" Living like this—in smelly digs. Having to pawn things when we want to enjoy ourselves. Counting every penny. Oh, one day I'm going to be so rich. Why aren't we like Primula and Stephanie ? " She named two of the débutantes in their class at the Academy.

" Would you seriously swop over with Stephanie ? And have a frightful mother like old Lady Myers and as much acting ability as a broomstick, just to be stinking rich ? "

" No, I suppose not," Lyn admitted, " but it would make life easier to have a bit more cash."

On Sunday morning they were up early and dashing about saying, " Oh, I know we'll never be ready by eight o'clock," although the whole day lay before them. They took it in turns in the cold bathroom, where chips of enamel came off the bath and stuck uncomfortably into one, and the plug didn't fit properly, so that after a few minutes one was left high and dry. The girls played at ladies' maids, and as they set about their mending Sandra said airily, " Oh, Jane, just run out and buy me half a dozen pairs of silk stockings, finest gauge, will you ? " and "Mary, ring up and make an appointment with the hairdresser, will you ? " said Vicky, plunging her red head into the basin. They were still thinking along the same lines at lunch.

" Pass the caviare, please," said Bulldog, holding out his hand for the cold mashed potatoes.

" Super venison, this," said Nigel, attacking yesterday's mutton that lay in colourless slices on his plate.

Although they had had all day there was still a scramble at eight o'clock when the taxi which they had ordered arrived at the door.

" Where's my collar stud ? " yelled Bulldog, frantically.

" Bother ! I haven't got a hanky ! "

" Oh, my stocking's laddered."

" No-one will see it. Come *on* ! The meter goes extra fast when the cab's standing still."

At last the six of them were bundled in, rather to the

horror of the driver, and they set off through the gaily lighted streets.

"Doesn't London look *different* from a taxi ? " observed Lyn, sitting back luxuriously, although Bulldog was almost on her knee, and Vicky's elbow was in her eye.

At "The Hotch-Potch" the commissionaire who opened the door of the cab for them was somewhat surprised to count six people extricating themselves from its depths. On the pavement the Blue Doors pulled themselves together, drew deep breaths, and walked through the canopied doorway.

They soon found themselves in a small softly lit room, with tiny tables crowded together and a minute space for dancing. Here they were shown to their table, ploughing their way through the dancers. The manager, a dapper little Frenchman, came up and greeted Bulldog, and told him to go round to the orchestra room just before nine. Bulldog was definitely scared by this time. He looked round anxiously at the diners, who all seemed very poised and sophisticated.

"It'll *never* amuse them," he thought desperately, and mopped his brow.

"Don't let's eat until I've had my first ordeal," he implored the others, and the waiter was not a little astonished to receive an order for six orangeades. The Blue Doors sat and stared at everything. The boys were intrigued by the band and the girls by the women's clothes.

" I think we look all right, though, don't we ? " whispered Vicky. Soon it was time for Bulldog to depart. Vicky straightened his tie for the tenth time. Nigel thumped him on the back, and Bulldog got up unsteadily.

" ' We who are about to die, salute you,' " he quoted.

" ' It is a far, far better thing you do,' " returned Lyn.

As he threaded his way between the tables Jeremy said,

" Poor old thing. Wouldn't be in his shoes for a thousand pounds."

" The back row of the courtiers for me, any day ! " agreed Nigel.

The first turn of the cabaret was a girl crooner, who received tepid applause. People talked all the time, and the Blue Doors began to feel very worried on Bulldog's account. Then the band did a fanfare, and the little Frenchman announced, " And now I present to you a new face—that young humorist, Bulldog Halford ! "

" Never heard of him," said someone at the next table.

Bulldog appeared in the spotlight, looking very red and shiny, and his evening dress worse than ever. First he did impressions of stage and screen stars which were clever, if not particularly funny, and then a sketch of two charwomen, with a different hat for each, which he whipped on and off as he spoke one part in Cockney and the other in North Country dialect. This amused the audience, who put down their knives and forks, and devoted their attention to him. The cries of " Encore " were so loud that the manager nodded and beamed, and Bulldog came back and sang a funny little song about an Irish country boy in London.

" Isn't he *delightful* ? " drawled a voice beside the Blue Doors.

" Heaven. I wonder why we've never seen him before ? "

" That's our Bulldog ! " Vicky whispered proudly. " Oh, I'm *so* relieved ! "

A few minutes later, when the dancing had begun again, Bulldog joined them beaming all over his face.

" Was it all right ? " he asked.

" You *know* it was ! " they laughed.

" Well, the manager liked it. Come on, let's eat."

He put away a simply enormous meal at the management's expense. The others ate less at their own.

" Must take nourishment when it's twice nightly," he said. " I'm on again at eleven, so don't get through dinner too quickly."

They danced between every course to make it spin out, but the floor was so crowded that it was more like marking time.

" I'm quite looking forward to the next session," Bulldog confessed, trampling on Sandra's toes. Sandra stood still to allow someone to get off the hem of her dress.

" Yes. So am I. Are you going to do the same things ? "

" I don't think I'll do the impersonations. I'll do the one about the cat burglar instead."

During Bulldog's second appearance Jeremy suddenly choked into his fifth glass of orangeade.

" Sh ! " hissed the rest of the Blue Doors. Jeremy recovered himself and began to whisper to them violently.

" Do be quiet, Jeremy ! Wait till afterwards ! "

But Jeremy kept on mumbling until he had gained their attention.

" Over there—Roma Seymore and Mr. Whitfield."

" *What* ! "

It was true. At a table on the far side of the room sat the director of the Academy and Roma Seymore, looking very distinguished in evening dress. They were watching Bulldog carefully, smiling occasionally, and making remarks to each other. Bulldog could not see them, as the tables were now in darkness and the spotlight blinded him. The whole act went with more of a swing than the first, and

Bulldog had to bow again and again. When he rejoined the Blue Doors at the table they got up to go.

" Are we going already ? " he asked, in surprise.

" Yes, I think we'd better, before the rush for taxis begins."

Outside, Nigel said to him, " Well, you're in a nice position now."

" What do you mean ? "

" Roma Seymore and old Whitfield were in there."

" Were they ? " said Bulldog calmly, then did a terrific " double take " " *Whaat ?* "

" Yes. Over in the corner opposite us. They recognized you, of course, and I think they saw us."

" Little fishes ! " said Bulldog. " That's done it ! They'll be livid to think I'm working."

" But ' The Hotch Potch ' is a very respectable place," objected Sandra.

" It's not that. It's just that it's a rule that students are not to do outside work during term-time," said Nigel.

" Oh, dear ! " sighed Bulldog. " I'm in for it."

Next day after prayers Bulldog was summoned to Mr. Whitfield's office. He went in with quaking heart.

" I enjoyed your little act last night at ' The Hotch Potch,' " said Mr. Whitfield, " but I should like to know why you are doing it when it is a rule that no professional work is to be done during term-time ? "

Bulldog cleared his throat.

" Well, sir, it's really on account of our parents. We don't want to ask them for any more money, and living in London is so expensive—so we've all got jobs for the evenings."

" All of you ? "

" Yes. Vicky's starting in the chorus of *Sit Tight* at the

Abbey to-night, and the others are walking on in *Gloriana* at Her Majesty's."

" I see. I suppose that was the reason for the influenza— last week ? "

" Er—yes, sir. I'm sorry, sir."

" Well, if the course here is proving too expensive for you and you are able to find professional work already——" began Mr. Whitfield, and Bulldog broke in with a horrified gasp.

" Oh, no, sir. It's not like that ! We're only doing these rather odd jobs to make money so that we can stay on at the Academy."

" I see." For a few minutes Mr. Whitfield tapped on the desk with his pencil, then he said, " Well, if it's really necessary, I can't stop you, I suppose. But I do disapprove strongly, and as it is a flagrant piece of disobedience I hope that you will not talk about it to the other students. And any work that the others miss through matinées will have to be made up, of course."

" Oh yes, sir. They're awfully worried about that."

" And next term you must try to live more economically. No more outings to 'The Hotch-Potch.' " His eyes twinkled. " How did you manage that if things are so bad ? " Bulldog hung his head and blushed.

" Pawned my watch."

Mr. Whitfield flung his head back and laughed.

" Poor Bulldog ! For your own first night ! Oh, what it is to be young." And Bulldog realized suddenly that Mr. Whitfield would have exchanged all his wealth and position to be young again, and he felt somehow superior and pitying.

" You can go now. By the way, I thought the charlady sketch extremely funny."

That night Vicky had her first glimpse of just how hard the chorus works. Up and down six flights of stone stairs she ran, changing from crinoline to bathing suit, from bathing suit to ski-ing clothes, and danced madly, ballet, then tap, then ballet on the enormous stage of the Abbey Theatre, to a jewel-bedecked first-night audience. As she took her make-up off, she felt as if she had been playing rugger. The chorus dressing-room was long, and had a double-sided mirror running down the centre, and lengthy dressing-tables. As they dressed, the forty dancers and show girls chattered like the occupants of a parrot-house.

"Coming out for a coffee?" Vicky's neighbour inquired in a friendly manner.

"No, thanks. I'm meeting some people."

"Coo—aren't you the gay one! Nice people?"

"Yes," said Vicky. "Very nice." She ran down the stairs, called good-night to the stage door-keeper, and was out into the lights of Leicester Square. In a little all-night snack-bar she met the four weary walkers-on.

"*Walk* on!" groaned Jeremy. "It's a day's march. Round and round that stage as soldiers."

"Did it go down well?"

"Yes. It's bad, really, but the audience loved it. How did yours go?"

"Fine. Audience lapped it up."

"But not like the straight theatre, is it?"

"No. It's exciting, but—I don't know. . . ."

They sipped coffee until Bulldog arrived.

"How's Mayfair?" they teased.

"Super! I had a wonderful dinner to-night."

"Beast. *We'll* have to eat at the Boshery." That was the name they had given Mrs. Bosham's.

They strolled home through the streets that were shiny

with freshly fallen rain ; the lights, reflected on the pavements, making them as gold as Dick Whittington believed them to be. At the corner of Tottenham Court Road there was a barrow of roasting chestnuts. They bought a bag each from the gay little Italian, and ate them all the way home, leaving a trail of empty shells behind them.

CHAPTER IX

PLANS AND PROBLEMS

MADDY walked quickly up and down Fenchester Station, partly because it was cold, but mainly to stop herself from dancing with excitement. " Life just *couldn't* be more thrilling ! " she reflected. Here she was, a film star over-night, through the success of *Forsaken Crown*. She had left Fenchester High School two days previously, at the end of the autumn term, and after Christmas she would accompany the Blue Doors to the Academy, where a junior department was being opened. And to-day all the Blue Doors were returning in force for Christmas, after a year's absence. She had last seen her sister Sandra on her runaway escapade to London, but she looked upon the other five as practically brothers and sisters. She opened her handbag, a newly acquired and very grown-up affair, peered in the mirror and removed a few smuts from her face, wondering why they always seemed so attracted to her. She tightened the ribbons on her fair plaits, and as she did so the train whistled round the bend.

The Blue Doors were hanging out of the windows, one dark head, two fair, and two carrotty ones. They cheered as they saw her, and she hopped from one leg to the other, pink in the face, grinning from ear to ear. They descended from the train in a body, and there was a pandemonium of kissing and back-slapping.

" At last, at last ! " cried Bulldog melodramatically. " Gosh, you've grown, Maddy."

" We've seen your film. It's heavenly ! "

" How's London ? "

" Where's a porter ? "

" Don't say you've started a handbag at last ! "

No-one could talk properly for excitement.

" Daddy's calling for you all in the car," said Maddy.
" But he said he'd probably be late, so we're to go into the refreshment room and wait for him."

They sat on their luggage in the crowded refreshment room and drank cups of tasteless tea and could not stop talking.

" Oh, tell me all about the Academy ! " begged Maddy.
" Do you know what age most of the Junior Class will be ? "

" Between twelve and fifteen," Vicky informed her.
" They've been having auditions for it these last few days."

" Why didn't I have an audition ? "

" They'd seen the film and were willing to take you on that, I suppose."

" Oh, how exciting ! For the first time in my life I'm longing for Christmas to be over."

" I'm not," sighed Bulldog. " I want just to eat and sleep and eat for weeks."

" Lazy as ever ! " teased Maddy.

" I've been working very hard, excuse me, madam ! " objected Bulldog. " But, of course—she doesn't know about our jobs, does she ? "

" Better tell her, I suppose. But keep it dark, Maddy."

Maddy's eyes grew round as saucers as she scented a secret.

" What's this ? "

" Well, we've been doing some jobs during the term to make some extra pocket-money. Vicky's been in the chorus at the Abbey, we've been walking on in *Gloriana*, and Bulldog has been doing a cabaret act in a night club."

" A cabaret act ? I thought that was something to do with the can-can ? "

" No, stupid ! I've been doing sketches and impersonations."

" In a night club ! Oh, Bulldog, was it very wicked ? "

" Wicked ? About as respectable as the Fenchester Ladies' Institute."

" That reminds me, how is our dear friend Mrs. Potter-Smith ? " Jeremy wanted to know.

" Don't mention that woman to me ! " Maddy made an awful grimace meant to resemble Mrs. Potter-Smith. " She nearly ruined the film, *and* my chances of seeing the première. And I don't think she's finished with us yet."

Bulldog giggled reminiscently.

" D'you remember the time when she took the part of the Greek goddess in that awful play the Ladies' Institute did ? "

They were in the middle of a flood of " D'you remembers " when Mr. Fayne arrived, kissed Sandra, and shook hands with all the others.

" It's good to see you back," he said. " The Avenue has been too quiet this last year."

After strapping a mountain of luggage on the back, they piled into Mr. Fayne's car and drove through the town which seemed so strange yet familiar after such a long absence. Their mothers were all hovering near their own front doors, and were out on the doorsteps as soon as they heard the car. There was more kissing and hugging and the Avenue was full of laughter and shouting once again. Heads appeared at the windows of the houses opposite, and more than one elderly voice said, with a mixture of interest and disapproval, " So *they're* back, are they ? "

While they unstrapped some luggage from the back of the car, Vicky took the opportunity to whisper to Jeremy.

" Look, I don't suppose there will be much chance for all of us to get together until after Christmas, so shall we say the morning after Boxing Day definitely ? "

" O.K.," said Jeremy. " Tell the others."

Christmas passed in a whirl of cooking, buying presents, putting up decorations, and, of course, eating. The Blue Doors glimpsed each other in the town as they accompanied their mothers on shopping expeditions, in church on Christmas Day, and when being taken to be shown to relations. But it was not until the day after Boxing Day that they could forgather in the Halford's dining-room and take stock of themselves. No-one had actually put into words what they were meeting for, but each felt that there were things to be settled.

" Well," said Nigel. " Here we are—back in Fenchester."

" And isn't it fun ? " said Vicky. " Everyone seems so much nicer than when we went away."

" And next time we come back," went on Nigel, " it may be for good. So I think we ought to start making plans for the reopening of the Blue Door Theatre."

" But listen," said Maddy, in an aggrieved voice. " When are you thinking of opening it ? "

" Next Autumn, I should think," said Jeremy. " Nigel will have had over two years at the Academy, and we shall have had about eighteen months."

" But what about me ? " said Maddy. " I shall only have had two terms."

" Oh, you'll have to stay on at the Academy and come to us in the holidays."

" Anyway," said Lynette, " once you get to London you'll probably be filming again soon, won't you ? "

" Don't know," said Maddy unenthusiastically. " Oh,

why am I *always* just this little bit behind the rest of you ! And I shall never catch up."

"All right, then," said Nigel. "That's settled. Except for Maddy, we leave the Academy after two more terms. Now the thing is—how large a company do we want, who's going to produce, what about salaries, and a hundred and one other things."

"I think," said Lynette, "that the seven of us should form the permanent company, and take it in turns to produce. We should employ permanent stage managers and scenic artist, but get extra actors down for odd weeks as we need them. But the question is—money."

"If we followed your suggestion, Lyn, how should we work out the salaries ? "

"Well, we could pay off our liabilities, salaries to stage management and to the artistes we'd called in, and share out whatever was left, after we'd paid for rent, lighting, scenery, advertising, et cetera."

"Doesn't sound as if there would be much left," said Bulldog glumly. "You know, it's a jolly big proposition." They were silent for some seconds, while the financial side of the question assumed gigantic proportions.

"You know," said Sandra, "there's an awful lot to be done before we dare to open the theatre professionally. I don't know what sort of condition it's in now."

"Let's go round and look at it," said Vicky eagerly. "Who's got the key, Maddy ? "

"I think it's still under the brick. I haven't been in for ages. The Bishop has used it once or twice for missionary meetings, otherwise it's still empty."

"But who *does* it belong to technically ? " asked Jeremy. "We call it ours, but it isn't really. We've never paid rent for it or anything."

" I think," said Nigel, " that in actual fact it belongs to the town council. I believe that is where the Bishop applied in the first place, when he got permission for us to use it."

" But if we're going to open it professionally, we shall have to pay rent for it, I suppose. But who to ? "

" The town council, of course."

" Oh, isn't it complicated ! Come on, let's go and have a look at it." They set out for the theatre, stopping to have a coffee at Bonner's on the way. Pleasant Street seemed narrower and grimier than ever, and the theatre, when they reached it, seemed even smaller than they had remembered it. The Seymore Trophy stood on its bracket rather forlornly.

" I *must* polish it," said Sandra. They looked round rather dubiously.

" We really ought to have tip-up seats, you know," observed Nigel.

" Those curtains are still a trifle odd. They're not heavy enough," said Bulldog.

" We could extend the stage," suggested Jeremy, " by putting on an apron in front."

" And *what*," said Lynette, " *what* about dressing-room space ? "

They groaned.

" We need several—if not many—hundred pounds," said Nigel. They sank down in chairs and pondered the situation grimly.

" Why didn't we ever think about this before ? We've been imagining that we could open it up—just like that."

" We didn't realize," said Lynette, " how much this theatre lacks that a real rep. must have."

" It's no good our aiming at something like Covent Garden," continued Nigel.

"If we can get it as good as the theatre at the Academy it will be all right to start with."

"But how can we get the several hundred pounds necessary?"

"Oh!" exclaimed Maddy suddenly. "I forgot. I've got several hundred pounds. More, I expect, from the film."

"Don't be silly!" said Sandra. "You know we wouldn't touch that. And anyhow, Daddy has put it into an annuity for you, so that you'll get a certain amount each year for the rest of your life."

"How dull!" said Maddy. "I wanted to squander it."

"Perhaps the Bishop——" began Vicky.

"Bishops don't earn much!" said Maddy. "I know because his housekeeper told me he only has cake one day a week."

"That's not because he can't afford it," said Nigel. "And anyhow, he's helped us enough already."

"I wonder," Jeremy began slowly, fingering the piano and finding it out of tune, "if the town council would help?"

"Why should it?" objected Lyn.

"Well, if Fenchester wants a theatre oughtn't the council to be willing to grant us a loan until we have got started and can pay it back? If the hall belongs to the council we shall be paying them rent as well, so it will be quite a good thing from their point of view."

"But *does* Fenchester want a theatre?"

"It needs one. Fancy a town of forty thousand inhabitants without a rep. It's ridiculous."

"Yes, but who on the town council would see that?"

"I'd vamp the Mayor, if you like," offered Maddy generously.

"Who's the Mayor now?"

" Barrington, the grocer. A horrid little man," Maddy informed them. " But Lord Moulcester, from Fennymead, you know, he's on the council, and Miss Gaunt. As she was our headmistress, she ought to help, now oughtn't she ? "

" It's our only hope," Lynette said finally. " And the only way of doing it independently. Because when we had paid it back we should be entirely self-sufficient."

" Not quite," said Sandra, " because as the hall belongs to the council we should always be somewhat in their power."

" Supposing "—Vicky sat up suddenly in horror—" supposing they won't let us open it at all ? " The thought was too awful to be grasped.

" No, no," said Lyn. " They couldn't stop us. Or, could they ? "

" Look here," said Sandra. " We're getting all het up about nothing. We must find out first if there's going to be any trouble before we start worrying about it."

" Let's go round and see the dear Bish," urged Maddy. " He's always a help, and I know he wants to see you."

As they came out of the theatre who should they bump into but Mrs. Potter-Smith. Her fur coat seemed shaggier, her hair more peroxided, and her hat more atrocious than ever.

" Well," she cried, widening her cow-like eyes and clicking her false teeth. " The dear things ! After all this time ! How you've grown ! I should hardly have known you. And you look—cleaner somehow than you used to," she laughed tinklingly.

" You look about the same," responded Maddy.

" Oh, you naughty wee one ! Yes, I've heard all about *your* escapades. Being a film star went to our heads a little, didn't it ? I hear you've had to leave your school ? " The Blue Doors seethed, but Maddy was imperturbable.

" Yes. They drummed me out. Miss Gaunt chopped off my form captain's badge with a sword while the school percussion band played *Land of Hope and Glory*."

" And where are you going to now ? " Mrs. Potter-Smith asked inquisitively.

" Oh, Borstal, I expect ! " said Maddy airily.

" Really, Maddy ! " put in Sandra. " No, Mrs. Potter-Smith, she left her school because a junior department is being opened at the Academy we go to, and she's coming there to join us."

" I see," said Mrs. Potter-Smith. " And what are your plans after that ? "

" I really think we should be getting along," said Nigel firmly, and almost dragged the others away.

" We must keep quiet about our plans," he insisted. " Old Potter-Smith could spoil everything if she got mixed up in it."

Ringing the door bell of the Bishop's house it really seemed like old times again—to be running to the Bishop for help. His poker-faced housekeeper, Mrs. Griffin, answered the door and betrayed no sign of welcome nor of recognition.

" May we see the Bishop ? "

" Who shall I say ? " she inquired.

" The Blue Doors, of course," said Maddy. " Don't you remember us ? We remember you." The house-keeper disappeared and returned to say that the Bishop would see them. He rose from his desk as they entered the study. He seemed a little older and a trifle bent.

" Hullo, Blue Doors," he exclaimed, smiling broadly. " I heard you were back in Fenchester and hoped you would call. How nice it is to see you all again ! Sit down, do ! I'll ring for some coffee."

" We've had some," began Sandra.

" But we could do with some more," added Maddy.

" Good. Well, let me look at you. Mm ! still the same, thank goodness. Well, how is the Academy ? "

" Wonderful."

" Heavenly."

" Lovely," they replied.

" And how much longer have you there ? "

" A couple of terms."

" And then ? "

" Well, that's what we've come to talk to you about, Bishop," began Nigel.

" Oh, dear ! You must think, Bishop, that we only come to see you when we want help," apologized Sandra.

" What else is a Bishop for ? " he asked simply.

" You see," said Nigel. " When we leave the Academy to open the Blue Door Theatre, the main difficulty will be money. We need several hundred pounds to buy new seats, alter the stage and equipment, build on new dressing-rooms, and hundreds of other things. Doubtless, when it gets started we should be able to pay back whatever loan was necessary for us to start, but where can we *get* that loan from ? "

" Yes," mused the Bishop. " I too have been thinking about this question for quite some time. Much as I should like to be able to help you personally, I'm afraid it is not possible. Also, I don't think that the Blue Door Theatre should be run as a private or commercial affair. It should belong in a sense to the town, so that the town will feel disposed to patronize it."

" Are we back at the subject of me vamping the Mayor?" Maddy asked, and was hushed up.

"I think that the best thing to be done is for me to approach the Town Council on your behalf to ask for a loan to turn the Blue Door Theatre into a civic theatre, with yourselves as their resident company."

"But *would* they?" queried Lyn. "Would they?"

The Bishop paused and thought hard.

"They might," he stated. "They might. One just cannot tell. There are so many factions on the council at the moment."

"How awful it will be if they won't," said Vicky gravely. "What should we do?"

"Don't think about it for the moment," advised the Bishop. "Here comes the coffee, so drown your sorrows, and tell me some more about your studies."

They told him about the Easter play tour and about Tutworth Wells, but omitted their evening occupations of the last term.

"Well, you're not sorry, then, that you have pursued theatrical careers?"

"What other careers *could* we have had?" asked Maddy. "Except, of course," she added politely, "being a Bishop. That must be rather fun. But they don't have lady Bishops, do they?"

They left the Bishop's house in a slightly more cheerful frame of mind, although he had not been over-optimistic. They were wandering along still discussing their prospects when Sandra looked at the new wristwatch she had been given for Christmas.

"Heavens! It's one o'clock! We must fly!"

"Why are we incapable of being in time for lunch?"

Over the lunch table Maddy said to her mother, "Saw Mrs. Potter-Smith this morning."

"I hope you weren't rude to her."

136

"*Yes*," *mused the Bishop,* "*I too have been thinking about this.*"

"I was. I told her she didn't look any cleaner than usual."

"Maddy! You know you must not be impolite to her, or to anybody else, for that matter. A great many people think very highly of Mrs. Potter-Smith, and she's getting to be quite an important person in the town. Why, she's even on the Town Council now."

"*What!*" Maddy and Sandra choked simultaneously over their soup.

"Yes. She was elected last time. What's the matter? Have I put too much salt in the soup?"

"Oh, Mummy!" Sandra was almost in tears. "That's done it!"

"What on earth are you talking about?"

"We're applying to the Town Council for permission to open the Blue Door Theatre and asking for a grant to start off with."

"*Are* you? Whose idea was it?"

"The Bishop's."

"Then it must be all right," said Mr. Fayne. "But I don't know if you'll get it. They're a funny crew these days."

"You're telling me!" said Maddy. "With Mrs. Potter-Smith as chief comedienne."

"We must do something to get round Mrs. Potter-Smith," said Sandra urgently. "What can we do?"

"Well, you know," said Mrs. Fayne, "I've often thought I ought to ask her to tea. She's always very friendly to me —gushing, in fact. I know you children don't like her, but if it'll do any good, I'll ask her round."

"But it must be from us," said Sandra. "May I write the note inviting her?"

"Certainly, dear."

" Talk about ' sacrificing all for one's art ' ! " said Sandra, as she got out her writing paper and pen.

" I think," said Maddy, " that I'll just write a little note to the Bishop telling him that Mrs. P.-S. is on the council now. I'm sure he doesn't know. And she is one of his deadly foes." So she too got out some paper and stretched herself on the hearth-rug. They were just finishing their letters when the rest of the Blue Doors came ringing at the bell.

"We hear that the mill-pond over at Fennymead is frozen, and we're going over to see if there's any skating. Coming?"

" Rather ! " exclaimed Sandra, " but I don't know if our skates are in very good condition. We won't be a minute. Here, Maddy, put my letter to Mrs. Potter-Smith into an envelope, while I go and ferret out the skates."

" I'll finish my letter to the Bish when I come back," remarked Maddy, skating having overshadowed all other considerations.

It was a long walk to Fennymead, but when they got there they found a good solid covering of ice on the mill pond, and people skating airily round or staggering at the edge. The Blue Doors staggered for the first few minutes, but then got used to it, and skimmed round happily. They met a lot of their old school friends, who greeted them with slight awe, now that they were on the stage. And now that Maddy had acted in a film she was, of course, looked on as something quite out of this world.

" Soppy dates," said Maddy scornfully, as two little girls stared and giggled at her.

Vicky was in her element on the ice, for all her ballet training came to the fore, and she was soon leaping and pirouetting as easily as if she were on dry land. Maddy got on quite nicely, but was inclined to fall down if she stood still.

After the long tramp home they were ravenously hungry, and the Halfords invited them all into their house for tea.

"I love just after Christmas," announced Maddy, her mouth full of iced cake, "because there's always so much food left over which people are glad for you to eat up."

"Well, whenever we want any eating up done," teased Nigel, "we shall know just where to come."

It was quite late in the evening when the Faynes returned to their house.

"Haven't you posted your letter to Mrs. Potter-Smith yet?" asked their mother.

"Yes. I posted it this afternoon."

"Excuse me, dear, but it's still on the table."

"It's not. I posted it with those others you gave me."

But there lying on the table was the envelope addressed to Mrs. Potter-Smith. Sandra picked it up, puzzled.

"Maddy, do you mean to say you posted an empty envelope?"

"No," said Maddy firmly. "I distinctly remember putting the letter in, addressing it in what I hoped looked like your best writing, and licking the envelope. It tasted rather nice.—Oh, gosh!" she cried, for her letter to the Bishop had disappeared.

"I think," she gulped, "I think I've sent the Bishop's letter to Mrs. P.-S."

"You careless girl!" scolded Mrs. Fayne. "If you were not so mad to go skating——"

Maddy turned quite pale. "Oh, dear!" she said. "Oh dear, oh dear!"

"Why, what's the matter?" asked Sandra suspiciously. "What did you put in the Bishop's letter?"

"It was to warn him that she was on the Town Council, and I said some rather nasty things about her."

" Oh, Maddy ! This is the last straw ! "

Sandra ran out of the house, banging the door, and went to tell the Blue Doors of their latest misfortune.

The following morning Mrs. Potter-Smith was rather puzzled to receive a letter which read :

" Dearest Bishop,

I must write to warn you that our deadly foe is at hand. In other words, that snake woman, Mrs. Potter-Smith, is on the Town Council, of all things. Isn't it stinking ? She'll never let us open up the Blue Door Theatre if she has anything to do with it, because she has always had her knife into us, hasn't she ?

We are starting a system of getting round her, and have invited her to tea. It will be awful. Her false teeth click so. But it's all for the good of the cause. Sandra says it is sacrificing all for our art, so I may even put on my new dress for her, though perhaps that is going a little too far . . . "

As Mrs. Potter-Smith threw the letter on the fire there was a nasty gleam in her eye.

CHAPTER X

COUNCIL CHAMBER

MRS. POTTER-SMITH, of course, did not come to tea. Instead, a rather puzzled Bishop turned up at the Fayne's house next morning to return a letter that began, "My dear Mrs. Potter-Smith."

"So I invited *him* to tea," said Mrs. Fayne afterwards. "You see, I'd just made a very special cake."

The Bishop helped to eat up the cake that afternoon, with Sandra and Maddy and Mrs. Fayne, and when they had finished and the Bishop had said firmly, "Not another crumb, thank you," Maddy ran round to fetch the rest of the Blue Doors.

When they were all crowded in, sitting on humpties and on the floor, the Bishop said, "I have here a petition I have drafted out for the town council. I want you to read it and see if it expresses your aims correctly, and if it does, to sign it, and I shall take it personally to the Mayor. I shall talk to him as persuasively as possible, and shall leave him the petition to be read at the next council meeting." He handed round several closely typed sheets of foolscap, which they read eagerly.

"Yes," said Lyn, when they had finished, "that's absolutely what we want to do, and the way you've put it, it reads as if we're doing a kindness to Fenchester, instead of *vice versa*."

"And then what happens? When they've read the petition, I mean?" asked Vicky.

"Then," said the Bishop, "they vote."

" Oh, I see. **How many** are there on the Town Council ? "

" Thirteen or fourteen."

" And Mrs. Potter-Smith is one of them ! " groaned Bull-dog. " Can't we ever be rid of that woman ? "

The Bishop smiled rather grimly.

" I've heard all about Maddy's unfortunate slip with the envelopes—and I'm afraid it won't help matters. What exactly did you say, Maddy ? "

But Maddy would not repeat it. She would only growl, " I could kick myself—but I could kick that old harpy harder."

" But still, that's only one vote against you," reminded the Bishop.

" We must canvas," said Bulldog. " Send flowers to the whole Town Council—and—and write letters to the local newspapers under different names, saying how badly the town needs a theatre."

" Why under *different* names ? " queried the Bishop. " There's nothing to stop you writing a perfectly honest letter to both the local newspapers, stating exactly what you want to do."

" That's a splendid idea," said Nigel. " We'll do that."

" And we could make Mummy get all her groceries at the Mayor's shop," suggested Maddy.

" And invite Miss Gaunt to tea," continued Vicky.

" And Lord Moulcester," added Maddy. " He wants to meet you all, because Sandra and I told him about you when we were filming. He's sweet, isn't he, Sandra ? "

" Yes, I think he'll be for us. He was on the stage for a little while once."

" And who else is there ? "

" There's Miss Thropple."

" Oh, yes, that arty-crafty old spinster. Mm ! She's a staunch Potter-Smithite."

" Those are all the ones we know, I'm afraid," Jeremy said. " The rest are unknown quantities."

" But surely," resumed Lynette. " Surely they'll *want* a theatre—who wouldn't ? "

" But they may not want to lend any money towards it," said Maddy sagely. " If we were offering them shares in whatever we make out of it, they'd probably jump at it."

" We can but hope," summed up the Bishop as he reached for his hat, prior to leaving. " I shall take the petition round to the Mayor this evening."

" Do *you* get your groceries from his shop ? " asked Maddy seriously.

" Yes," laughed the Bishop, " and at Christmas he sends me a calendar, which I always give to Mrs. Griffin to hang in the kitchen."

" That's all right, then ! " sighed Maddy.

All the following week, whenever she was sent out shopping, Maddy would go straight to Barrington's, the Mayor's shop, and indulge in long, friendly conversations with Mrs. Barrington in between the serving of customers. But the Mayor was never visible.

" Too busy mayoring, I suppose," thought Maddy.

Nigel composed a very impressive letter which he sent to both the local papers, and which appeared in one of them. It read :

" DEAR MR. EDITOR,

" We, the undersigned, are desirous of opening a repertory theatre in Fenchester, at the premises of the one-time All Souls Brethren Chapel, later the Blue Door Theatre, which is the property of the Town Council.

We feel that a town such as Fenchester, which has a large percentage of intelligent inhabitants interested in the Arts, is sadly lacking in having no theatre. A repertory theatre would provide good plays weekly or fortnightly at prices within the reach of all, and would put Fenchester on the map as an art-loving town. And who could be more suitable to launch this project than seven young Fencastrians, who, having had the best possible training and considerable experience, are now anxious to return to their native soil ? In short, Mr. Editor, we hope to enlist your support in this scheme, and to request your readers to convey their approval of it to the Town Council."

Here followed their names in full. The Blue Doors read it when the paper came out on the following Thursday, and thought that it looked very well, but they were not prepared for the storm of protest and approval that it brought forth. All day the telephones in the three neighbouring houses rang, and people they had never heard of before said :

"But what a *mad* scheme ! . . ."

"Fenchester has needed a theatre for years. . . ."

"It is a lot of nonsense. . . ."

"We shall certainly support it. . . ."

"Well, what *do* people want ? " cried Sandra in despair. "The people who *don't* want a theatre needn't be so irate about it. They just needn't come, that's all. No-one will force them to."

It seemed hardly safe to go out. First they were attacked by an old lady who waved an umbrella at them and shouted, "I'd like to give you—theatre ! What you all need is a box on the ears and a little hard work for a change."

"Hard work ! Hard work ! " seethed Lyn. "I'd like her to do a stiff rep. season and see how she'd like it."

Maddy giggled. " She'd be rather difficult to cast, wouldn't she ? "

But perhaps the people who approved of the idea were the worst. They gushed.

" And now, I've got a little niece who's a lovely little actress. Never had any training of course, but I wondered if you would be able to give her a start."

" Give her a start," groaned Jeremy afterwards. " Let's get *our* start first, for goodness' sake. If things don't get a move on it will be time to go back to the Academy and we shall have settled nothing."

They moped about, going to the cinema too often and trying not to talk about the Blue Door Theatre in case it should all fall through. They felt hurt and baffled somehow, to think that after taking it for granted all these years it should suddenly present so many difficulties. And then they heard that the next council meeting was to be held one afternoon just before they departed for the Academy.

" But shall we *know* before we go back ? " Vicky asked.

" I wish we could be there," said Nigel, " and hear all the nattering that will go on."

" Let's hide ourselves behind the curtains of the council chamber, and at the most dramatic moment run out and fling ourselves on our knees at their feet," suggested Maddy.

" Why bother to hide ? " said her father. " There's a public gallery where you are perfectly entitled to sit and hear the whole proceedings."

" *Can* we ? Oh, how lovely. How awful it will be, though ! As bad as it was waiting to hear the results of the Seymore Contest."

" Yes. For just as much, if not more, will depend on it," agreed Lynette.

" What shall we wear ? " asked Vicky, returning to the eternal feminine question.

" We must try to look very, very grown-up," said Sandra, " otherwise they won't think we are capable of such an undertaking." The girls all pinned their hair up, except Maddy who was not allowed to, so she compromised by tying it back tightly, to look as much like a bun as possible.

They even wore hats to look respectable, and the boys put on dark lounge suits instead of their usual shapeless corduroys. They were glum and silent as they walked to the Town Hall.

" What an ugly building it is ! " observed Lynette. " All that red brick—and those turrets ! "

" Shall we be allowed to speak ? " asked Maddy, as they mounted the ornate marble staircase.

" No ! " said Sandra firmly. " If you as much as open your mouth, I shall take you home."

" But there's so much I'd like to say."

" Wouldn't we all ! "

" If Mrs. Potter-Smith sits directly below us, I shall want to drop something on her, I know I shall," threatened Maddy.

" This is terrible," said Lyn, after they had sat in silence on the hard wooden chairs for some minutes. " Like waiting to hear one's own death sentence."

All round the walls of the lofty hall were enormous oil paintings of past councillors of Fenchester, wearing robes of office and clasping scrolls.

" What a batch of stooges ! " observed Maddy. " I hope the present lot are a bit better."

At this moment the councillors began to troop in and take their places round the long table in the centre of the hall. They were *not* a better-looking lot than their predecessors. Except for Miss Gaunt and Lord Moulcester they all looked rather dreary. And when Mrs. Potter-Smith sailed in, beaming all over her plump face, the Blue Doors hissed softly under their breath.

" What an entrance ! " observed Lynette.

" What a part ! " rejoined Nigel.

After much coughing and shuffling, the meeting began by the Town Clerk reading out the minutes of the last meeting. During this, which was long and boring and quite inaudible, Maddy sneezed loudly, and one of the lady councillors, looking up at the public gallery, saw the Blue Doors sitting there. She turned to her neighbour and whispered, and soon the news had gone right round the table.

" Like that party game," observed Vicky. When Mrs. Potter-Smith heard the news she gaped up at them, quite taken aback.

" Now she realizes she can't say all the rude things behind our backs that she had intended," said Maddy. The flower on the top of Councillor Potter-Smith's ridiculous hat quivered ominously.

There was quite a lot of business to be settled before the question of the Blue Door Theatre was brought up, and the seven in the gallery fidgeted and sighed and worried, with heavy frowns on their faces. At last the Mayor said, " And now I have here a petition handed to me by the Bishop on behalf of seven young Fencastrians." He read out the petition that the Blue Doors had signed, asking for the use of the Blue Door Theatre and for a loan to be granted. Immediately a buzz of opinions went round the table. Bald heads and matronly hats got together in conclave.

" I should like," said the Mayor, " to have your views on this separately. For my part I—er—feel that we have got on quite well without a theatre all these years." The Blue Doors groaned inwardly. Then Miss Gaunt got up and spoke. The Blue Doors felt a wave of deep affection for their ex-headmistress.

"I think that this is one of the most exciting pieces of news Fenchester has had for a long while," she began. "How it has happened that a town of this size should still be without a theatre I cannot imagine. I can vouch personally for the integrity and ability of the seven young people concerned, and I think that a theatre would add considerably to the attraction of the town, both for tourists and the country people from round about, as well as providing a much-needed cultural interest. Should this excellent idea be carried out, I shall myself be a patron of the theatre."

"Good old Gaunt," breathed Bulldog.

Next, a very old gentleman got up and announced that he didn't hold with the theatre, and what on earth were the Council doing, considering lending money to a lot of play-actors?

"You'd never see it back again," he finished in an aggrieved manner. Maddy jumped up, pink with rage.

"Oh, yes, you—" Sandra clapped a hand over her mouth, and pulled her down into her seat. "You little idiot! You'll ruin everything," she hissed.

Then Lord Moulcester rose, his little goat beard sticking out at an aggressive angle.

"Mr. Mayor," he said, "I wish to state that if the council refuses this chance of a first-class theatre, they will be very foolish, for there are plenty of other towns that will jump at the opportunity, and to one of those towns this company of young professionals will certainly turn if we refuse them. When you consider how much more prosperous the town has been since the film *Forsaken Crown* was made at Fennymead, surely it must be realized that a little publicity and a go-ahead spirit are needed here."

" Good old Lord Moulcester," said Maddy. " And he used to be such an old stick-in-the-mud."

" There are plenty of funds that could be diverted to the loan that would be required at the start," continued Lord Moulcester. " The Education Committee surely could do something, and we could stipulate that every so often the repertory company should do a play suitable for children, and give matinées for the schools."

There were a few " Hear, hears ! " from some corners of the table, and the Blue Doors crossed their fingers.

" Finally, I should like to say," concluded Lord Moulcester, " that I too know these young people, and if anything should happen to prevent them repaying the loan, I should have pleasure in personally vouching for the amount required."

" The dear thing ! " whispered Maddy, wriggling in her seat. " I told you he was a duck."

But then the worst happened. Mrs. Potter-Smith rose, bridling with determination.

" I really cannot understand," she began, clasping her plump white hands affectedly, " how the council can consider spending money on such expensive luxuries as a theatre, when there are so many necessities still lacking. What about the new hospital—the repairs to the alms-houses—and the rebuilding of the public conveniences ? "

" My goodness ! " sighed Lyn. " I think we've had it."

" When I think," Mrs. Potter-Smith's voice softened dramatically, " of all the poor sick people needing hospital beds, all the dear old people seeking a haven in which to spend the autumn of their days, and of—well—all that sort of thing—I cannot understand how you can contemplate such a rash move. Surely there is enough amateur talent in the town, without letting a professional company monopolize one of the few public halls. I'm sure we all remember what chaos the film people caused in the town. Surely we don't want the same type of person to be amongst us regularly ? "

There were some noises of agreement, and the Blue Doors registered their agony of mind in varying ways. Maddy hissed audibly, Lyn banged her forehead with her fist, two tears rolled slowly down Vicky's face, Sandra sat very still and prayed hard for something to happen to make Mrs. Potter-Smith shut up. Bulldog said all the bad words he knew under his breath. Jeremy got out his empty pipe and sucked at it feverishly, and Nigel buried his face in his hands.

"Finally, I should like to say," said Mrs. Potter-Smith, shooting a malicious glance up at the gallery, "that I too know these young people." And she sat down heavily, while the rest of the council coughed in a somewhat embarrassed way, conscious of the Blue Doors in the gallery.

Then Miss Thropple got up.

"I agree with everything that Mrs. Potter-Smith has said," she twittered. "Everything." And she sat down again, breathing hard.

"I can't stand this much longer," said Lynette. "I shall just get up and scream."

"What a yes-woman that Thropple is," breathed Bulldog.

The ex-mayors of Fenchester looked down at them without pity, the sky over the glass roof began to darken, the lights were lit, and glared into the anxious eyes of the Blue Doors. The little group of people down below seemed to be the only people in the world, for on them the future depended. The voices rambled on and on, arguing and contradicting, politely and interminably.

At last the Mayor rose to his feet and said, "As there seems to be some difference of opinion on this matter, I think we had better put it to the vote. Who will propose the motion that we allow the Blue Door Company the use of the theatre and grant them such loan as they and we may deem necessary ? "

Lord Moulcester raised his hand.

" I propose it," he said.

" And I second it," said Miss Gaunt quickly.

" Those in favour ? "

Some hands were raised, and the Blue Doors leaned forward counting earnestly.

There were seven in favour.

" And those against ? "

Seven hands were raised against.

" Oh, gosh ! " cried Vicky. " What now ? "

There was an empty chair at one end of the table, and at this moment who should hurry in but the little antique dealer from near the Blue Door Theatre.

" It's Mr. Smallgood and Whittlecock ! " cried Maddy delightedly. " Oh, *dear* Mr. Smallgood and Whittlecock. He'll vote for us, I know he will ! "

" But will he, will he ? " Lyn repeated wildly, fixing the grey little man with an hypnotic stare. The motion was hastily explained to Mr. Smallgood and Whittlecock, and he was asked whether he were for or against the project.

Maddy stood up and waved violently, mouthing " Yes ! Yes ! " but he did not appear to see.

"Well, er—I really don't know—" he began.

" Your vote, please," said the Mayor, who was beginning to be tired of the whole subject.

" Oh, well—by all means——"

" In favour ? "

" Er—yes——"

" Then the motion has been carried that we should allow

the Blue Door Theatre Company the use of the hall as a theatre, and grant them a loan for the commencement. And now we must turn our attention to the subject of drainage."

There was a scuffle from the public gallery as the Blue Doors shot out of the door like arrows from a bow, laughing and shouting maniacally. Down the marble stairs they danced, Vicky tapping madly, Maddy sliding down the banisters. The boys fought playfully on the mat at the bottom, and they talked at the tops of their voices.

"Now then, now then," said the little man in uniform at the door. They were so excited that they had to run and run through the dark streets to the milk bar where they had first drunk to the success of the Blue Doors.

"*What* a narrow shave!" cried Lynette, as they gulped down their milk shakes. "Bless little Mr. Smallgood and Whittlecock! We must take him some flowers or something in the morning."

"I knew he'd help us," said Maddy.

"Don't be silly," said Jeremy. "He didn't even know who we were. He was just thoroughly dazed and vague, and said the first thing that came into his head."

"Thank goodness it was yes!" sighed Sandra. "Oh, how lovely life is! Now there's *nothing* to stop us. We can go straight ahead with plans. It's too heavenly for words."

For a long time they were so crazy with relief that they could not settle down to discuss plans sensibly, but ordered all the different coloured drinks they could find on the menu and mixed them indiscriminately.

"Bovril is lovely with orangeade," announced Maddy.

"I think we ought to go back to the town hall, and as they come out say 'thank you' to the people who supported us" suggested Sandra.

They walked more soberly back, each thinking how terrible it would have been if their plea had been unsuccessful. They surrounded Miss Gaunt and Lord Moulcester and pumped them by the hand.

"Thank you! Thank you!" they all cried. "Oh, isn't it heavenly?"

"It is indeed," agreed Lord Moulcester. "And when are you going to open?"

"Next September, sir," Nigel told him. "All being well. I want to go into rep. elsewhere next Easter holidays, and learn about the business side of it."

"Very wise, my boy, very wise. Ah, well, I envy you considerably, and I wish you every success."

"So you're leaving me next term, Madelaine," Miss Gaunt remarked.

"Yes. Aren't I lucky?" said Maddy.

"Maddy!" cried Sandra. "Oh, Miss Gaunt, she doesn't mean it that way!"

"Of course she does. And I quite understand. The Academy should provide her with just what she needs."

"And I'm sure she's no loss to you," smiled Jeremy.

At this moment little Mr. Smallgood and Whittlecock came out and started off down the road, a bent little figure. Maddy ran up behind him, and embraced him violently.

"Thank you a thousand times!" she cried.

"Er—the same to you," and he passed on completely bewildered.

The Blue Doors laughed until their tummies ached. It was time to go home and tell their parents the glad news. They received it enthusiastically, glad to know that now there would be no reason for their children to be away from home once they had left the Academy.

Next day Nigel set about the problem of getting an

architect to consider building on the dressing-rooms in the waste space behind the theatre, and they both crawled about on hands and knees, measuring with footrules.

"It's going to cost an awful lot," Nigel said at lunch-time. "I must go and see the secretary of the Education Committee and find out how much we can borrow."

The remainder of the holiday sped by in a whirl of plans and arrangements. They went round to all the local shopkeepers from whom they hoped for support, asking for commodities to be supplied to the theatre at special rates.

"We'll have to arrange about the new seating when we're in London," said Nigel. "And the curtains."

A local builder was to put up the dressing-rooms and enlarge the stage. There seemed to be a hundred and one details to be considered, and they dashed about like mad things, right up to the time of their departure to London once more.

"We shall need another holiday to get over our holidays," observed Bulldog.

Maddy was nearly crazy with excitement. She had been allowed to spend some of her film earnings on new and more grown-up clothes for the Academy, and was very proud of a pair of red slacks, a green dancing-practice dress, and her first pair of shoes with heels that were not absolutely flat. Her mother had given her a beautifully bound *Shakespeare* and her father a large wardrobe trunk.

"I really *feel* like an actress now," she sighed happily, as she repacked it for the hundredth time.

On the day of their departure they had quite a crowd of friends and relations to see them off.

"Life is all arrivals and departures," said Lyn.

"What a lot of them we've had already——"

"And it's nice," said Maddy, "not to be one of the people who are left waving on the station, and have to turn round and stooge home !"

As the train pulled out Vicky leaned from the window, and shouted to the receding streets of the town :

"Good-bye, Fenchester. We'll soon be back !"

Chapter XI

JELLIED EELS

MADDY in London was like a cat on hot bricks. She was all over the place all the time, and at such a speed that Bulldog told her she would meet herself coming back one day, if she were not careful. Every morning she was up at six or seven, long before the others had yawned and turned over for an extra half-hour. She would bound out into Regent's Park and feed the swans with bread, or, if she had none, cheat them with pieces of wood until they flapped their wings and squawked angrily. When the others came down to breakfast she would be polishing up her lines for the day, and would greet them cheerily.

"For goodness' sake don't be so hearty, woman!" Jeremy snarled. "You look like an advertisement for Eno's."

She was at the Academy long before anyone else, practising tonic sol-fa at the piano, doing acrobatics on the roof, and poking about the wardrobe, getting in Mrs. Bertram's way and dressing up in anything she could lay hands on.

In her class, the "Babies" as they were called, she was the undisputed leader, and whenever they were left to rehearse by themselves the role of producer automatically fell to her. She was the class representative for the Students' Council, a sort of trade union that discussed problems and arguments among the pupils. And already she had a student production in rehearsal. The other members of the class ranged in age from twelve to fifteen, and although several of them had been on the stage ever since they could get licences, they held Maddy somewhat in respect, as her film *Forsaken Crown* was still attracting crowds to the Palaceum, Leicester Square. It was Maddy's one grumble that the " Babies " were only allowed theatrical lessons in the morning. In the afternoon they had to settle down to fractions and spelling, just as at Fenchester High School. She was always in trouble for concealing a copy of a play under her desk, and often, as her lips moved silently as if working out an arithmetical problem, she would be in reality swotting up her lines.

When the Academy was over for the day Maddy would disappear with a swarm of the " Babies," and they would wander over the face of London, causing havoc wherever they went. They had competitions in running up down-ward-moving escalators, and played " last into the tube train." Sometimes they went roller skating, and Maddy returned covered with bruises and dust. Sometimes they went to a news cinema where there was a good long Disney programme and not too much news. Other nights they stormed the box offices of theatres where they knew the shows were doing badly, and occasionally a kind manager would agree to let them in for nothing, as they were from the Academy, and in return they would clap like mad, however bad the play. Sandra found it impossible to coax Maddy into staying in to do her mending and write letters home, and usually had to do them for her.

" I don't know what our poor mother would say," sighed Sandra, " to see her running wild like this."

" Oh, leave her alone. She's having a wonderful time. And working hard, too," said Jeremy. " There's no doubt as to who is top dog among the ' Babies.' "

Maddy was playing Peter in *Peter Pan*, one of the Merry

Wives in *Shakespeare*, and the maid in a gay little scene of *Le Bourgeois Gentilhomme* in the French acting class.

"Such bounce," sighed Jeremy after hearing her lines through. "I can't think where you get it from."

"It's sheer relief at not having a lot of lights and cameras around when you're trying to act," replied Maddy.

"Do you really prefer the Academy to filming?" Jeremy asked.

"Of course," Maddy replied stoutly, "and besides you're all here too."

"But you don't see all that much of us."

"No, but you're around. I can borrow money from you, and get Sandra to wash my hair and all that sort of thing."

The term seemed to fly by on wings. No sooner had they arrived at the Academy on a Monday morning than it seemed time to go home on Friday afternoon and make plans for the week-end. The money that they had saved while working during the previous term eked out their allowances, so there was no need to look for further employment until the Easter holidays.

"I must get into a rep. this Easter," said Nigel firmly, "otherwise I shan't have the slightest idea how to set about the business side of the Blue Doors when we open up."

Once more he started writing letters and sending photos round to all the companies, and even visited some of the theatrical agents, sitting for hours in the tiny waiting-rooms, watching the stream of teddy-bear-coated actors and fur-coated actresses that went in and out. Everywhere he met with the same answer—"Come back when you've had some professional experience." He found that having studied at the Academy meant next to nothing, in fact some agents seemed to bear a grudge against him on account of it.

" A few years' experience would have done you twice as much good," he was told by an unpleasant little Cockney agent with a red face and a large cigar.

" And yet," thought Nigel, " one is told there is no chance on the stage nowadays unless one is trained."

At last came the welcome letter from a rep. in Scotland to say that they would take him as assistant business manager, if he would walk on occasionally.

" That's terrific ! " he crowed. " I'll learn all about front-of-house management now, and how to make a simply stupendous profit out of the Blue Door Theatre."

" Wouldn't it be heavenly if we did," mused Bulldog, " so that we could build a really terrific theatre with a revolving stage and everything."

" But what are *we* going to do ? " asked Lyn. " This Easter there are no Academy tours going out that would suit us."

" Let's stay in town," suggested Vicky, " and get whatever work we can. We might get some filming or something."

" Yes, let's stay," said Maddy, " I haven't really had time to explore London properly."

" You know it better already than we do."

The day after term ended Nigel departed for Scotland.

" Bring us back some haggis," they shouted at Euston Station after they had loaded him with comics, and Maddy had bought him some very sticky toffee.

" Isn't it horrid being split up ? " grumbled Sandra. " Thank goodness we shall never have to be again, once we get back to Fenchester."

Next day they began their search for casual work. There were quite a few students staying in London with the same idea, and the Academy was proving helpful by posting up in the foyer every day a list of who was wanting what and where. By this means the Blue Doors found themselves working four or five days out of every week. They went down to the Pinetree Park Studios several times as extras on a stupendous historical film about the Great Fire of London—all except Maddy, whom they would not allow to accompany them, as it might do harm to her career to be recognized in the crowd after having starred in *Forsaken Crown*.

" Oh, what a nuisance," she grumbled, " I did want to come too."

" That child has no notion of prestige or position," remarked Jeremy.

" It's incredible."

Lynette and Sandra and Vicky had a few days' work as photographers' models, posing for hours in such beautiful clothes that it was a wrench to exchange them for their own shabby garments when the day was over.

" Well, couldn't I advertise some children's clothes ? " Maddy wanted to know. " I had lots of offers when I was making *Forsaken Crown*. Toothpaste, too."

" No," they told her, " it's quite out of the question."

" But, why ? " she wanted to know. " If you can, why can't I ? " It was impossible to make her understand that she had a reputation to keep up.

" You go out and enjoy yourself to-morrow," they told her, when they had got another day's crowd work.

Maddy found that exploring London by herself was beginning to pall. All the " Babies " had gone home for the holidays, and she felt a little lost without someone with whom to paddle in the Serpentine or feed the monkeys at the Zoo.

" I wish I could get a job like the others," she mused.

The following week, when the others had got a commission to walk on in a Shakespearean season in Regent's Park, they asked Maddy if she would like to come along too and see if the producer could use her.

"Oh, no," she said sarcastically, "surely it's below my dignity. And anyhow, I've got a job."

"You've got a job?"

"Yes. I must fly now, or else I'll be late." And putting on her coat she ran out and banged the door of No. 37.

"The little brat—she's up to something," remarked Jeremy.

"I hope it's nothing too terrible," sighed Sandra. "You know what Maddy is."

That night they walked on as citizens in *Julius Cæsar*, and from the bushes that served as wings watched the scenes they were not in. The play was all very familiar to the boys, who had toured in it.

"I wonder," mused Bulldog, "if it's a step up from being a soldier to being a citizen? But at least it's nice to have one's knees covered."

It was getting dusk as they walked home, and people were coming out of the Gala, a theatre which seemed to have strayed somewhat off the beaten tracks of theatre-land and was hidden in a back street of Soho.

"Isn't it nice," said Lyn, "to think that they are the public and we're not."

The gay lights of the theatre lit up the darkness of the mean street, and a barrel organ jangled away, playing musical comedy tunes of the 'twenties.

"How nostalgic these tunes are," remarked Jeremy, "even to us, and we were not even born then." An old man was turning the handle of the machine, nodding his head and long grey locks in time to the music.

"Isn't he heavenly ? " cried Lyn. "Oh, do let's give him some money."

They looked around for his collecting hat or plate. A little girl appeared to be collecting from the crowd which streamed from the theatre.

"Are you his little girl ? " a large lady in a sable cloak asked the child.

"Oh, no," said a voice that was extremely familiar to the Blue Doors, "his great-granddaughter. There are seven of us."

The lady turned to her companion. "How nicely spoken ! " she said. "Gladys, give her ten shillings." But before the crisp slip of paper was placed in the hat, Sandra had pounced.

"Maddy ! " she cried. "Come home at once ! Oh, how could you."

"Oh, hullo. Told you I'd got a job, didn't I ? "

"You little idiot ! " ranted Jeremy. "Supposing some-one recognizes you ? " and he dragged her roughly away by the arm.

"Hi—wait a minute. I must give the money to Mr. Chubb." She bounded across to the old gentleman and handed him the hat. He counted its contents rapidly with one hand, while the other churned out *Velia*. Then he pressed some of the money into Maddy's palm.

"Thank you, Missy, kindly," he said. "Sorry you can't stay."

"So'm I," said Maddy in an aggrieved tone. "I was having a lovely time. Bye-bye." All the way home they scolded her.

"If you ever do anything like it again I shall tell Mummy and Daddy, and they'll make you go home at once. What-ever made you do it ? "

" Well, you'd all got jobs, so I didn't see why I shouldn't.
And I bet I've made more than you to-night." She jingled
her pocketful of coppers and sixpences. " Mr. Chubb was
such a nice gentleman."

" But however did you *meet* him ? " expostulated
Lynette.

" It was like this," said Maddy. " Someone at the
Academy told me that a friend of his had hired a barrel organ
for some charity or other, and told me where you could get
them, so I went along there, but they wouldn't let me have
one. Then just as I was going away I saw Mr. Chubb and
he had just got his organ, so he said I could go along
and help him. And what do you think we had for
supper ? "

" What ? "

" Jellied eels."

" Oh, Maddy, you'll be ill."

" No, I shan't. They were lovely. We ate them at a
stall—a lovely stripey stall."

" Oh, you little horror ! Thank goodness term starts
next week. It'll keep you out of mischief."

" Our last term," sighed Jeremy. " Isn't it awful to think
of ? How quickly the time has gone . . ."

" People say," said Vicky, " that schooldays are the best
days of one's life. But they're wrong, because at school
one has to sit through so much that is boring. I'm sure
that the really happiest time is spent during the specialized
training that comes directly after schooldays."

" How lucky we are," observed Jeremy, " to have the
Blue Door Theatre to return to, so that all this scrapping
about looking for work is fun, and not stark necessity."

Gradually the thought of their return to Fenchester filled
their horizon. Nigel returned from Scotland with a very

thorough idea of how the Blue Door Theatre's finances should be managed.

"We must find a really dependable person to work in the box office," he announced.

"When the box office has been built," added Bulldog, under his breath.

"Not just someone capable of taking in the money, but a sort of a secretary with an eye to business," went on Nigel.

"Let's advertise in *The Stage*," suggested Lyn. "It'd be fun to be putting in an advertisement, instead of scanning the 'Artistes Wanted' column."

"And also," continued Nigel, ignoring the interruptions, "we must encourage permanent bookings by all our friends and relations—you know, keeping the same seats for a family on the same night each week."

"If we could almost fill the theatre in that way," said Sandra, "we should have nothing to worry about."

"We can write to Terry at Tutworth and warn him to be ready to leave there about September," said Vicky.

"Yes, if you're sure he's really good at scenic design. We can't employ anyone just for friendship's sake."

"Of course not, but Terry's every bit good enough," the girls reassured Nigel.

And then began the discussion as to which of their fellow students they should invite to join the company.

"We want about three," said Nigel. "An A.S.M., a stage manager, and a character woman. To save salaries we shall have to employ other people by the week as we need them."

"Obviously we should take Myrtle, if she'll come," suggested Jeremy. "We'd never find a better character actress, and, after all, Fenchester is a little better than Wigan."

"Just a little . . ."

Next day Nigel approached Myrtle and told her about the Blue Doors' scheme.

" So if you're interested," he finished up.

" You mean—you're offering me a job ? " she inquired incredulously.

" Yes. I'm afraid the pay won't be much, but we're going to try to do interesting work."

There were tears in Myrtle's blue eyes.

" I'd take it if *I* had to pay *you*," she announced. " The thought of having to start off round the agents again at my age was killing me. And after the heavenly time I've had here at the Academy. . . . I'll never be able to thank you enough, deary."

Somehow the news soon went round the Academy that the Blue Doors were opening their own company, and they found themselves suddenly the most popular people in the school. Invitations to lunch and dinner and to parties and theatres and picnics simply swamped them. They accepted them all and lived on the fat of the land until people realized that no bribes could influence their decisions. For stage manager they had decided on Ali, the Indian boy, who had resolved to give up acting and go in for stage-managing professionally. He promised to come to them for six months to gain experience before looking for a West End position. As assistant stage manager they decided to have Billy, on condition that he did not expect to be given any parts, for his time at the Academy had in no way lessened the impediment in his speech.

" Yeth," he said, " I know I lithp, tho I might ath well thtage-manage."

" And we'll jolly well pay him a bit better salary than *we* had as A.S.M.'s," said Vicky, " and treat him like a human being."

Their advertisement in *The Stage* for a box-office secretary with some theatrical experience produced the most extraordinary selection of people. They called at the Academy every day between four and five o'clock all that week, and Nigel interviewed them in the foyer, feeling madly important and rather embarrassed. They were nearly all women; some were faded, dejected spinsters with a fervent desire to "keep up appearances," others were ex-actresses and chorus girls whom Nigel felt sure could not add two and two correctly. Of the few men who applied each seemed to have something wrong with him, cross eyes, or no roof to his mouth.

"It's no good," sighed Nigel, when the last one had been interviewed, "we couldn't have employed any of them. They're just not *us*."

For the next few weeks they kept their eyes on the "Situations Wanted" columns of the newspapers, but none of the advertisers sounded of the right type.

"They all sound either too 'refaned' or else absolute scoundrels," objected Jeremy.

Then one day Maddy said, "Nigel, dear——"

"Yes? I presume you want something?"

"I want you to see a friend of mine whom I think would do for the box-office bloke."

"Who is he?"

"Wait and see. When will you meet him?"

"Tell him to call round at the digs to-night. Is it someone from the Academy?"

"Oh, no. A very dependable sort of person."

"Well, I don't promise anything."

That evening as Nigel and Jeremy sat writing letters in the dining-room of No. 37 Mrs. Bosham put her head round the door.

" A gentleman to see you, Mr. Nigel."

" Show him in, please, Mrs. Bosham."

In came an elderly, grey-haired gentleman in an old-fashioned suit that smelt slightly of mothballs. He bowed with old-world courtesy.

" Mr. Halford, I presume ? "

" Yes," said Nigel. " You're a friend of Maddy's, I hear."

" Indeed, I am. And she has told me that you are looking for a front-of-house manager for your theatre. Now, I have had many years of experience in that line. I began as a chartered accountant, and then took to the boards as a tenor singer, following which I toured abroad for many years with my own company."

" I see," said Nigel. " You could produce references, I suppose ? "

Out came a sheaf of dog-eared yellow papers, all testifying to the complete integrity of their owner. Nigel explained what the duties would be, and that all the financial side of the theatre would be his responsibility.

" And your age ? " Nigel inquired, feeling rather impertinent.

" Fifty," said the old man, without batting an eyelid. Nigel mentally added on another good fifteen years, and said, " Well, I shall have to think it over, Mr.—er—what was the name ? "

" Chubb."

Jeremy, who was sitting quietly in the corner, looked up sharply.

" Well, Mr. Chubb," concluded Nigel, " if you'll leave me your address I'll get in touch with you."

" Care of the General Post Office, Leicester Square," was the reply, as the visitor bowed himself out of the room.

Jeremy saw him to the front door, and as he watched the

bent figure down the road a chord seemed to strike in his memory. And the name . . .

" Chubb—Chubb," he murmured, and suddenly recalled Maddy's voice saying, " Mr. Chubb was *such* a nice gentleman."

"Well, I'm blowed ! " And he ran to tell Nigel, who had been in Scotland during the barrel-organ incident.

" Maddy ! " Nigel yelled up the stairs. " Come here at once."

" I'm in the bath ! " she replied.

" Well, get out."

In a few minutes Maddy, clad in a bath towel and with a pink and shining face ran down the stairs.

" Did you like him ? Isn't he nice ? "

" What on earth do you mean by sending that old ruffian round for the job ? " Nigel demanded angrily.

" But I think he's so suitable, somehow. He's been a gentleman, he says, but he's fallen on bad times. I think it would be lovely to set him on his feet again. I lent him the money to get that suit out of pawn. Doesn't he look lovely with his hair cut, too ? "

"Oh, Maddy," groaned Nigel. "The friends you make !"

" But don't you think he'd look lovely in the box-office ? Sort of imposing ? "

" But how could we trust him to handle all our money ? Don't forget it's not even *our* money. It's the Town Council's."

" But he's been an accountant. A chartered one, too," pleaded Maddy.

" Well, why isn't he still ? " Nigel wanted to know. " He probably got kicked out."

" He wasn't," Maddy cried hotly. " He left to go on the stage. Surely you can understand that ? "

He bowed with old-world courtesy.

" Oh, Maddy, you're incredible. . . ."

Over supper Nigel told the others of the reappearance of Mr. Chubb, and they were all exceedingly intrigued.

" If only we could be sure about him," said Vicky. " He was certainly a striking-looking old man. And being fairly old he would sort of add weight to the company. Because, after all, we are terribly young to run a company, aren't we ? "

" It's the kind of thing one would love to do," agreed Lyn, " to take someone from the gutter and give him a fresh chance. But dare we do it ? "

" Let's have a look at his references," said Sandra, and read them all carefully.

" Gracious ! " she cried. " This one is signed E. Moulcester—I wonder if that's Lord Moulcester ? Is his initial E., Maddy ? "

" Yes—Ernest. There, I said Mr. Chubb knew all the best people."

" Then we'll write to Lord Moulcester straight away," said Nigel, " and find out about Mr. Chubb." The letter was posted that night, and two days later a telegram arrived that said, " Edwin Chubb my old schoolmate. Please employ."

" That's settled, then," said Nigel. " If he's not trustworthy Lord Moulcester can answer to the town council."

" Of *course* he's trustworthy," Maddy expostulated. "Look how he gave me my share of the barrel-organ earnings. *And* he paid for the jellied eels."

Mr. Chubb was overcome with delight when he next visited the Blue Doors, and sat drinking coffee with them in the dining-room, toasting the success of the Blue Door Theatre. It was only when he crossed his legs in a lordly manner that Nigel noticed the newspaper that padded the worn-through soles of his highly polished shoes. "Yes," thought Nigel, "I think he needs this job enough to make a go of it."

The last term sped by, and because they knew that the time was so short, everything about the Academy seemed miraculously dear. The long hours spent sunbathing on the roof, supposedly learning lines, and then going in to the dark and coolness of the underground theatre ; walking round the sunny square arm-in-arm with friends, indulging in long psychological discussions in the dressing-rooms, they were conscious of a " never again " feeling that added sweetness to the summer days. Lyn sometimes stopped to think, " These are, and have been, the happiest days of my life. This is what it is to be young. And so soon it will pass. And other people will be leaning on this parapet looking out over London and thinking how happy they are, and listening to the ballet class piano in the distance and eating strawberries bought from the fruit stall in the square. . . ."

And there was nothing to be done about it.

CHAPTER XII

PUBLIC SHOW

"I HOPE," said Maddy firmly, "that you will all win something in the Public Show. I shall be most ashamed of you if you don't."

"We'll do our best, ma'am. But it all depends what parts we're given. Someone's got to play the uninteresting parts, and if it's us—we're done for," said Bulldog.

"Nonsense!" replied Maddy. "Felicity Warren says that an actress should be able to recite the alphabet backwards, and still make it sound interesting."

"Don't be silly," said Lyn. "How would you win the gold medal if you just had to play a maid, and say, 'The carriage awaits without'?"

"I'd fill it simply chock full with meaning," said Maddy. "Think how many ways there are of saying it. You can say it gaily—'The carriage awaits without'"—she bared her teeth in what she hoped was a vivacious smile—"or you can sweep on and declaim it melodramatically, like this." She swept across the room, with her hands clasped tragically, and wailed, "The carriage awaits—*without.*" For a long time they played this new game, until every way of announcing the carriage had been exhausted and they were weak with laughter. But although they joked about it, the question of what parts they would be allotted in the Public Show was an important one, for so much depended on it.

"If only one could win that gold medal," sighed Lynette. "It would be a start—such a start."

"What good would a gold medal be in Fenchester?"

asked Bulldog. " People like Mrs. Potter-Smith would merely ask if it were made of real gold."

" But if one of us got it, it would justify us to our parents, and show the Town Council that one at least of us was dependable."

" When we hear the cast lists we shall know our fates," said Vicky. " It is quite obvious that whichever of Lynette and Helen gets the better part will also get the medal."

The rivalry between Lynette and Helen still existed. As each developed in her own way, their styles of acting grew even more different. Now that they were in the Finals, and persons of importance, the Academy was split into two followings, Helen's and Lynette's. Lynette's satellites accused Helen of being too stark and " arty," and Helen's upholders regarded Lynette as too flighty and artificial in her acting. And yet the two girls themselves were always on excellent terms. Although not exactly friends, the secret that they shared about Helen's job as waitress in the low café during the first term seemed to bind them together.

" You can tell," thought Lynette, " that the theatre is in her blood. So many things that I have to be taught she knows by instinct."

And then came the fateful day on which the parts for the Public Show were announced. Roma Seymore and Mr. Whitfield were sharing the producing, but it was Miss Smith who read out the list in her clipped, emotionless voice.

" Scenes will be performed from *Major Barbara*, *The Merry Wives of Windsor*, *Hay Fever*, *Uncle Vanya*, *Othello*, and *Hamlet*."

" Hamlet ! " breathed Jeremy, already visualising himself in black tights with a touch of white at the neck.

"Major Barbara!" breathed Vicky, imagining how much a Salvation Army bonnet would become her.

"Uncle Vanya!" thought Lynette. "Let me see— Sonya? Or Ilena? Which do I want?"

But then the list was read, and the Blue Doors turned to each other helplessly, white with disappointment.

"Of course, there's no reason why we should be given all the good parts," murmured Lynette, completely stunned, for she was playing Jenny, a small part of a pathetic little Salvation Army girl in *Major Barbara*, and Jeremy was not playing *Hamlet* but a vaguely comic diplomat in *Hay Fever*. Sandra was playing a decorative but dull widow in the same comedy, and Vicky was playing a Merry Wife, which she had done before, and Bulldog was playing Falstaff, also for the second time. Nigel had a good part in *Major Barbara*, Bill Walker, the Cockney thug. But as they listened to the rest of the casting, they realized that all the plums had fallen to the lot of other people.

"I think that either Ali as 'Othello' or Helen as 'Sonya' in *Uncle Vanya* will get it," prophesied Lynette.

They went home through the drizzling rain, dragging disconsolate feet.

"We must just make the best of it," said Sandra with an attempt at cheerfulness. "Come on, let's go down to the library and try to get hold of copies of the plays."

"Can't be bothered," said Jeremy. "Couldn't care less about the part."

"Oh, come on. Don't be such a drear. We'll have to learn the parts whether we like them or not."

"It really is a little thick," grumbled Lynette. "We sweat for months and months, studying as hard as we can, and then, when we get a chance to prove ourselves, to be given such bad parts!"

" Oh, I don't know," said Bulldog cheerfully, " they might be worse. One girl has only got three lines, you know."

" It's all right for you," retaliated Lyn. " You couldn't have a better part than Falstaff. It's absolutely you."

" Type-casting, of course," agreed Bulldog. " But all the same it wasn't the part I wanted."

" Oh, you're never satisfied ! " Maddy scolded them. " At least you haven't got to announce the carriage."

The atmosphere in the Finals' class was extremely tense during these last few weeks. Everyone was so deeply immersed in his own particular little bit for the Public Show that the team spirit usually apparent had entirely disappeared. There was constant friction among the students and between the teachers, and every day produced its own tears and scenes. Nigel and Lynette quarrelled bitterly over their scene in *Major Barbara*, and Sandra and Jeremy were so bad that they were threatened with having their parts taken away from them.

" What a climax to our brilliant careers at the Academy ! " laughed Jeremy cynically. " However we dare to think of opening a professional company I can't imagine ! "

In order to give everyone a scene it meant a tremendously long programme that was difficult to rehearse in the few short weeks that were left of the term, and they were kept late at the Academy nearly every evening. The days were very hot and stuffy, and at night their rooms at No. 37 were almost unbearable. One extremely hot night the three boys could stand it no longer, and got up and carried rugs into Regent's Park, where they slept under the starry sky until a policeman prodded them in the ribs at seven o'clock next morning, and it was time to hurry home for a bath and breakfast before work.

This year, as the weather was stormy, it was not to be an out-door show, but would take place in the little theatre, which had been newly decorated, ready for the occasion, and smelt sickeningly of fresh paint.

"I shall really be glad to leave, after these awful rehearsals," said Lynette at the end of a particularly bad session that lasted until seven o'clock in the evening and left everyone exhausted and hot and bad-tempered.

"Unless you all improve considerably," Mr. Whitfield had thundered. "We shall have to cancel the show. In any case it will be the worst we have ever put on."

"He says that every year," Roma Seymore told them.

Maddy had been asked to distribute programmes, as she was the youngest, yet the most distinguished pupil of the Academy.

"They're just showing her off really," Lynette confided to Sandra. "Everyone will recognize her from *Forsaken Crown*."

"Well, I hope she'll wear something respectable," said Sandra. "She's been going round like a little tramp lately."

The careless clothes affected by some of the students had captivated Maddy, and she now lived in a pair of shabby corduroys, sandals that were always coming to pieces in the street so that she had to stop and take out needle and thread to mend them, and shapeless jumpers that came down almost to her knees. When she heard that she was to be present at the Public Show to give out programmes she was delighted.

"Oh, good!" she cried. "Now I shall be able to lead the applause whenever one of you makes an exit."

"Don't you dare," warned Jeremy.

"Well, at least I'll be able to listen to what everyone says about you."

"It will probably be horrid," moped Jeremy.

179

An air of depression hung over them and everywhere they went. No. 37 seemed even more squalid than usual.

"It will be nice," said Vicky, surveying the bath with distaste, "to get home to civilization again." And yet they well knew that when the day came to leave London and the Academy they would be heart-broken.

There were notices in all the papers that the Academy's Public Show was about to take place, and mentioning the names of the many distinguished theatre people who were to be the judges. The Blue Doors, knowing how bad they were in their parts, winced at the list.

"If only we'd been eligible at the last Public Show, when we did *The Importance*," Lynette moaned.

The last-term students were already on the look-out for jobs, and people were liable to be absent from rehearsals for an hour or two, and then appear, radiant, after a successful audition, or dejected, after a tramp round the agents. The Blue Doors were chafing at their inability to get on with things at Fenchester.

"We'll be lucky if we open in September," Nigel observed. "There's still oodles to be done."

He and Mr. Chubb, who was proving a tower of strength, went down to Fenchester for several week-ends, and returned to report favourably on the building of the dressing-rooms, and the new seating accommodation.

Lynette was in an odd state of dissatisfaction. She was bored with her part in the Public Show, and wishing the term over, and yet she could not bear the thought of leaving London. And suddenly the years that she had spent in constant company with the Blue Doors seemed to catch up on her, and she went out of her way to avoid them, going out in the evenings for long walks by herself, or going to the cinema with other students, whom the Blue Doors considered "outsiders." She quarrelled with Nigel more than ever, snubbed Maddy, and avoided the other two girls, and although she knew that she was doing it, she could not help it. There seemed to be some problem at the back of her mind that she could not quite face up to. When plans for the Blue Door Theatre were discussed she maintained a remote silence, as though they did not concern her.

"Anyone would think you were longing to be anything but an actress," complained Maddy. "I should be terribly thrilled if I were ready to leave the Academy and come back with you. I'm always behind the rest of you—and I'll never catch up. Still, it will be fun to be all on my own up here."

"I dread to think what mischief you'll get into," said Sandra. "But still, it won't be my responsibility."

"Mrs. Bosham has promised to 'look after me like a mother,'" said Maddy. "I jolly well wish she could cook like my mother."

There was a dress rehearsal of the Public Show which all the students attended, and never was a dress rehearsal worse. It lasted five hours with long waits between acts. The curtains jammed and they had to get the boilerman to come and unstick them, and a piece of scenery fell on Bulldog's head.

At supper-time Nigel said to Maddy, who had made no comment on the performances, "Well, let's have it."

Maddy took a large mouthful of college pudding and said through it, "You were all lousy."

Lynette flared up. "I'd like to see you do better. On a stage that stank of the paint that was still wet on the scenery, and with a houseful of giggling juniors in front."

"Don't wonder we giggled," retorted Maddy. "That Salvation Army bonnet of yours—golly!"

Before Maddy could be more annoying, Sandra said

firmly, " Hurry up and finish your supper. I'm going to wash your hair so that you'll look nice for to-morrow."

" Oh, don't bother," said Maddy. " I'll probably have a scarf round my head."

" Oh no, you won't," said Sandra firmly. " Nor will you wear slacks."

" Oh yes, I will."

" Oh no, you won't."

This continued until Sandra plunged Maddy's head into the soap suds.

Later in the evening they became conscience-stricken, and had a hurried rehearsal of their pieces for next day, and did voice production exercises as they undressed for bed.

" Moo, mah, may," intoned Vicky.

" That won't win you the gold medal," Maddy told her.

" It's too late now."

They all had troubled dreams of going on in the wrong play, or in the right play but the wrong clothes, until Mrs. Bosham brought them up cups of tea.

" As it's a special sort of day," she explained.

It *was* an odd sort of a day, thundery and sunless, with a red glow in the sky at breakfast-time. As they walked to the Academy there seemed to be a breathless hush over the streets. Vicky clutched her tummy and her head in turn.

" Oh, I feel sick. Oh, I've got such a headache. I'll never get used to appearing in front of an audience—never. How I hope to be an actress when I get such stage fright I can't imagine."

A large striped awning had been put out in front of the doorway of the Academy, and there were flowers in all the windows.

" Doesn't it look gay ? " said Sandra.

" Quite Continental," said Vicky.

" Gay," grumbled Lynette. " I feel it should be draped in black to celebrate the funeral of so many young ambitions."

" You're becoming neurotic, my girl," Nigel told her.

" Well, at least I *know* how bad I am in the show," Lyn told him rudely.

" Miaow," squawked Bulldog.

Chaos reigned inside the Academy. There was a buffet tea being laid in the refectory, and students had to lunch out. Roma Seymore, wearing a turban, ran round in circles, trying to be efficient.

" Bet you she's got her hair in curlers under that scarf," said Vicky.

Mr. Whitfield was looking very smart in a tailcoat.

The Blue Doors bought some sandwiches and ate them, sitting in the square, feeding the fluttering sparrows and scraggy cats that frequented the patch of sun-dried grass. As they were not on until the second half of the programme, they stayed to watch the audience arrive. In cars they came, Rolls Royces, and shooting-brakes, in taxis, and on foot— smartly dressed West End actors and actresses, artily clad producers from the out-of-town reps., and a few parents, obviously wearing their best clothes for the occasion. Mrs. Bosham, plus feather boa, was on the pavement to watch the arrivals, clasping her stumpy umbrella, and viewing all that went on with eyes that goggled with excitement. She spotted the Blue Doors and waddled across to them.

" What a collection, eh ? " she exclaimed. " Best lot o' celebrities they've 'ad for years. Now, can you slip me in somewhere ? I always like to see my young people performing."

Nigel took her across and explained to Miss Smith who

she was. Miss Smith took a doubtful look at the feather boa, and then recognized its wearer.

" But of course ! Mrs. Bosham comes every year."

And radiant with achievement, the happy landlady was led to a seat of honour in the stalls, behind London's most influential dramatic critic, and next to a popular matinée idol. Maddy came bouncing up to supply her with a programme.

" Hullo, Mrs. Bosham. I'm glad you got in all right."

" Never miss a public show, if I can 'elp it."

" Will you try to keep that seat next to you for me when I've finished giving out programmes ? " asked Maddy, and Mrs. Bosham laid her umbrella forbiddingly across it.

The stalls filled up with a rush. There was much bowing and smiling, and " I really don't know why I bother to come to these things, my dear. They bore me to tears usually, but one always hopes." A few press cameras flashed, and everyone started to put on their best smiles. When the lights went down Maddy slipped into the seat beside Mrs. Bosham.

" The gang don't come on until the end of the show," she whispered, " but all the best scenes come first, I'm afraid."

By the first interval there was a feeling that the Gold Medal had already been won, for Helen had given a performance of " Sonya " in *Uncle Vanya* that made everyone sit up and rustle programmes to discover her name. All the sultry fire of her personality was poured out, and her terms at the Academy had taught her a precision and restraint of feeling that she had not had in the early days. Hearing the applause, Lyn stood in the dressing-room, " Yes, she's got it. And she deserves it. I think that in time to come we shall be proud to say that we were in the same class as Helen." And she jammed her ugly Salvation Army bonnet on to her head with a gesture.

The second half of the programme was rather an anti-climax. The *Hay Fever* scene was not really very funny, though Sandra and Jeremy tried hard with an unhelpful team. Bulldog had a moderate success with his Falstaff, but over-did it as usual, and Vicky was nervous, and a little inaudible.

" Well, I never ! Fancy Mr. Bulldog," was all that Mrs. Bosham could say.

Maddy heard the eminent critic in front of her remark, " I should say that this young boy was very Falstaff, only more so." " How rude !" she thought. " Or is it ? "

Then came the *Major Barbara* scene. Maddy sat forward on the edge of her seat, hanging on to every remark of the aged critic, and breathing rather hard on his bald head. When Lynette entered he glanced at his programme and mumbled to his companion, " Yes. I remember this girl from last year. Got something."

Lynette did her best with her few lines, and looked sweet and striking and pathetic. Nigel was too loud and mono-tonous, and a few people left before the end of the scene, as it was long past tea-time.

" No," Maddy said sadly to Mrs. Bosham. " She hasn't got it. I was afraid she wouldn't."

" *I* nearly joined the Salvation Army one time," was the inconsequent reply.

When the curtain had come down finally and the visitors had hastened upstairs to fall hungrily on the buffet tea, the ten judges went into a huddle in the stalls to decide on the prize-winners. Maddy, on the pretext of collecting the used programmes that were scattered on the floor, hung about appearing to be engrossed, but with her ears nearly on stalks to overhear all that went on. It was decided unanimously that the Gold Medal must go to Helen, but there were numerous other smaller awards to be considered. They decided on Myrtle for the Comedy prize, and one of the old Etonians for Diction.

" Now, what about the prize for Grace and Charm of Movement ? " said the matinée idol, scratching his beautifully waved head with a gold propelling pencil. There was considerable disagreement over this. Some stood out for one of the Roedean girls, who had played " Sorel " in *Hay Fever*.

" What about the little red-haired ' Merry Wife ' ? She wasn't very good but she was graceful." Maddy sat on the floor under one of the plush-covered seats with her fingers crossed.

" Good old Vicky ! " she thought.

" No. I think the dark girl who played ' Jenny ' in *Major Barbara*," said the critic firmly. " She wasn't consciously graceful, but she put up a very good show. I think she ought to get *something*, and that's all that's left." Because the critic was by many years the senior of the judges, they accepted his suggestion.

" All right, then. What's her name ? Lynette Darwin. O.K. We've finished now," and thankfully they made their way teawards.

When they had gone up, Maddy swung between the rows of seats, chanting joyfully, " Grace and Charm of Movement—Grace and Charm of Movement."

Miss Smith put her head round the door and said, " Still here, Maddy ? You have worked hard to-day."

" Yes, Miss Smith," agreed Maddy smugly.

" Well, if you're not too tired to go up and hand round cakes you can help clear up whatever is left." Soon Maddy

186

was burrowing her way through the crowds of sweetly perfumed women and cigar-smoking men, holding out dishes of dainty cakes with the nicest one farthest away from the visitors, in the hope that it would be left to be " cleared up " by herself. Several people recognized her and asked her if she were Madelaine Fayne. To some she said " Yes," and enjoyed being told how much they had loved *Forsaken Crown*, and to the others she said gravely, " No. My name is Gladys Smelly," and enjoyed seeing them choke into their dainty cups of tea. When everyone was full of éclairs and meringues and hoarse with talking, the prize-winners were announced.

" Maddy," said Miss Smith. " Run down to the dressing-rooms and fetch Helen, Lynette, Richard, Myrtle, and Jane." In the girls' dressing-room there was a hubbub of chatter and a smell of removing cream. But when Maddy shouted, " They want the prize-winners upstairs," there was immediate and breathless silence.

" Helen, Lynette, Jane, Myrtle."

" Who's got what ? Who's got the medal ? " people shouted, but Maddy only shook her head and ran off to call Richard from the boys' dressing-room. Shiny-faced from removing grease-paint, and somewhat sheepish, the prize-winners went up to the refectory. The eminent critic made a rather long but witty speech, shook hands with them, and presented the prizes. The gold medal that Helen received was worthless in itself, but to her it opened up gates to further achievement. The minor prize-winners were given books. Lynette received a nicely bound copy of Ellen Terry's *Memoirs*, which she already had, but she made a mental note to exchange it with Nigel for his *Collected Works of Shaw*, of which he possessed two copies. The critic said to Lynette as she was about to go out of the door :

"In fifteen years' time, my dear, you *might*—note I say *might*—be beginning to learn something about the art of acting, and except for the Gold Medallist, I would say that nearly all the other performers this afternoon will by that time be rearing healthy families in Chiswick." Lynette was very cheered by this rather mixed compliment, and walked back to No. 37 not feeling too bad about having failed to win the Gold Medal.

Maddy sat among the array of half-empty plates left after the departure of the guests, picking a crumbled tart from here and a squashed cream bun from there.

"I bet I've enjoyed myself to-day more than anyone."

The day after the Public Show started off in a very ordinary way. Kippers for breakfast at No. 37, buying the morning papers on the way to the Academy to see what was said about the Public Show, and a long post-mortem on the subject between themselves.

"You weren't as bad as I feared," Maddy told them. "In fact you didn't disgrace me at all."

"Thank you. As long as I pleased you and the critic of the *Daily Tribune*."

The Academy looked rather drab without the striped awning, and with the flowers dying in the windows.

"What a boring day this will be," remarked Lynette. "Everything over, and yet we can't go home for another week."

"Can't think why we've bothered to come to-day," said Bulldog.

As Lynette entered through the swing doors a junior running up the stairs called out, "Lynette, darling—there's a telegram for you in the rack!"

"Thanks." Lynette thought as she took it, "Suppose

Mummy and Daddy are coming up to town, or something."

At first the words did not make sense. She turned it over and looked hard at the back, on which, of course, there was nothing.

" Please call at the Tiller and Webb Productions Office, Charing Cross Road, this afternoon at three," it read.

Chapter XIII

OPPORTUNITY IS A FINE THING

JEREMY saw Lynette's face grow pale, and said quickly, "Is it—anything from Mum and Dad?"

"No," said Lyn. "Oh, no. No, it isn't."

"Well, what is it then, you soppy date?" Maddy snatched the telegram from Lyn's nerveless hand and read it, her eyes and mouth widening.

"Tiller and Webb! Gosh! Lynette! It must mean a job."

"Yes," said Lynette, abashed and exhilarated. "Yes. Perhaps it does." The telegram was handed round the six of them, and their excitement made other people come over to inquire what was up. Soon the whole Academy knew that Lynette was to have an interview with the most important theatrical management in town.

"It's probably only a walk-on," Lynette kept saying, and everyone replied, "Yes. But with Tiller and Webb." The rest of the morning she walked about in a daze, occasionally turning to Sandra to say, "What do you think I should wear?" or "How ought I to do my hair?" She went to Roma Seymore to ask if she might be absent from class that afternoon, and Mrs. Seymore seemed to know all about it already.

"Yes," she said. "They rang up after the show yesterday to inquire if you would be free to consider an engagement."

"Consider!" exclaimed Lynette. "Do you know what it is?"

" No, dear, I don't exactly, though I believe it's a very nice little part. But don't get too excited about it yet, will you ? So many things can happen."

" No, no, I won't count on anything," vowed Lynette, but with fast beating heart. After lunch she hurried back to No. 37, ironed a crisp summery dress, and brushed her long hair until it shone.

" Now, ought I to wear gloves ? " she pondered. " Yes, of course I ought." And she plundered Vicky and Sandra's drawers to find a white pair. There were some dirty spots on them which she tried to cover with powder, dropped the powder box, and laddered her stockings as she bent down to clear it up.

" Thank goodness I left plenty of time to get there," she thought. She snatched up a large straw hat, tied the ribbons under her chin, and let it fall down onto the nape of her neck. She surveyed herself in the fly-blown mirror that distorted your reflection if you stood too close.

" Not bad," she thought, " but terribly young. Much too young for anything."

At last she was swinging along Charing Cross Road, the sun beating down, seeping through her thin clothes, and a hot smell of petrol and melting tar from the busy roadway. She was pelmanizing herself, saying loudly inside her, " I mustn't be nervous, I must be poised, and collected and— suave—and svelte—and talk confidently—as if all the managements in London were wanting me."

The clock of St. Martin in the Fields was striking three as Lyn reached the Tiller and Webb offices, which were in a tall business block at the Trafalgar Square end of Charing Cross Road. There was a notice saying " Tiller and Webb Offices, 5th Floor," and a lift by which to ascend. She didn't quite know how to work it, so decided to walk.

The stairs were stone and rather steep, and the air struck chill after the brilliant sunshine. By the time she reached the top she was out of breath, panting and shivering with excitement. " Calm yourself, calm yourself ! " she murmured, and opened her handbag to powder her nose.

" Gosh, what a face ! " she thought. " *I'd* never give me a job," and then she marched boldly through the door marked " Inquiries." The little waiting-room was empty, but there was a hatch with a notice that read, " Please ring." She rang, and a secretary pushed up the hatch and said peremptorily, " Well ? "

" I have an appointment," said Lynette firmly, " for three o'clock."

" Who was it with ? "

" I don't know," said Lynette. " I just had a telegram."

" What is the name ? "

" Darwin. Lynette Darwin."

" Oh, yes," said the girl, glancing at a notebook. " For Mr. Cathcart. But you'll have to wait."

For three-quarters of an hour Lynette sat on the edge of an easy-chair and read back numbers of *The Stage*, while the secretary informed the trickle of job-seekers who came into the office that Mr. Cathcart was ill, away in the country, or not back from lunch.

" How funny that it's called ' Tiller and Webb's,' yet there doesn't seem to be any Mr. Tiller or Mr. Webb around," Lynette pondered. At last the hatch was flung up again and the girl said, " Mr. Cathcart will see you now," as she unlocked a secret sort of door in the wall for Lynette to pass through.

Beyond the secretary's office was the inner sanctum, with " C. K. Cathcart, Casting Director " painted on the door. The secretary threw it open and announced, " Miss Darwin," so there was nothing for Lynette but to walk in. She thought of Daniel in the lion's den, and of the early Christian martyrs, and then found to her relief that Mr. C. K. Cathcart looked very much like her own father. In fact, he appeared to be as nervous as she was. They both said " Good afternoon," and he told her to sit down. Then he looked at her for a long time without speaking, and Lynette wondered whether she should remark what a lovely day it was. Then he said, " Well, Miss—er—Darwin, in September we are putting on a new show in which there is a part that Mr. Duncan De Whit, the producer, thinks might suit you. He saw your Public Show yesterday and liked your performance."

" Oh, yes," said Lynette in a rather squeaky voice.

" So I'd like to hear a few details about you, if you don't mind. How long have you been at the Academy ? "

For the life of her, Lynette could not remember, so she smiled vacantly and said, " Quite a time."

" One year—or two ? "

" In between." (" Bother," she thought, " why am I being so dopey ? ")

" And have you done *any* professional work ? "

" Yes. I've done some rep. at—at Tutworth Wells."

The name sounded rather like Nether Wallop or Little Muddington-in-the-Marsh to Lyn's nervous ears, but Mr. Cathcart nodded as if he had just about heard of the place.

" Oh, well, that's good. We couldn't employ you if you were completely inexperienced." Lynette blessed the days of toil at Tutworth Wells.

" And how old are you ? " Lynette added on a few months and said, " Eighteen."

" Oh, dear. You're very young, aren't you ? " he said accusingly.

193

"I'm sorry," said Lynette miserably, and he laughed kindly.

"The part is of a girl of seventeen, but it's very tricky and emotional—not at all easy to play. To be quite frank with you, I should have plumped for a really experienced actress for the part, but then Mr. De Whit has seen what you can do, and I haven't. In a few minutes' time he will be coming to hear you read a bit of the part." Lynette gulped, feeling quite ill with the desire to succeed. "You're really a very lucky girl to have attracted De Whit's notice. Every *ingénue* in London has been after this part, but he hasn't been able to find the right person."

He handed Lynette a fat typewritten script in an orange cover and said, "You'd better have a look at it until Mr. De Whit arrives. Read any of 'Nita's' speeches that you like. The best ones are in the scene with the mother. That's the leading part. Marcia Meredith is playing it for us." He went out of the room, and Lynette stared at the script. The type danced up and down in front of her eyes, and not a single phrase would make sense. She found herself gazing out of the window, and listening to the striking of clocks and the hum of traffic from the street below. Then the door was flung open and Duncan De Whit entered like a whirlwind. He was loaded with books and papers and a dispatch case, had a gay silk scarf flung carelessly round his neck, and the lightest grey suit Lynette had ever seen.

"Ah," he said expansively, grinning broadly across a nutcracker face with beady bright eyes. "Lynette Darwin. Yes, I prefer you minus the Salvation Army." Lynette laughed nervously. He walked round her appraisingly, then said to Cathcart, who had followed him in, "Told you she looked just right for Nita, didn't I? Not pretty-pretty, but interesting—and the right age!" Lyn flushed with pleasure.

" Not pretty-pretty, but interesting."

" Well, I suppose you're free to take an engagement ? "

" Oh, yes," said Lyn eagerly.

" Well, we'd like to hear you read. Have you got a copy of the script ? I'll give you a brief outline of the plot. You're a very nervous, highly strung young girl who comes back from school in France, to find that your mother, whom you worship, a woman of forty or more, has suddenly gone very gay and refuses to grow old gracefully. It sounds rather hackneyed, but it's been treated in a very original manner by the author, who is quite a young man. Look, read this speech at the top of page ninety."

Cathcart sat at his desk toying with the inkwell, while De Whit wandered aimlessly round the office, straightening pictures on the wall, and looking at himself in the mirror. Lyn took a deep breath, stood up, and began to read. It was an extremely emotional speech, and to plunge straight into it in cold blood was very difficult. Her voice sounded metallic and false, and she could have wept with mortification at ruining such a lovely speech.

When she had finished neither of them said anything. They just looked questioningly at each other. Lynette shuffled and coughed and wished she could sink through the floor. Finally Cathcart said, " Very well, Miss Darwin. We'll let you know what we decide, if you'll leave your address and phone number." Lynette's heart sank, but she smiled politely and said, " 37 Fitzherbert Street," and gave the phone number. They were very charming as they said good-bye and showed her out, and De Whit said, " Well, let's hope it's ' au revoir.' "

All the way along Charing Cross Road Lyn remembered that " Let's hope it's au revoir." " Was he merely being polite, or did he mean he wanted me to have the part ? He liked me. Cathcart wasn't so sure. Oh, I read it so badly."

She walked blindly in the hot sun, oblivious of the heat, the traffic, and the people, wrangling with herself as to whether she had got the part or not.

"If I'd got it they'd have told me. No, they wouldn't. They must discuss it between themselves. And perhaps with Marcia Meredith—Marcia Meredith! To act with her—I'd never dare. She's so famous. And so brilliant." She found herself in St. James' Park, gazing intently at the ducks, who swam and flapped and caught flies coolly on the dark water. The shade of a willow tree looked inviting, and she flung herself under it and fell asleep from sheer mental exhaustion.

The week that followed was torture. Every morning she woke early and ran down to wait for the postman. She saw him come slowly along Fitzherbert Street, popping letters through letterboxes, with maddening precision. Sometimes she ran along the street where the shadows of the houses were long on the pavements, and asked him breathlessly if there were anything for No. 37, and was presented perhaps with a catalogue for Mrs. Bosham. Other mornings she made herself stay in the dark hall and wait for the flap of the letterbox to be lifted, and a cheery letter from one of their mothers to flutter in. Whenever the phone rang she rushed to answer it, and she watched the message rack at the Academy with an eagle eye. Her temper became shorter and shorter, and she did not join in any of the end-of-term horseplay that went on. No work was ever done in the week that followed the Public Show. Mostly they lazed on the roof in their bathing costumes, playing silly acting games like "Charades" and "Proverbs," and carried on a feud with the medical students at the college opposite, throwing missiles of every sort across at them. The other Blue Doors were kindly and sympathetic, and never failed to ask "Heard anything?"

when they saw her, but they could not understand the over-whelming importance it held for her.

" Forget about it," advised Sandra sensibly. " Then when you *do* hear, it will be a nice surprise."

" Forget it ! " groaned Lyn. " If only I could ! "

On the seventh day of hearing nothing she decided that she must pull herself together. She was looking pale and tired, and was not sleeping well. She forced herself to think what fun it would be when the Blue Doors opened up at Fenchester again.

" Much better experience than a West End show," she told herself. " To play a new part every fortnight will do me the world of good. We'll probably do *The Constant Nymph* again, and we might do *The Importance* and *She Stoops to Conquer*—oh yes, it will be grand." She even joined in a conclave with the others, to decide on their first show. Then, on the day before the end of term, Roma Seymore called her out of class and said, " Lynette, dear, I wonder if you're free at tea-time to-day ? "

" Yes, Mrs. Seymore. Can I do anything for you ? "

" Well, I'm having tea with Marcia Meredith, who is an old friend of mine. We were at this Academy together many, many years ago, and she has asked me to bring you along, as they are considering you to play the part of her daughter."

" Are they *still* considering me ? " gulped Lynette.

" Yes, I think so. Haven't you heard anything ? "

" Not a thing."

" Well, come along with me this afternoon, and if Marcia likes you that will be half the battle."

Lyn reeled back into the classroom.

" How shall I behave ? What shall I wear ? " she de-manded of the Blue Doors.

"Don't look too glamorous if you want her to like you," advised Vicky. "I should try to look madly young and rather plain."

"Easy," said Maddy.

"You be quiet, Miss Fayne. And should I talk or listen?"

"Listen admiringly," advised Jeremy, "and laugh at her jokes, if she makes any."

Once more Lynette spent most of the afternoon on her toilet, borrowed a dab of perfume from Sandra, stockings from Vicky, and some money for a taxi from Jeremy. The meeting was to take place at a little Belgian *pâtisserie* called "Chez Bertrand," in Soho, where the Blue Doors had often popped in for a cup of coffee and a sticky cake.

"Funny," thought Lynette, "that the most important interview of my life should take place in such an ordinary little café." She paid the taximan and went in. Immediately she saw Marcia Meredith, for she was the most colourful thing in the room. She was a large woman, dressed in black with a smart crimson hat at an extreme angle. She had large striking features, enormous burnt-out eyes, and dark hair in an elaborate coiffure. Although beautifully made-up, her age showed in lines at the corners of the mouth, and a conscious lifting of the chin to defy any suggestion of sag. Beside her Roma Seymore seemed almost pastel-coloured and motherly. Roma introduced Lynette, and Marcia Meredith said in a rich husky voice with a break in it, "My dear, how are you? Excuse my fingers being rather sticky, but we're simply *wallowing* in these delicious cakes! Sit down and have some. Those are especially delicious."

Marcia kept up a vivacious monologue throughout the meal, and Lynette was relieved to find that she had only to say "Yes" and "No" at intervals and to look pleasant.

The actress gave vivid impersonations of all her friends, and Lyn came to the conclusion that she gave an even better performance off stage than on. Finally, Marcia drained her cup with a gesture and said, " My dear, I must fly—I've got to change and get to the Savoy by eight-thirty." She kissed Roma affectionately on the cheek, leaving the imprint of her lipstick, and extended a gracious hand to Lynette. " Good-bye, you dear thing. I know we shall meet again in the near future," and she made a terrific exit from the little café, bestowing sweet smiles on the beaming proprietor and waitresses. Lyn sank back exhausted.

" Phew ! " she said, and Roma smiled.

" Yes, she does affect one that way, but one can't help admiring her."

" Did she like me, do you think ? " Lynette asked anxiously. " I hardly said anything."

" Yes. She liked you all right. If she hadn't, it would soon have been quite obvious, I'm afraid. Marcia doesn't bother to be polite." Lynette reflected that no mention had been made of the play.

But next morning at breakfast-time the 'phone rang, and Mrs. Bosham hurried into the dining-room.

" There's a gent on the phone for Miss Lynette. Says 'is name is Pee Whit or something."

Lyn swallowed several baked beans whole, and ran into the hall. The stag's head and the late Mr. Bosham stared at her accusingly as she picked up the receiver with trembling hands.

" Hullo, Miss Darwin," came Mr. De Whit's cheery voice. " Wonder if you could come down to the office ? Little matter to discuss."

" Yes, why yes," said Lynette. " What time shall I come ? "

" Oh, between eleven and twelve. I shan't be there, but Mr. Cathcart will deal with you."

Lyn returned to the breakfast table thinking, " A little matter to discuss—oh, what does that mean? And how long will this uncertainty go on?" She couldn't wait to titivate herself. On the stroke of eleven she was ascending the stone stairs, talking to herself almost incoherently. "It doesn't matter really if I don't get it—nothing I can do now will alter anything. Oh, I must, I must." In Mr. Cathcart's office she sat on the edge of the chair, and he discussed the weather. As if it mattered ! Then suddenly he whipped a sheaf of papers out of a drawer and pushed it across the desk.

" I wonder," he said, " if you would be interested in signing this." It was some seconds before she realized that it was a contract.

" Now, I must read it carefully," she thought, " as if I were used to signing contracts and not too eager." But the legal terms defeated her, and she merely looked to see what her salary would be. The sum made her gasp.

" I'm not worth it," she thought as she signed. It was all over so soon.

" We start rehearsing on the fifteenth," said Mr. Cathcart, " but I shall probably be in touch with you again before then."

On wings, Lynette ran down the stone steps, out into the sunshine and noise of Charing Cross Road. She wanted to stop passers-by and say to them, " What do you think ? I've just signed a contract—I'm really going to be an actress. I'm the happiest girl in London." Her feet did not seem to touch the ground as she sped along. Everything suddenly seemed to be more highly coloured than usual. The sky was a Mediterranean blue, the dumpy taxis that rattled by were gaily painted, and the women's dresses as varied as a rainbow. Everyone seemed to be smiling, and Lynette wanted to smile back, and say, "Isn't it a lovely day? Isn't London wonderful? I'm so happy, aren't you?" She wanted to celebrate madly, to do something really rash. She went into a milk bar and ordered an enormous sundae with strawberries on top.

"It'll cost the earth—but it doesn't matter."

On, up to Cambridge Circus she bounced, and walked down Shaftesbury Avenue to look at the theatre at which she was to appear. It was the St. Christopher's, an old theatre with a fine history. At the moment it housed a detective play. Lynette stood and looked up at the posters and the photographs outside.

"Soon it will be me—soon it will be me."

She retraced her footsteps into Charing Cross Road.

"The most lovely road in the world," she thought.

At Foyle's she stopped and went in, fingering enviously the sweet-smelling books. Rashly she bought a beautifully illustrated ballet book, and went out again hugging it. The trolleys clanged in Tottenham Court Road, the buses were red and sailed heavily round the corners. The sun struck the fragments of quartz in the paving stones and they flashed goldenly. Lynette's heart bubbled in her throat with joy. She gave pennies to beggars, bought some sweets and presented them to a ragged little boy, and cut through the square towards the Academy. Suddenly she realized that it was the last day of term, and she sat down on a green-painted seat to think about it. The lions on the doorway grinned as hard as ever, the pianos were tinkling ballet music, and on the roof dark figures fenced wildly, their foils glinting in the sunlight.

"What a wonderful thing to have happened on my very last day!" she thought. "It's the only thing that could make up for leaving the Academy." She watched the stream of students coming in and out of the swing doors. She knew them all, had chatted on the stairs with them, walked down Tottenham Court Road with them, sat with them in Raddler's.

"How exciting it will be to come back here to visit them," she thought. "When I'm playing at the St. Christopher's !"

The clocks struck two and Lynette got up and stretched and sauntered across to the Academy, savouring the satisfaction she would receive from telling her news to the others. There was the usual end-of-term excitement, people rushing about asking, "Are you coming back next term ?" "Where are you going for the holidays ?" She looked everywhere for the Blue Doors, and finally found them in the wardrobe, helping Mrs. Bertram. As soon as they saw her they dropped the armfuls of costumes under which they were staggering.

"Well ?" Radiant-faced Lynette announced, "I've signed my contract. We rehearse on the fifteenth." There was silence. On the faces of the Blue Doors every emotion played, amazement, joy, disappointment, envy. No-one said anything. The seven of them stood and looked at each other. Bulldog had been trying on a policeman's helmet, which was perched at a rakish angle on his red head. At last Maddy said rather shakily, "We—we didn't think you would—take it."

"Why not ? "

"Well—the Blue Door Theatre. . . ."

"Oh ! " Lynette sat down suddenly on a heap of old curtains, deflated as a balloon pricked by a pin. Slowly she said, "I'd forgotten. Yes, I'd forgotten that."

"We *can* get on without you," said Nigel. "But we

didn't want to. We haven't got a really strong actress without you."

" But you're quite right to take this opportunity," Sandra put in, rather too quickly. " I mean, it's a very lucky thing. I mean . . ." She trailed off into miserable silence.

" I hope you don't feel," said Lynette slowly, " that I'm letting you down in any way."

" Why, no ! " they chorused in a somewhat forced manner. All except Maddy.

" I think you are," she said. " You're an idiot to go straight into the West End. Mr. Whitfield says everyone should have four years' rep. first. And what about our parents and the Bishop ? We promised them we'd all come home."

" But—but surely they'll understand," stammered Lynette. " I mean—an opportunity like this ! " Maddy looked at her coldly and walked out of the wardrobe. Lynette said brokenly, " Of course—Maddy has had even better offers than this—for films—and turned them down. Oh, what shall I do ? I've signed my contract ! "

" Of course you must keep on with it," insisted Nigel. " It's the chance of a lifetime. We're not expecting you to back out now."

" But you did hope that I wouldn't accept it. Didn't you ? " The Blue Doors shuffled uneasily. " Yes, you did. But don't you see—I couldn't. It's a wonderful part. It's London—it's good money ! " Suddenly she burst into tears, crouching in the folds of the old blue velvet curtains. They comforted her, and told her that it was selfish of them to make her unhappy when she'd had such a piece of luck, but Lynette sensed that behind their kind words they were remembering the offers that Maddy had turned down in order to stay with the Blue Doors in their precarious venture

at Fenchester. Vicky ran and fetched her a cup of tea from
the canteen and Sandra lent her a handkerchief, and Bulldog
put on an act with the policeman's helmet to cheer her up.
Mrs. Bertram appeared and told them that they must go into
the theatre for the end-of-term ceremonies.

Everyone was rather over-wrought, and there were more
tears from people who were leaving when Mr. Whitfield
said the little prayer about " worthy citizens of London."
Then they sang the National Anthem, cheered the staff, and
surged up into the dressing-rooms to pack their make-up
cases, their practice clothes, books, and all the odd belongings
accumulated in their lockers during a year and a half.
Addresses were exchanged, vows of reunion made, and
promises of " See you on Crewe Station on a wet Sunday
train call." There was terrific hand-shaking, kissing, and
embracing, and the six of them stood on the mat marked
B.A.G.A. and looked at the swing doors, none of them
wishing to be the first to make so final an exit. Then,
" Excelsior ! " cried Bulldog with a gesture, and they walked
out into the square.

The doors swung to behind them.

Chapter XIV

"BELOVED VIPER"

ALL through the hot nights Lynette tossed and turned and wondered if she were doing right. She had a letter from her mother which read, " Dear Lynette, Daddy and I were very surprised at your piece of news. It is certainly very fortunate for you, but I cannot pretend that we are really glad about it. We were looking forward so much to having you home and settled down in Fenchester once more. The Blue Door Theatre won't seem the same without you. I'm sure the Bishop will be very upset about it. But just the same we wish you all the best of luck in your new venture. I don't know if Daddy and I will be able to get up for the first night, but we will try to come and see it as soon as possible. . . ."

" They don't understand," Lynette thought miserably. " How *can* they understand that this is the chance of a lifetime. It might never happen to me again."

The Blue Doors, with the exception of Maddy, continued to be sweet, yet distant. They were wrapped up in plans for the opening of the theatre, and were out all day, dashing round London, buying sets of plays, furniture, and properties. They had received a nice fat cheque from the Fenchester Town Council and were having a wonderful time buying all the things that they had longed for for their theatre for years. The boys gloated over the new lighting equipment they had acquired, and the girls over several long mirrors for the new dressing-rooms.

Lynette received by post a script of her play ; *Beloved*

Viper it was called. She spent several days alone at No. 37 looking over her part.

"Gosh, it will be awful here without the others!" she thought, "I think I shall move—a little room in some nicer district—a flatlet, perhaps—I shall be able to afford it."

The time approached for the Blue Doors to depart. Mr. Chubb was already installed at the theatre, and had been introduced to the Bishop by Lord Moulcester and thoroughly approved. Every day Nigel had long and involved telephone conversations with Mr. Chubb, the Clerk of the Town Council, and local printers and newspapers at Fenchester. Then at last one night he announced, "Well, it's time to get moving. There's nothing more we can do in town. The next thing is to get down to Fenchester. And, gosh, the amount of work that's waiting to be done there!"

"When do we leave?" asked Maddy eagerly. "I'm all packed and ready."

"Two days' time, I should think," said Nigel. "If that suits everyone?"

"O.K. by us."

"Oh, dear," sighed Lynette, "I shall miss you so."

There was a silence, then Maddy said coldly, "Well, you know what you can do——"

"Be quiet, Maddy," Sandra checked her. Maddy tossed her head and went out.

"I'm sorry, Lyn," said Sandra. "She doesn't mean to be unkind. She is honestly disappointed that you're not coming back to Fenchester."

"I see," said Lynette slowly. "I'm sorry."

"When do your rehearsals start, dear?" asked Vicky.

"The day after you leave."

Mrs. Bosham was heart-broken to know that she was losing her lodgers.

" Well, I don't know," she said tearfully. " House won't seem the same without you lot. Miss Lynette and I will be real lost without you."

" However shall I tell her that I want to move ? " thought Lynette. " But I won't bother until the show is open."

The night before they left they gave a party at No. 37, inviting all the rest of their class from the Academy, and Mr. Whitfield and Mrs. Seymore. Mr. Chubb was up in town from Fenchester and appeared wearing a faded greeny-black opera cloak. Mrs. Bosham really rose to the occasion, and the food was wonderful. It was a buffet supper, with a marvellous array of cold meat and pickles. Sandra had made lots of little savouries out of cheese biscuits and potato crisps, and anchovy and olives and cucumber, and everything she could lay hands on. Jeremy had evolved a cider cup, into which he flung slices of orange and apple and cucumber, with bottled cherries floating on top. Everyone talked very loudly, and the room was full of smoke and laughter, so that they had to open wide the windows that gave out on to the tiny patch of cat-ridden backyard with a fine view of the drain, the meat-safe, and the dustbin.

After everyone had eaten and drunk as much as they were capable of, they sat on the floor on cushions, and Mr. Chubb did some dramatic monologues, *If* and *The Green Eye of the Little Yellow God*, and did not seem to mind that his audience laughed immoderately.

" Ah, it's good to be back among one's fellow Thespians," he intoned as he sat down amid wild applause. Then they turned on the wireless, which was inclined to crackle, and pushed back the heavy Victorian furniture and danced to the late night orchestras. Bulldog whirled Mrs. Bosham round in a wild polka until she had to sit down on her favourite horse-hair chair and sniff some smelling salts. Mr. Chubb and Myrtle were getting on splendidly together, swopping stories of their old touring days, finding that they remembered the same digs and landladies from Sheerness to Dunoon.

All the rest of the class who were not accompanying the Blue Doors to Fenchester expressed their envy of Ali, Billy, and Myrtle, and made Nigel and Mr. Chubb promise to employ them for odd weeks whenever possible. Lynette, of course, was the object of greater envy, and promised to invite everyone who was staying up in town to tea in her dressing-room on matinée days, once the show was started. They drank to the success of the Blue Door Theatre and to a long run for *Beloved Viper*.

"But how could it fail ? " demanded Mr. Whitfield, " with Marcia Meredith *and* Lynette Darwin ? "

Maddy was so excited she could hardly keep still. To-morrow it would all be starting—the theatre that they had dreamed about for so long, and although she would be coming back to town for term time at the Academy for another year or so, she would at least be in at the Fenchester opening.

Lynette was happy, and looked round at everything, trying to imprint it on her mind and hold it there, yet somewhere there was a feeling of guilt and slight trepidation.

The sky was massed with scarlet-tinted clouds as the guests took their leave.

" Shepherd's delight," said Vicky, as they closed the door behind Mr Chubb, the last to leave. " A good omen."

Next morning there was chaos at No. 37. Such packing and yelling up the stairs and telephoning, that one would have thought a regiment were departing. Their trunks and suitcases full to overflowing, they had to resort to carrier bags and brown paper parcels strapped on to the sides of their luggage. At the last minute, when every available cubic

centimetre of space was as full as it could be, Mrs. Bosham
appeared with large packages of sandwiches for all of
them.

" Oh, thank you, Mrs. Bosham. Liver sausage—how
delicious." When she had gone Maddy said, " Well, the
only space I've got is inside me," and sitting down on the
bed she began to demolish her packet. " Yes, I think it's
the only way. And we've got some time to spare."

The empty rooms looked very melancholy, now that the
bookcases were cleared, the gramophone records no longer
stacked in the corners, the framed pictures of actors and
actresses taken from the walls.

" As if we've never really been here," remarked Vicky.

" But we have," said Maddy. " Oh, yes. Look, there's
the mark where Bulldog spilled his hair cream. And there's
where your Dégas picture was nailed up."

" Does the train go at five- or twenty-five minutes past ? "
Sandra inquired suddenly.

" Five past."

" Gosh, we must hurry," and immediately there was a
stampede to say good-bye to Mrs. Bosham.

" Go and find a taxi," yelled Nigel, and Maddy and Bulldog both ran out at the door. Within a few minutes they
had both got one, and were considering sending one away,
when they realized that six of them *and* their luggage could
not possibly get into one vehicle. Lynette stood out on
the doorstep with a strained smile, helping them in with the
endless luggage, and trying to wise-crack with them.

" We probably won't be able to get to your first night,
but we'll be thinking about you," said Sandra. " And all
the best of luck for it."

" And—and good luck to you, too," said Lynette foolishly
as if they were strangers.

At last they were all stowed away in the taxis with cases on the roofs, and Maddy leaning half out of the window to wave.

" Cheery-bye—cheery-bye ! " shouted Mrs. Bosham, waving a large blue-spotted handkerchief. The taxis started up, and groaning under their heavy load, crawled down Fitzherbert Street and round the corner out of sight.

" Oh, dear ! " sighed Lynette, leaning against the dusty iron railings.

" Come along, ducky," said Mrs. Bosham. " We'll 'ave a nice ' cupper,' shall us ? "

Down in Mrs. Bosham's basement, sipping an enormous cup of almost black tea, Lynette tried hard to overcome the depression that engulfed her.

" I shouldn't be miserable," she told herself. " I'm one of the luckiest girls in London. I should be bubbling over with joy. Oh, but I'm not."

She took her script out with her for a walk. Just to carry it about seemed to help her to know the part. And even a glimpse of the bright orange script cheered her up. The more she read of the part the more she realized what a gem it was.

" If only I can do it," she thought. " It would be so easy to make her into a sloppy little prig. She must be played so as to be credible." Already the thought of the first rehearsal next day produced a quaking feeling in the pit of her stomach. To have to rehearse with an experienced and famous actress like Marcia Meredith. Terrifying !

The following day she dressed with great care and a trembling heart, and setting out with plenty of time to spare, walked down to the St. Christopher's in Shaftesbury Avenue. The friendly old stage door-keeper directed her down the stairs to the stage, and she made her way through the gloomy passages and through a soundproof door. Draped over the furniture of the detective thriller that was still playing at the theatre were some other members of the cast. Lynette said good-morning to them shyly. There was a handsome, elderly actor of about sixty with steely grey hair, an extremely glamorous blonde with a hair-style that looked as if it had been sculptured on her head, and a young man whom Lynette recognized as Vivian Conroy, an up-and-coming film actor.

" Are you the girl who is playing ' Nita ' ? " demanded the blonde, in an extremely " Mayfair " voice.

" Yes. My name is Lynette Darwin. How do you do ? "

" Hullo. My name is Loraine French. This is Mr. Roger Revere, and Mr. Vivian Conroy." Lynette smiled at each of them, and sat down on the arm of a chair.

" What do you think of the play ? " demanded Mr. Revere.

" I think my part is a lovely part, but I'm not sure of the play as a whole," said Lynette truthfully, and looked round hastily to see if the author were about.

" That's how we all feel about it. Still, it's always difficult to judge a new play. It's up to us to *make* it a good play, of course."

" And Marcia will drag in the audience," added Loraine French. " She has an enormously large following, you know."

Lynette looked round the stage. The curtains were closed, making the fourth wall, and the set was cosy and cheery.

" I'll be acting on this stage," she thought. " Night after night. Until it will seem like home——"

There was a sudden commotion in the wings, laughter and loud voices, and on sailed Marcia, wearing a wonderful mink coat and a sensational hat. Behind her came Duncan De Whit, overflowing with energy and good temper, and last came a fair, pale young man with a slight stoop.

" Good-morning, good-morning, good-morning," cried De Whit. " How nice to see you all so bright and early. May I introduce our author, Mr. Timothy Carew." The young man blushed a deep shade of beetroot and shook hands with everyone, obviously too nervous either to hear or care what anyone's name was. Marcia flung herself into a chair, stretching her magnificently long legs.

" But I'm exhausted already ! I've not been up so early in the morning for months. Oh, work, work, work ! It fascinates me. I could sit and watch it all day long."

" Now, who is there left to come ? " said Duncan De Whit. " Our stage director is around the theatre some-where, I believe, and there's old Weatherby, who's playing the butler, and the girl who's playing the maid. Oh, here they are . . . " A very old man and a young girl about Lyn's age entered somewhat timidly and were introduced. The girl's name was Joan something or other, and Lyn thought she seemed rather nice.

"Well, I think," said Mr. De Whit, " that we'll have a little read through just sitting down comfortably, shall we ? Then I think it will be time for a coffee."

" Good idea, Duncan, dear boy," said Marcia. " I missed my breakfast, I was so late this morning."

They went through the first two acts of the play, and it sounded much better read aloud. The young author sat watching them breathlessly, blushing gratefully if anyone laughed at the humorous lines. Marcia was quite ruthless towards the weaker spots of the play.

" Hey, Timothy, I can't say that line. Now, can I ? I ask you ? "

" Well, what would you rather say ? " Timothy would ask, and the line would be altered to suit Miss Meredith. About twelve they went out to the little *pâtisserie* in Soho where Lynette had been introduced to Marcia, and had some coffee and squashy cakes. Lynette found herself at a table with the author, the girl who was playing the maid, and the old character actor. At the next table Marcia, De Whit, and Loraine were making a great deal of noise and laughter. Conversation at Lynette's table was more pedestrian. The young author was painfully shy, and the Joan girl was quiet but self-possessed, so they listened to a long monologue of how Mr. Weatherby had had a very bad journey from Norwich to Newcastle-on-Tyne one Sunday before the Great War. At last De Whit said, " Well, boys and girls, back to our work. There's just time to finish reading the ' opera ' before lunch."

" I like this man," cried Marcia. " He measures life by meal-times, which is something I do appreciate. Producers who break for ten minutes at lunch-time and expect you to exist all day on a bun and lemonade are my *bête noire*." They trooped back to the theatre. On the way Timothy Carew fell into step beside Lynette.

" I say," he said, " may I talk to you ? I feel so terribly scared of all these people. They're all so frightening—except you."

" Yes," agreed Lynette, " they are a little overpowering. I expect it's only just at first, though."

" I thought that the day my first play went into rehearsal would be the happiest day of my life," confessed Carew. " But it's not, I'm so scared. I wish I'd stuck to the Civil Service."

Lynette laughed.

" You don't really. You know you don't. Think of

the thrill when you see people queueing up to watch a play that you've written. It will be wonderful."

" But do you really feel it's all right—as a play, I mean. I've been having terrible doubts about it lately."

" I see no reason why it shouldn't run for years," Lynette told him, " but one just can't tell what will tickle the fancy of the public. It must be good, otherwise a management like Tiller and Webb would never have accepted it."

This seemed to pacify the author considerably.

" It's very kind of you to be so comforting," he said. " Why are you so—so untheatrical ? "

" Am I ? " asked Lyn, surprised.

" Yes. You're not artificial like the others."

" Perhaps it's because I've only just come out of dramatic school," laughed Lynette. " This is my first real West End job, you know."

" I'm terribly glad they've chosen you for the part. I wasn't allowed any say in the casting," Timothy told her, " and I was afraid they'd get some hard, grown-up type for the part and that would have ruined it. You're so right."

" Thank you," said Lynette gratefully, and having bolstered up each other's egos they went back into the theatre slightly reassured.

At lunch-time Marcia said, " I must fly if I'm to get to the Berkeley in time."

" I'm going to the Ritz, so can I drop you ? " said De Whit.

In solitary state Lynette ate her lunch in Lyons, wishing that she had arranged to meet one of her friends from the Academy. " I'm sure I shall never get out of the habit of eating cheaply," she thought, and got a peculiar satisfaction out of the procession of workaday faces that passed by.

And it was lovely to think that after her coffee she would have some real hard work to return to.

They finished reading through in the afternoon and were left with an overpowering urge to get some life into it.

" Now run off to your tea, girls and boys, and get a good night's rest, and I'll see you at eleven o'clock to-morrow morning," cried De Whit.

Lyn obeyed his directions, and after a solitary cinema she retired to bed in a very lonely and quiet No. 37. It was so odd not to hear the boys coming in late, giggling on the way upstairs, and the murmur of the girls' voices in the next room.

The following weeks of rehearsal were a mixture of excitement and depression, exhilaration and despair, and enjoyment and boredom. Gradually the part began to take shape. By dint of learning her lines on buses, and trains, in the bath and in bed, Lynette soon knew them perfectly. The moves were more difficult, and several times De Whit came near to losing his temper when she turned up in the wrong place. On these occasions Lynette would retire to a corner to nurse her wounds, and the memory of his hard words would rankle for many a day. But at other times De Whit would say, " That's terrific, darling. That's fine," and beam at her jovially, so that she would feel warm all over. She got tremendous satisfaction out of trying to do what he told her. He would give her an inflection, saying, " No, dear. Not like that—like this," and when she got it correctly at last, " That's right. Clever girl." And Lynette's heart would sing with achievement.

Marcia was sweet to her and would take her out to coffee in the mornings, and keep up an amusingly scandalous monologue about all the other members of the company. She also gave Lynette many helpful hints about her part.

" There are some things that a man producer can't see in the playing of a female part. Now, if you don't appeal to the feminine members of the audience you're losing seventy-five per cent. of your public. It's the suburban matrons who make up the audiences in the long run."

Timothy Carew continued to make Lynette his confidante, running to her whenever anyone had complained about a line or refused a suggestion that he had made.

" I should never have started coming to rehearsals," he moaned.

" How could you have stayed away ? " Lynette demanded.

" Yes, you're right. I must see that the parts are played as I meant them to be. One little alteration and the whole sense of the play is lost." He was now working on a long semi-autobiographical novel, and every night returned home to write until one or two in the morning, appearing pink-eyed at next day's rehearsal.

" If only this play is a success I can sell my novel without any trouble."

Lynette felt great sympathy for the shy, pale young man, for he had given up being a Civil Servant four years previously to devote himself to writing, and for two years had lived on air without a single success. Now things were beginning to look up, and this play might be the turning-point of his career.

Some days everything seemed to go wrong. People forgot their lines, made wrong moves, and could produce no emotion whatsoever. Over and over again they would do one or two lines in order to get them perfect. De Whit was ruthless in his methods.

" You're not in rep. at Little-Oozing-on-the-Mud now," he would roar at Lynette, so that she would have difficulty in restraining her tears. Gradually, through much toil and tribulation the character of "Nita" became real to Lynette, so that she felt as if she knew her as well as the Blue Doors.

There were big excitements when they had to go to an extremely exclusive fashion house in Bond Street, where the clothes were to be made. Lynette saw Marcia floating about in exquisitely lacy underwear, and felt ashamed of her own schoolgirlish undergarments. But the fitter was complimentary about her figure. "A sight easier than wangling things for Miss Meredith," she said cryptically.

Lynette spent many of her evenings flat-hunting. She saw lovely little flatlets in large blocks, small mews flats, large studio rooms in Chelsea, and expensive suites in Mayfair completely beyond her means. And yet she was loath to make the break with all the old associations of No. 37.

"And Maddy will be coming back for next term. Perhaps I won't leave the Boshery until Maddy has finished at the Academy."

She had regular letters from the others telling of the hard work and fun that was going on at Fenchester, and wrote back in detail all about the progress of rehearsals. Some of the Academy people looked her up, and they had tea and talked about "the old days" as if these were years ago. Helen, in her seventh heaven, rang Lynette up to tell her that she was going to Stratford-on-Avon to play small parts in the Shakespeare season.

The summer got hotter and hotter. They had to have glasses of iced water in the wings to soothe their parched throats as they rehearsed, and whenever they were not needed they would hurry to the stage door for a breath of fresh air, and sit on the little stools that were put down for the gallery queues.

"If we run as long as this thriller has," said Marcia, "We shall be doing well."

"I think we shall run," said Lynette optimistically. "The public always lap up anything with a villainess in it, and the title of this will get them too. *Beloved Viper*—it's a terrific title."

"And what a Viper," thought Lynette. In the striking clothes that had been designed for her, all in varying shades of green, Marcia looked as slinky and dangerous as any woman could. Beside her, Lynette in innocuous pastel shades would appear angelic.

Sometimes after rehearsals Lynette and Timothy would stroll through the hot streets, talking, talking, talking, and always with the same theme—the show. It filled their horizon. There was nothing else in London, nothing else in the world. Everything pertained to it. The weather must not be too fine, nor too bad, or the audiences would not be good. They bought newspapers to see if any advance publicity were out yet; they went to see other plays that they feared might rival the popularity of *Beloved Viper*. They went round to the studios where the set was being built, and all the time, the show—the show—the show was all that mattered.

"Oh, Lynette!" cried Timothy. "What's going to happen to us?"

"We must wait and see," was all there was to be said.

CHAPTER XV

PRELUDE TO SUCCESS

ONE morning Lynette was going up the escalator at Leicester Square tube station when something caught her eye so that she exclaimed aloud. It was the first poster of *Beloved Viper*, and there was her own name as large as life for all to see—" Lynette Darwin." She flushed and looked round to see if anyone had noticed it, but everyone else on the escalator was either reading the morning paper or discussing the hot weather. She hadn't really had a chance to see the poster properly, so when she got to the top of the escalator, she went down again on the other side in order to be able to ascend once more and have a real look at it. It certainly looked nice. Two girls behind her remarked on it this time.

" Coo—look at that, Ethel. What a title, eh ? "

" Ooh, Marcia Meredith ! She's ever so lovely. We *must* see that ! "

" Well, that's two people for the box office," thought Lynette.

At rehearsal that day they went straight through the play, and it was not until the end that they realized that De Whit had not stopped them once to comment or criticize. He had been sitting in the gloom at the back of the stalls, and now he walked slowly down the gangway between the seats and addressed them across the footlights.

" Well, what was wrong with that ? " he demanded. They thought hard.

" Too slow," suggested Marcia.

" Underplayed ? " asked Lynette.

" No. No, there was nothing wrong with it. If you can do it like that a week to-night, I shall be perfectly satisfied. You remembered everything I've ever told you. Now let's have lunch."

They glowed with pride for the rest of the day. But after that they began to get stale. People missed entrances and the whole thing became over-rehearsed.

Poor Timothy almost went crazy with anxiety for his play. " Oh, it seems so dull," he complained. " However will anyone sit through it ? "

" That's a kind thing to say," Lynette rebuked him, " when we're all doing our best."

" Oh, I don't mean you—I mean the play."

" It's only because you've seen it rehearsed so many times. I should stay away until the dress rehearsal, if I were you."

" Of course, if you want to get rid of me . . ."

" Why not go away for a few days and take your novel with you ? " suggested Lynette.

" Yes, perhaps I will. I can't stand much more of this."

Later in the day De Whit said, " You're all being so dull and boring me so much that I can't bear the thought of seeing you again to-morrow, so I think you'd all better take a long week-end and I'll see you on Monday. That will give us three days before the first night."

" Thank goodness," cried Marcia, " I can have a good morning's sleep again."

" Tell you what," suggested Timothy to Lyn, " I'm going down to stay at Roehampton with some friends. Why don't you come down to-morrow and we can go swimming in the pool ? "

They spent a lazy day in the sun, reading and dozing,

eating sandwiches and drinking fizzy lemonade, and plunging into the pool at intervals to cool their sunburnt limbs. The sun soothed and drugged them into forgetfulness of all the ordeals of the next week. They repeated the day's programme on the two following days, and it seemed as if they had never done anything but lounge in the sun.

" Oh, this is the life for me ! " cried Timothy, stretching and wiggling his toes ecstatically. " When you've made my fortune for me in this play I shall spend the winter in the South of France."

" Gosh," said Lynette, " I'm so sunburnt I shall hardly need any make-up. I'm afraid I shan't look as pale and ethereal as I should. In fact, I shall be a somewhat lobster-tinted *ingénue*."

When she returned to No. 37 on Sunday night she suddenly had a feeling that she had forgotten her lines, and had a hurried study to reassure herself.

Monday began a very busy week. The costumes were brought round to the theatre for a final fitting under the lights, so that De Whit could alter any effects that he did not care for. There was slight trouble because Lynette was wearing a pale green dress when Marcia was also wearing green.

" Quite impossible," said Marcia in a final tone. " There's enough green already with me wearing it all the time. No-one else can possibly wear it."

" Perhaps you're right," agreed De Whit. " But what can we do ? Either she has to wear the same dress as in the previous scene, or she'll have to get something ready-made." At last the *couturier* agreed to get another dress made hurriedly for Lynette, exactly the same, but in pale mauve.

There were photographs to be brought to hang outside the theatre, her make-up to be looked over, and her dressing-room equipped. She had a charming little room on the second floor with yellow walls and chintzy curtains. Round the mirror she pinned a photo of the Blue Door Theatre, her favourite Van Gogh, and a portrait of Ellen Terry. She bought a little pink cloth for the dressing-table, and was rather rash over a new house–coat to match the room. When it was all ready, with her make-up laid out on the table, and Ellen smiling down benignly, she walked slowly round it with her hands clasped in joy. Catching sight of her ecstatic face in the mirror she laughed aloud.

" A dressing-room—a dressing-room *all of my own* ! " She remembered the crowded dressing-rooms at the Academy, on the schools tour, and at Tutworth Wells, where somebody else's make-up was constantly getting mixed up with hers, and a favourite stick of make-up apt to disappear if left lying about for a second. Her dresser was to be Mrs. White, a sweet, grey-haired old lady, who seemed so old that Lynette felt that she could never let her wait on her. Mrs. White was very much touched by Lynette's enthusiasm.

" Ah, yes," she sighed, " I remember how excited I was before my first London first night."

" You—you were on the stage ? "

" Yes, Miss Darwin. Many years ago, of course. On the musical side. A dancer, I was." It was hard to imagine that the stiff old limbs beneath the faded black dress had ever been filled with music.

" And I ? " thought Lynette. " What is there to stop me ending up as a dresser ? " And she looked around her room again with more sober eyes.

On Tuesday, the day before the dress rehearsal, they went straight through the play in the morning and afternoon, and were given all day Wednesday off. The set was to be put up during the day, and at six-thirty the dress rehearsal would commence. It was to be a semi-public affair, with an audience of friends and relations especially invited.

" Sort of trying it out on the dog," as De Whit put it. Lynette had invited Helen, Mrs. Bosham, and Miss Smith and Mrs. Bertram from the Academy. Mr. Whitfield and Roma Seymore would be at the first night.

On Wednesday morning Lynette stayed in bed very late, and Mrs. Bosham brought her up an egg for her breakfast.

" Must fatten you up," she said.

" For the kill," added Lyn mentally in a morbid manner. She played soothing records on the gramophone, but her stomach was turning over with nerves.

" To-night is really as bad as the first night," she thought, " but thank goodness the Press isn't being allowed in until to-morrow."

She got up in time for a rather dreary lunch, with Mrs. Bosham telling her stories of plays which she had seen that had been booed off. The one bright spot was the arrival of an illustrated magazine containing a lovely " candid camera " photo of a rehearsal at the St. Christopher's, showing De Whit explaining something to Marcia, Lynette, and Vivian Conroy. The caption underneath said, " Producer Duncan De Whit discusses a tricky point with his stars, Marcia Meredith, Vivian Conroy, and Lynette Darwin." Marcia was leaning on Lynette's shoulder in a friendly manner.

" Gosh, I must send this home," thought Lynette.

In the afternoon Lyn went to the theatre to take a few more oddments for the dressing-room. On the stairs she bumped into Joan, and they went out to have tea together.

" I do envy you your part," exclaimed Joan over waffles and ice-cream. " It's so compact and dramatic. Mine is so ragged. I keep popping on and popping off."

"It's a lovely part," Lynette agreed soberly. "If only I can do justice to the play—and to Timothy."

"Don't let Marcia intimidate you," said Joan. "She's inclined to over-shadow you, you know."

"But of course!" cried Lynette. "She's supposed to. She couldn't help doing so."

"But don't let her have it all her own way," insisted Joan, and Lynette thought this over carefully. Perhaps she *was* a little colourless beside Marcia's verve and brilliancy!

Back in the theatre she pottered round the dressing-room until it was time to make up and get dressed for the first act. Her pale mauve frock was the most beautiful garment she had ever worn, and she surveyed herself almost with awe. She didn't look like Lynette, the untidy schoolgirl, nor Lynette dressed up for a Blue Door show, nor like the typical Academy student. She looked like——

"Why, yes, of course—I *look* like Nita!"

She thought about her part as hard as she could and then Timothy knocked and came in, and started getting her in a dither because he was so nervous himself. At last she said, "Timothy, please go. *I've* got to go on that stage and act to-night—not you, so please keep your nerves to yourself." And she bundled him out of the door. "Good luck, dear," he shouted as she shut it.

Her dresser did the back of her hair for her, "overture and beginners" was called, and Lynette ran down the stone stairs. The rest of the company were in the wings all looking surprisingly more handsome and pretty with their make-up on. Marcia looked absolutely ravishing, and was laughing and joking as if entirely carefree. Only the cigarette that trembled between her fingers gave her away.

"It's only a dress rehearsal," they kept assuring each other. "Nothing to be worried about. No-one important

Marcia was laughing and joking.

in front at all." And yet they patted their hair and rearranged their dresses, and paced up and down the set with peculiarly hunted expressions. The set was beautiful ; creamy white, and so solid-looking that it was difficult to believe it was only canvas and wood. De Whit came up and gave them a few bits of last-minute advice and then departed to watch from the front. The panatrope played a few bars of overture, and the heavy curtains slid apart and up. Lynette was not on until half-way through the first scene. She stood with Vivian Conroy in the wings, listening to the appreciative chuckles from the audience at the witty lines.

"*Doesn't* an audience make a difference ?" he remarked.

"And don't they love Marcia ?" said Lynette. "What a round she got on her entrance !"

Lyn's cue came nearer. She had feared that the enormity of appearing on the stage of the St. Christopher's would overpower her and she would find herself tongue-tied and helpless as in so many nightmares, but once she was on, the weeks of rehearsal made it seem as normal as walking on to the stage of the Pavilion, Tutworth Wells, or of the Academy theatre. Immediately she sensed the friendliness of the audience, and knew that she had created a good impression. This first scene was happy and amusing, with the relationship between mother and daughter quite care-free. Lyn was happy, bubbling over with joy inside her, and her nervousness gone. Behind the layers of other important thoughts in her mind—carefulness for her moves and voice and thoughts belonging to the part—there was a little phrase that kept cropping up, "At last I'm where I've always wanted to be. I must make the most of it." And she did, getting every ounce that there was to be ex-tracted from her part, matching up to Marcia in quality and strength. It was as if the steps of a difficult dance had suddenly become easy to her. It was like suddenly learning to swim or to ride a bicycle. At the end of the scene, when the curtain had fallen, Marcia kissed her lightly on the cheek.

" Good little creature," she purred. " But be careful not to upstage me, won't you ? "

" Oh, yes. Sorry," said Lyn, dancing off to change into her next dress.

" It's going lovely," her dresser told her, waddling about the room fetching and carrying. " Watched some of it from the flies. You were a real treat."

The next scene was somewhat more emotional, and Lyn had to get rid of some of the buoyancy that she was feeling. She sat in a corner before her entrance and tried to think of awful things, of how she would feel if the same situation occurred between herself and her own mother. She was thinking so hard that her cue came before she was really ready for it, and she had almost to run to get on to the stage in time. The audience were hushed and still during this scene as the true nature of the woman Marcia was portraying became apparent. Occasionally someone made a little exclamation at some of the more pointed lines. Lyn had a rather long speech of which she had been frightened, but it went without a hitch. Her last line came :

" Well, Mother, is it peace or war ? "

" War," was Marcia's almost inaudible reply as she stubbed out her cigarette and the curtain fell. The first act was safely over.

De Whit bounced round and said it was going over wonderfully well.

" Keep it up, boys and girls, and we've got a sure success."

When Lynette had changed into her pale blue suit for the second act Timothy came in, pink to the ears with excitement. "It's terrific. You're stupendous. It's amazing," was all that he could say.

The second act was the most difficult of the three. Lynette had a rather tricky love scene with Vivian Conroy, who, although handsome, was not a good actor, but to-night he outshone himself, and as they made their exit together there was a spontaneous round of applause.

In the third act Lyn had a quick change from a dressing-gown and pyjamas into a coat and hat, and this she had to do in a little quick-change room at the side of the stage. She had been scared of this for a long time, for she had had so little rehearsal with the actual garments. But Mrs. White was a tower of strength, fastening her up and tidying her hair. There was even time to repowder before entering for her longest and most emotional scene. In this scene Marcia was truly the " viper " of the title. In her slim-fitting green dress she was incredibly serpentine, and Lynette was filled with an almost genuine fear and horror at her raging temper. The scene mounted up to a crescendo of hysterics. To-night it was easy for Lyn. She was so strung up that any outlet was a relief. She sobbed and screamed in the complete abandon that De Whit had bullied and pleaded out of her. When the curtain fell she was almost exhausted. The remaining scene was one of pathos and aftermath. The dispirited, dejected little figure in a grey dress as she wandered round the empty room after her mother had gone, saying " Mother " over and over again brought a flutter of handkerchiefs and a burst of applause at the final curtain.

Everyone came on for the curtain call, and the audience clapped and clapped, and Lynette could see dimly the front row of faces in the stalls and noticed that they had the beaming, escaped sort of look of people who have been taken out of themselves and away from their own worries and tragedies for a little while. Marcia stepped forward to acknowledge her applause, and then held out a gracious hand towards Lynette, who blushed and bowed. They took six curtains and then retired. Lynette was nearly dropping with exhaustion. Timothy helped her gallantly up the stairs, telling her how good she was. He was brimming over with delight.

"They liked it, Lyn," he kept saying. "I was standing in the foyer and I heard people saying, 'What a good play,' and 'Oh, I did enjoy it.' Lynette, I think it will be all right. Oh, you were lovely—simply terrific. You made *me* cry, and I ought to be hardened by this time." He whispered in her ear, "You were better than Marcia. Do you know that?"

"Don't be stupid," said Lynette tersely.

"Everyone was asking who you were. And De Whit says he wishes we'd asked the Press to-night, as it's gone so well. He's afraid the first night won't be so good, as the dress rehearsal went so amazingly well."

"Oh, that's just superstition," said Lynette confidently.

The call-boy came running up. "Oh, Miss Darwin, Miss Meredith requests any of the company who are not otherwise engaged to have supper with her at the Wiltshire Grill."

"Oh, thanks. How lovely."

She ran along to her dressing-room, and before she had got very far with removing her make-up Helen, Miss Smith, and Mrs. Bertram and Mrs. Bosham arrived. They were all enthusiastic about the play. Helen shook her hard by the hand and said gruffly, "Didn't think you could do it." Miss Smith said, "Excellent, Lyn. Mr. Whitfield and Mrs. Seymore will be so pleased with you." Mrs. Bertram told her that she had looked the best-dressed person on the stage, and Mrs. Bosham said, "What a luverly play, eh? Oh, I did 'ave a good cry. Enjoyed meself something chronic."

In Marcia's dressing-room a crowd of Marcia's satellites surrounded her, mainly one-time actresses, who had either married and left the stage, or in some way had not quite made the grade.

"Lovely, darling," they told her, and enveloped her in embraces redolent of fox fur and Chanel Number Five. And then some seconds later, "But who's this new girl ? She's very good." One of them said, "Of course, dear, you have a very unsympathetic part. Do you think it's a good idea ? Do you think that the public will like it ? "

"Yes," joined in another, "I mean they're used to seeing you being your charming self, not a poisonous type of harridan. That girl has got the sympathetic part. She's the person that the matinée matrons are going to coo over."

"But it's a good idea to have a change of part occasionally," put in Marcia. "It's fun."

"Yes, dear. But is it wise in your position ? " ("At your age" was implied.)

Marcia pretended not to listen and changed the conversation, but all the rest of the evening it was churning backwards and forwards in her mind. At the Wiltshire Grill she was gay and entertaining. Most of the company had come along, and many of their friends. They ate hungrily and talked a lot, filled with relief and exhilaration. Marcia watched Lynette, who had a flush of excitement in her usually pale cheeks. She looked so young. And it was this child, no more than a schoolgirl, whom people came first to congratulate. "You stole the show, my dear." Marcia heard De Whit tell her. And while she ate and drank and talked there were thoughts coiling like vipers round the brain of the ageing actress.

Lynette was having the time of her life. She was thankful that she had thought to put on a fairly decent dress that day, and could dance on the tiny floor space when invited. Everyone made a fuss of her, De Whit called her his " honey child," and introduced her to several of his friends as his discovery. Timothy claimed her attention whenever possible, but he was suddenly being treated as the eminent young author by everyone. A gossip column writer came up and chatted with them all.

" Oh, I know all about Miss Meredith, don't I ? " he laughed, and turned to Lynette. " Now, little Miss Darwin, if you could let me have some details about your career."

" What do you want to know ? "

" How you started—all that sort of thing."

" How I started ? "

Lynette suddenly realized that here was a wonderful chance of boosting the Blue Doors, and she started to tell him some of the stories of their early amateur days. Half an hour later she was still talking, and the whole table was listening in delighted silence, with occasional bursts of laughter.

" I must go home now," Lyn said at last, anxious for a good night's rest.

" Just one more dance," Timothy pleaded. As they danced a press camera flashed, and Timothy said to Lyn, " I think we've done it. I think we're a success. Thank you for being so brilliant to-night."

" Thank you for writing such a lovely part," retaliated Lynette. They danced as happily as they could on the crowded, smoky floor. Lynette closed her eyes to savour her happiness.

" I might still have been at school," she thought, " swotting to pass exams that would have got me nowhere. Oh, I'm lucky, I'm lucky."

At last she managed to break away from the merry party.

" Good-night, darling," cried Marcia. " Sleep well. You look very tired, poor dear."

" I think you look smashing," Timothy told Lyn shyly.

They caught a bus home, watching the flashing neon lights from the top deck. Lyn felt strangely as if she had been through a critical operation and recovered. Everything that had been blunted and jaundiced by anxiety had regained its savour. They sang silly songs going down Fitzherbert Street, and Lynette had to knock on the door of No. 37 because she had forgotten her key. Mrs. Bosham appeared in an incredible woolly check dressing-gown, with a scarf tied round her head in a bow under her chin as though she had toothache.

" This is Mr. Carew," said Lyn.

" Oh, the author, eh ? Come in, do, and I'll make you a cupper tea."

They sat in Mrs. Bosham's basement by the fire, for it had turned chilly, and Mrs. Bosham raved over the show.

" What a clever young man," she kept on saying. " And you look such a baby, too. Well, well."

When Lynette saw Timothy out of the door he said, " Be as good again to-morrow, won't you ? "

" I'll try," said Lynette. She watched him down the road, then looked up at the starry sky. " I'll try with all my might."

CHAPTER XVI

FIRST NIGHT

LYNETTE dreamed that it was exam time at school, and she woke with that sick feeling in her stomach. The rain was beating greyly down and her porridge was lumpy. Then she remembered that she was lunching with Timothy at a famous theatrical restaurant. It was the first time that either of them had dared to go there, for one had almost to produce one's pedigree to secure a table. While she was dressing there was a phone call for her. She ran down the stairs in her house coat. Maddy spoke from a long way away.

"Hullo, Lyn. I'm speaking on behalf of the Blue Doors, your parents, my parents, the Halfords, and the Bishop, and —oh, ooms of people in Fenchester. We just want you to know that we're thinking about you—and wishing you all the best for to-night. They wanted us to ring you this evening at the theatre, but we knew you'd be in an awful flap by then."

"It was awfully sweet of you to think of it," said Lyn gratefully.

"How did the dress rehearsal go ? "

"Fine. Terrific."

"Good. We saw a lovely picture of you in that magazine."

"How's the Blue Door Theatre going ? "

"We're nearly ready to open. Gosh, we've been working like niggers."

"What are you opening with ? "

" We're not quite sure. But we're going to do all the things we know first."

They chatted for a long time, until the pips became too insistent, and Maddy rang off with final wishes for good luck.

" Gosh," thought Lynette, " I'm glad Maddy has come round a bit. She had every reason to feel a bit mad at my letting them down."

She dressed in her best dress, and Timothy called for her at mid-day. As ever, he was in a state of nerves, but she managed to calm him down enough to enjoy his lunch. The restaurant was crowded with actors and actresses, writers, painters, and musicians, and they had such fun picking out people that they did not realize that people were looking at them and wondering who they were. The lunch was delicious : *pâté*, and pheasant, and an enormous ice-cream trifle, and black, sweet Turkish coffee. They sat over their empty cups talking for a long time. De Whit, with a crowd of friends, came over to speak to them.

" Hullo, children. Stoking up for to-night ? "

" Yes, rather ! "

" Mind you have a rest this afternoon, Lyn dear. You look tired."

" Yes, I'm going home to rest now."

" Good girl." And off he shot to chat and laugh at all the neighbouring tables.

Lyn walked slowly back to No. 37 and put her alarm on for four-thirty. " And, please, Mrs. Bosham, knock me up as well. It would be awful if I overslept." But she did not sleep at all. There were so many thoughts and images and worries and fancies in her brain that she just lay on her back and studied the cracks in the ceiling that she thought looked like a rabbit, and that Maddy had held strongly were a lion.

Before four-thirty she was up and dressing again in her best in case they should go out afterwards to celebrate. She took a taxi to the theatre, thinking, "After all, it's a day on which to be rash." The doorkeeper greeted her with, "Nice batch o' telegrams for you, miss." She fell on them and carried them up to her room. They were from the most surprising people. People whom she thought had forgotten her years ago, vague aunts and distant cousins. There was one from Terry, the scenic artist at Tutworth, another from Miss Gaunt, her old school mistress, and piles from people at the Academy. She put them up round her mirror and surveyed them happily, then began to get made up. De Whit popped round to tell her that the house would be packed out and even some people standing.

"A very distinguished audience, too," he remarked. "Good luck, dear."

Others of the company came in to wish her good luck, and she popped along to Marcia and Vivian Conroy. Marcia, apparently completely unconcerned, was already entertaining some of her friends, talking sixteen to the dozen as she put on her make-up. When Lynette returned to her dressing-room she gasped with delight, for there was a mass of flowers which Mrs. White was arranging.

"Aren't they beauts?" the dresser said happily. "I've left the cards on them so that you can see which is which."

There were yellow roses from De Whit, red roses from Timothy, chrysanthemums from Helen, and a pathetic bunch of Michaelmas daisies from the garden of No. 37 from Mrs. Bosham.

"How kind people are," she thought, and began to put on her first act dress with Mrs. White's assistance. It was then that the full realization of what was before her rushed over her.

"Last night was all right. But that doesn't help to-night. Gosh, I *must* be good. There are so many people I mustn't let down. Timothy, and the Blue Doors, and my parents." She was trembling all over, and when Timothy came round to wish her luck he too was shaking so much that they just looked at each other and roared with hysterical laughter.

The calls came with relentless regularity, the half, the quarter of an hour, five minutes please, overture and beginners. Lyn kept thinking of the enormous auditorium—row upon row of hungry faces, ready to criticize her, to ruin her, or to make her. She ran down into the wings, her coat thrown round her shoulders to stop the shivers. In the wings there were more hurried wishes of good luck from the stage management and stage hands. The overture was blaring out, and then it began to fade. Lyn found herself wishing desperately that it would continue.

The music disappeared altogether, there was a few seconds of breathless silence, filled only by the thumping of Lynette's heart, and then the curtain rose. There were murmurs as the audience admired the set, late-comers banged and shuffled into their seats, and then Marcia entered. There was a vigorous burst of applause, and the show had started. Lyn's cue came, and she walked on, icy cold, and more frightened than she had ever been in her life. She did not remember saying the first five minutes of dialogue, but she must have done, for Marcia sailed gaily on, playing up with verve and charm, and all the tricks of her trade. To-night's audience were definitely more sticky than the previous evening's, and the laughs were not so frequent. When Lyn ran up to change for the second act she was still shaking and uncertain.

"Oh, yer 'ands are cold, Miss Darwin," cried Mrs. White. "Here, stick them under the hot-water tap."

Neither Timothy nor De Whit came round between the

acts. "That means they're—not sure," Lynette thought fearfully.

It was when she entered in the second act that she realized something was wrong. In the wings everyone had had a rather strained appearance, and when she began to act with Marcia she realized why. The leading lady had entirely changed the reading of her part. Instead of a poisonous, difficult harridan she was playing the role of a delightful, middle-aged woman ; in fact, the kind of part that she always had played previously, the part in which the audience knew and loved her. All the unsympathetic lines she played with a delicious gurgle in her voice that turned them into comedy lines, and the audience roared with laughter. Consequently all Lynette's lines, in fact her whole character, missed fire, and she knew that she was going for nothing, that Marcia was acting her off the stage. All the tricks and wangles that the ageing actress had ever learnt came into play. She edged up-stage, so that Lynette had almost to turn her back to the audience to address her, she cut all Lyn's best lines, she did bits of comedy " business " during Lyn's longer speeches, and the characters turned into a lovable, witty-minded mother, and an unsympathetic, spineless, dreary daughter. Soon Lynette was completely put off her stride and disheartened. Tears were not far off, and her voice was muffled and indistinct. Marcia continued to charm the audience and carry them with her, to take the centre of the stage, and to play to the gallery. In the wings the little stage director was literally dancing with fury, and the company looked on aghast. At Marcia's exit there was terrific applause, and Lynette heaved a sigh of relief.

" Now, perhaps, I shall have a chance," she thought. But poor Vivian Conroy was so put off by the extraordinary performance he had witnessed that he fluffed and dried and perspired heavily under his make-up. The audience were obviously not interested in any other character but the mother, and there was even a loud yawn from the gallery. They hurried through their scene, and at last the second act curtain fell. Vivian Conroy sat heavily on the sofa.

" What on earth has come over the woman ? " he demanded, wiping his face with his handkerchief. Lynette could not speak. She walked dimly up the stairs, conscious of alarmed whispering round every corner.

" Why, ducky ! " cried Mrs. White as Lyn entered like a ghost.

De Whit flew in, seething with rage, his spectacles glinting furiously.

" I'm so livid—so livid. Oh, you poor darling—but, dear, you *must* play up. This act will be agony if you don't."

" But what *can* I do ? " Lyn asked, breathlessly calm. " She won't let me do anything."

" I know, dear, I know. She's ruining the play, even if she is snatching a rather precarious success for herself. I've tried to talk to her, but she won't even open her dressing-room door. Oh, Lynette, you must be a brave, brave girl," and he darted off to try to calm everyone else. A deathly pale wraith then appeared in the doorway. It was Timothy. They stood and looked miserably at one another. Then Timothy sank down on a chair.

" I can't watch any more," he said brokenly.

" I'm sorry. So sorry," said Lyn softly.

" It's not you ! It's that—viper ! How could she ? How could anyone ? "

" Act three beginners, please," shouted the call boy in a maddeningly cheery voice.

" I can't," said Lynette pathetically, frightened and feeble.

" You must, I suppose."

" Yes, I must."

On the stairs, members of the cast were standing looking at one another, horror-stricken. Marcia was still in her dressing-room. When she swept on to the stage for the first scene of the third act she got another round of applause. But soon even the audience realized that there was something wrong. The third act was written so strongly that it was completely ruined by Marcia's refusal to play in any other way than sweetly and whimsically. Everyone attributed the faults to the play, and Lynette's attempts at emotion and hysteria became entirely unnecessary and out of place. Marcia purred and laughed and used her most endearing charms, but of no avail. The audience began to shuffle and cough and several seats banged as people got up to go out.

Lynette tried so hard. She pretended that she was back at the Academy, acting with someone who was doing it all wrong, but she must not let it affect her. And yet, when she did manage to get her words out as they should have been, they made the play even more senseless. The third act wore on, and Lyn, Loraine, and Roger Revere did their best to restore a little balance, but by this time the audience had lost patience. Lyn just did not bother to scream and sob as she should have done, for inside her she was cold and dead as stone. Left alone on the stage she panicked and made her exit before the curtain fell instead of holding the stage and waiting for it. They took their bows stiffly, all except Marcia, who was smiling as graciously as ever. Someone in the gallery shouted out, " A lot of rot." And the curtain fell and did not rise again.

" Only one curtain call ? On a first night ! " Marcia complained.

De Whit strode on to the stage.

"Yes," he shouted. "And that's more than you deserve, Marcia Meredith."

Lynette fled from the noisy scene that followed. As she ran up the stairs the tears began to fall, and she collapsed in a chair, her head down on the dressing-table among the make-up and grease-paints.

"Don't," said Timothy, who had sat in her room throughout the last act. "Don't, dear. It's not your fault. We're just—unlucky."

"Well, what a scandal!" said Mrs. White. "Come along, deary. It wasn't as bad as all that." But Lynette could only weep. "Here, deary, lie down on the couch for a bit." For a few minutes Lynette seemed to lose all consciousness and they fetched sal volatile to revive her. At last she was able to remove her make-up, slowly, with rending sobs. De Whit came in and sank down on the couch.

"That woman—that woman!" was all he could say. "What are we going to do?"

"I can't possibly go on to-morrow night," said Lynette, a sorry sight with swollen eyes.

"You'll have to, dear. Your understudy isn't ready at all. But I don't even know that there'll *be* another night. I've not seen Cathcart or anyone belonging to the management yet."

"What has Miss Meredith to say?" Timothy asked dully.

"She won't admit that there's anything wrong. She just says, 'But they loved it,' and is giving a cocktail party in her dressing-room."

"Incredible—incredible," gasped Timothy. "Doesn't she realize what she's done to me—to Lynette—to you?"

"I don't think she does," said De Whit weakly. "She is just a silly, vain, selfish old woman."

"Thank heaven no-one has come round to see me," sighed Lynette. "That means it *must* have been bad. Mrs. Seymore and Mr. Whitfield haven't come round."

"Duncan, can't you tell her that she's got to play it properly to-morrow night?"

"It won't matter if she does. The Press were here in full force to-night, and they're just going to slaughter it."

"Of course," said Timothy dully.

One by one the company came to find De Whit to ask in a bewildered fashion what was happening.

"I don't know. I only know we're done for," was all he could say.

They condoled with Lynette and made a fuss of her, but she knew that kind words could not mend the ruin of her first West End first night.

"It was all so unnecessary," was all she could think. "It could have been a success for us both, if Marcia had only kept her head."

"Come out and have something to eat," suggested De Whit. "We'll go somewhere quiet. We'll all feel better when we've had something to eat."

They went into the snack bar of the little pub opposite and ordered steak and chips. Lyn could not touch hers; to her it tasted like sawdust.

"Our lovely play!" groaned De Whit. "Last night it was—it was brilliant. Wasn't it? You all knew it was."

Timothy was sitting white and silent, looking strangely like a disappointed small boy. And then from over the partition that divided them from the smoking-room came the loud voice of a playgoer who had just come out of the St. Christopher's, and a friend who had not seen the show.

" Well, what was it like ? "

" Pretty bad. Pretty bad. Marcia was all right. Same as usual, of course. But it was a very weak play. Can't think why Tiller and Webb ever bothered to put it on. Their stuff is usually so good."

" What was this new girl like ? "

" Which girl ? "

" Derwent—or some such name."

" The daughter ? Oh, pretty bad. The worst Academy type. Obviously inexperienced. The Meredith wiped the floor with her."

Lyn rose unsteadily to her feet.

" I must go," she said in a little voice.

" I'll come with you," said Timothy quickly.

" No. No, I don't want anyone."

" But it's raining," said Timothy stupidly.

" I know." Lynette pushed her way out of the crowded snack bar and out into the cool evening air and the steadily falling rain.

" The worst Academy type—obviously inexperienced." And that was what the papers would say next day. She walked blindly through puddles, across roads, regardless of the traffic. It was a grey evening, turning into a black night. The passers-by looked despairing and down-trodden in macintoshes, galoshes, and hoods. Lyn longed to be able to go home to her mother, to tell her all about it and to be put to bed with a hot drink. She was suddenly so tired that she had to lean against a lamp-post and gasp. She stood and watched the cars and people, trying to find some meaning in it all.

" Why ? Why ? " she cried inside her. And the roaring traffic and the drip, drip of the rain gave no reply. Detail by detail the whole panorama of the awful evening spread out again in her mind, from the first line on which she had noticed something wrong with Marcia, to the last overheard remark, " The worst Academy type . . . Meredith wiped the floor with her." Her feet were soaked with rain and she felt she could walk no farther. A policeman spoke to her. " Everything all right, miss ? "

For a ridiculous moment she wanted to say, " Well, you see, it's like this," and tell him all about it, but then she realized that the failure of another show could mean nothing to him. " After all—it's only acting," she knew he would think, and she laughed rather hysterically up at him. " No, thank you. I mean, yes, thanks," she stammered, and got on a bus. The top deck was deserted, and she fell into a front seat and watched the lights with a reeling head and a heavy heart, seeing London through a mist of rain and tears.

Chapter XVII

PRODIGAL'S RETURN

THE show ran for just over a week. Without a doubt
they were the most unhappy days of Lynette's life.
She hardly dared to go out for fear that she would bump
into someone she knew who had not happened to read the
notices and would ask cheerily, " How's the show going ? "
Or was it worse to meet someone who *had* read the notices
and would carefully make no mention of the show ? The
newspapers had really been quite kind. They slated the
play for its apparent lack of point and balance, praised
Marcia, and most of them were polite enough to ignore
Lynette. One of them called her a " bread-and-butter
miss," which rankled for a long time. And the elderly
critic who had awarded Lyn the prize for grace and charm
of movement merely said, " I prefer to draw a veil over
Thursday night's performance of *Beloved Viper*."

At the theatre the atmosphere was unbearable. Marcia
spoke to no-one and no-one spoke to her. She was playing
the part more or less as it should have been played, but the
houses were so thin that she soon hardly bothered to give a
performance at all. Lynette gave a good performance every
night, but it was too late to save the show. De Whit and
Timothy stayed well away from the theatre. Mr. Cathcart
buzzed around the dressing-rooms trying to pacify everyone
by telling them that if only they would hang on for a few
weeks after this show was closed, the management would
soon be casting something else in which there might be parts
for them. But Lynette's mind was made up.

Over supper with Timothy after the second night's show she said, " No, I shan't stay in town. We finish on Saturday week, and the next day I shall go back to Fenchester. For at least two years. Next time I get a part in the West End I intend to be experienced enough to hold it down, come weal, come woe ! "

" Come Meredith," added Timothy, who had cheered up somewhat now the ordeal was over and it was definite that his play was a flop. " Yes, I think you're wise. And please may I try out my next play down at Fenchester, to see if it's fool-proof ? I must never write another that can be ruined so easily."

" But of course," cried Lynette. " That's a wonderful idea. Have you got any others that haven't been performed yet ? "

" Yes, but I'm a bit doubtful about them."

" Well, once we see that we've got a regular sort of audience it will be fun to try out new plays."

" I'll be back," vowed Timothy, eating chips with great determination. " Just you mark my words. Within five years I'll have written a play with a star part for you, and we'll be back at the St. Christopher's going strong. What do you bet ? "

" I don't bet," said Lynette stoutly. " I intend it to happen."

" That's the spirit. They can't keep us down, can they ? "

But most of the time it was difficult to be cheery. To realize that she had had her chance—and lost it, and with it the dreams of having a little flat somewhere and going each night to the theatre, and entertaining friends to matinée teas —it was all very bitter. Especially as it was not her fault at all.

" Marcia can afford to have a flop. She'll soon have another success and be as popular as ever. . . ."

Mrs. Bosham was heart-broken at losing Lyn.

" Well, Miss Maddy will soon be back to keep me company for a while."

" But, Mrs. Bosham, you'll have lots more Academy students soon, won't you ? "

" Oh, yes. They come and they go. . . ."

" They come and they go," thought Lynette. " How true."

She spent the days mooching around London, seeing all the things that she had meant to see during her two years in town. There was something soothing about visiting the Tower of London, the British Museum, and Kew Gardens.

" Makes me feel like a tourist, and that will make it less bad having to leave."

But her heart ached for all her shattered dreams. She realized that it was the first real failure of her life. Always previously she had been lucky and successful, so that this set-back had come as an extra shock. Timothy came to tea after the Wednesday matinée, and brought her a book about Chekhov, illustrated with fascinating old photographs. He said shyly, " I've marked a bit that I think might be cheering." She flipped through the pages until she found a paragraph marked with red pencil, and beside it the word " Us " and an exclamation mark. It read :

" Art, especially the stage, is a region in which it is impossible to walk without stumbling. There are before you yet a good many unsuccessful days, and even whole unsuccessful seasons ; there will be great doubts and immense disenchantments ; but you must be prepared for all that, you must expect it, and without looking aside must stubbornly go on, fanatically bending it all to your will."

"That's what Chekhov wrote to his wife, Olga Knipper," Timothy explained.

"It's terrific!" cried Lynette, with shining eyes. "It will be a great comfort."

They made tea on the gas ring, and ate crumpets dripping with butter which Mrs. White had popped out into Soho to buy. Lyn looked round the cosy little dressing-room and wished that it were to be hers for longer.

"They come and they go." She remembered Mrs. Bosham's words, and sighed heavily. Timothy seemed to read her thoughts.

"Of course," he said, "you could have gone into an office in Fenchester. Two or three pounds coming in regularly each week, knowing you'd have Saturday afternoons off and Sunday, and a fortnight in the summer. And think of that nice bank clerk you could have settled down with."

"Shut up!" laughed Lynette. "I'm not regretting anything—only that such a woman as Marcia Meredith was ever born."

The days slipped by, and everyone was impatient for the show to come off. Already another company of artistes were rehearsing for the next show, lounging over the set of *Beloved Viper* as if it belonged to them.

"It's awful—awful," a little voice inside Lynette kept saying, while she put on a brave face to the rest of the company.

"You're lucky to have something to go to," Joan told her, "even if it's only rep. I shall have to start parking myself on the agents' doorsteps again. What a life."

From the Blue Doors Lyn had condolatory letters, all of which ended up by saying that they couldn't help feeling glad that she would be coming to them after all. And Nigel put at the end of his, " We have finally decided on opening with *Little Women*, so as to give Maddy a nice part before she has to go back to the Academy. Will you play Jo and produce it ? I feel that it is more of a woman's play from a production angle."

" How sweet of them," thought Lynette. " They know that's a part I've been wanting to play. And they think that a new part and producing as well will take my mind off it all. It will, of course." And already her mind raced ahead towards the casting and the costumes and the scenery for *Little Women*. " Yes, it's a good show to open with. It will draw in the family audiences."

" I envy you," said Timothy. " Some work to start on right away."

" Yes, I'm lucky. But you can come down and see us whenever you like and discuss which of your plays we can try out."

" Thanks. Writing is an awfully lonely occupation, you know."

" It must be. But rather restful," observed Lyn.

" Restful ! Gosh, after what I've been through these last few weeks——"

" But that was unusual."

" Most unusual, thank goodness."

The last night approached. The show was to come off very quietly, no party, for there was nothing to celebrate. The Saturday matinée audience was poor, but at the Saturday night performance it was the fullest house they had had since the first night.

" Of course," Marcia Meredith remarked to nobody in particular, " I think the management are crazy to take it off now. We're just about beginning to pick up."

But no-one trusted himself to reply. As they took the curtain with Marcia extending a modest hand towards the company to acknowledge the applause, Lyn felt hot tears rushing into her eyes.

" I didn't think I *could* cry any more," she thought as the footlights, the applauding audience, the sweeping line of the circle, the upper circle, and the gallery swam before her eyes in confusion as she bowed. And suddenly the injustice of the whole thing swept over her again. On her way upstairs she paused outside the dressing-room that had a gold star painted on it, and Marcia's name in large letters. Then she walked in without knocking. Marcia was putting on a glamorous white house coat.

" I just came to tell you that if you think you've ruined my career you're quite wrong. You've merely given me a wonderful example of how not to behave when one is successful. Good-bye. I hope I never have to set eyes on you again."

Marcia's face was almost laughable in its amazed horror. Lynette went out and shut the door, then ran all the way up to her dressing-room with trembling knees. " It was undignified—but worth it," she thought.

In the dressing-room Mrs. White was bustling around packing up her things. Regretfully Lyn took off the little grey dress. The management had offered to sell them all their clothes at very reduced rates, but Lynette had refused hers.

" I could never bear to look at them again." So Joan was to have Lyn's.

" Terribly useful for rep.," she had remarked. But Lyn was too much of a sentimentalist to take this into consideration.

" Now, don't you fret, miss," said Mrs. White, kissing

her good-bye on the cheek in a motherly fashion. "You'll be back."

"Yes," sniffed Lyn, "I'll be back." Her belongings filled one large suitcase and a hatbox. It was awful to have to take down the picture of Ellen, the Blue Door's photo, and the Van Gogh. And then in came De Whit carrying her photos that had hung outside the theatre.

"You'd better have these. You'll be wanting them soon, won't you?"

Lyn packed them in her case and did up the fastenings, not quite knowing what to say.

"Now, you're sure you're doing right," he persisted, "in going back to—er—wherever it is? If only you'd hang on a bit longer I'm sure we'd find something for you."

"It's very kind of you," Lynette said firmly. "But I really can't. You see, I sort of—broke a promise by playing in this at all, so perhaps that's why I've been so unlucky."

"I see. You're a very sensible girl, I think. But I know that we shall work together again soon. In this business when you've worked with a person once you're bound to again."

"I hope so," said Lynette. "I really did enjoy rehearsals tremendously. And learnt a lot."

"By the way," said De Whit, grinning broadly, "I've heard what you said to Marcia, and I couldn't be more pleased."

"How did you hear?" gasped Lynette, flushing.

"Her dresser was outside the door."

"Oh, dear, it'll be all over the theatre."

"And a good thing, too. She's got off far too lightly, to my mind. Well, good-bye, dear." He kissed her affectionately on both cheeks, and turned at the door to say, as on their first meeting, "But let's hope it's au revoir."

The rest of the company drifted in to say good-bye, and try to hear the details of her scene with Marcia, but Lynette was not talking. Then the faithful Timothy appeared to carry her cases to the stage door, and look for a taxi. Lyn chatted to the stage door-keeper while she waited.

" I'm right sorry to see this show come off," he said sympathetically. " Saw some of the dress rehearsal, I did. And cried like a baby. Usually I don't fancy a play much. Prefer the pictures, myself——"

Lynette giggled at the thought of a stage door-keeper not caring for plays. She tipped him and said good-night as Timothy appeared with a taxi. She dreaded saying good-bye to Timothy, for that would be the last link with the show and everything, but as he helped her into the taxi he said, " I'll see you off to-morrow. What time are you going ? "

" Eleven-five."

" O.K. I'll be there."

" Thanks a lot. Cheerio." As she sank back on the leather seat she caught a last glimpse of the illuminated lettering on the theatre. " Marcia Meredith in *Beloved Viper*," and underneath in little letters " Lynette Darwin." And even as she looked at them the lights went out.

Mrs. Bosham comforted her with a somewhat odd-tasting steak-and-kidney pie down in the basement, and they listened to a music-hall programme on the wireless. Lyn huddled by the fire, looking into the flames.

" Evenings drawing in a bit, aren't they ? " observed Mrs. Bosham.

" Yes, they are—drawing in—I think I'll go to bed, Mrs. Bosham."

Despair stalked in the cold, shabby bedroom, so she decided to pack that night instead of the following morning.

Everything she packed brought a fresh twinge of nostalgia.
Her worn-out ballet shoes, copies of all the plays they had
done at the Academy in the past two years, the dress she
had worn when she first went to the Tiller and Webb offices.
The effort of shutting the trunks and cases tired her out,
and at last she was able to sleep.

Next morning all was a hustle and a bustle. So many
oddments had been left out, and Mrs. Bosham kept adding
things that Lyn might need on the journey—a packet of
sandwiches, some back numbers of *Woman's Chat*, some
milk in a medicine bottle. As Lyn kissed her plump cheek
good-bye she reflected sadly how *over* everything was. If
and when she came back she would probably not return to
No. 37, and she mentally said a long farewell to the blistered
front door, the iron railings round the area steps, and the
shabby lace curtains at the windows. And then it was all
gone, and the taxi driver was rattling away down Tottenham
Court Road whistling happily, as if this were a day like any
other. And Lynette realized that he was going to pass the
St. Christopher's Theatre. "Oh, no," she thought, and was
about to direct him another way, but then she told herself not to be so sentimental. Already the posters for the
next show were up outside the theatre. New names—new
faces—fresh music—more laughter. . . . There was no stopping it.

At the station Timothy was already waiting with a little
buttonhole of rosebuds for her, and all the theatrical magazines to read on the journey.

"Why are you so sweet to me ?" Lynette demanded as
they struggled with her luggage, "when I've been instru-
mental in ruining your play ?"

"Because," said Timothy, "I see in you my future
leading lady. You have inspired ideas in me for at least six

255

plays, in the last six weeks. That's why I carry your cases for you."

The train was crowded, but at last Lyn found a seat, stowed her luggage in the guard's van, and got out on to the platform again to talk to Timothy. They were deep in a discussion on Bernard Shaw when the whistle went, and Lyn had to dash back into the train. She smiled while she waved, but as the figure of Timothy became smaller and smaller her smile disappeared gradually, until she was leaning out of the window staring at the rails that slid relentlessly by, taking her away from London. For how long ?

" Can't we have that window shut ? " grated a pernickety voice. Lyn turned a face of such acute despair to the speaker that she added :

" Oh, aren't you feeling well ? "

" No," quavered Lynette, and pushed her way out of the carriage to the toilet.

" Train sickness, I suppose," agreed her fellow-travellers.

But it was heart sickness that Lynette suffered in an atmosphere of disinfectant and train wheels. Fragments of wisdom came to her aid—" Progress on the stage is often crab-like. . . ." " Without looking aside, you must stubbornly go on, fanatically bending it all to your will. . . ." " You'll be back. . . ." " I see in you my future leading lady. . . ."

At last she was able to face the carriage full of sandwich-eating, newspaper-scanning travellers, and she buried herself in the books that Timothy had given her. The carriage got stuffy and smoky and full of snores, and Lynette lapsed into a miserable semi-coma.

About three o'clock the scenery became familiar. She recognized Fennymead Castle and began to tidy herself. Already London seemed far behind and a new chapter begun.

She had not let anyone know what time she was coming, so there was nobody to meet her. She left her luggage in the cloakroom, had a wash and brush up, and decided to walk through the town via the Blue Door Theatre, to see if anyone were there. It was a clear autumn Sunday, with the children coming out of Sunday School. Fenchester seemed clean and small and quiet after London. She noticed that Mr. Chubb was making a good job of the publicity, for everywhere there were posters advertising the opening of the theatre in two weeks' time, and in the photographer's window were large portraits of all the company. At last she was in Pleasant Street, and there was the theatre, bright and clean as a new pin, with a little box-office built on to the front. In it sat Mr. Chubb, looking as proud as a captain at the wheel of his ship. He was going over some accounts and looked up when Lynette tapped on the window pane.

"Ah, dear young lady! How very nice to welcome you home. We've been half expecting you all day. They're having a little read through on the stage."

"I'll go in, then," said Lyn. "Doesn't the theatre look lovely? And you've got out some awfully good posters."

"Colourful, aren't they?" agreed the business manager proudly.

Inside, the theatre seemed much larger, and the tip-up seats had taken away all resemblance to the chapel that it used to be. The six Blue Doors were up on the stage reading *Little Women*. Myrtle was there too, and Ali and Billy were doing something on step-ladders at the back of the stage. Lyn stood and watched. They were too engrossed to notice her. She sat down and looked around her. Yes, this was where she belonged all right. She looked around the walls, at the Seymore Trophy on its bracket, the photos of previous

257

productions of their amateur days, and she sighed. Maddy glanced up.

" There's Lyn ! " she shouted. Everyone peered into the dimness of the little auditorium.

" So it is," said Nigel. " Hi ya ! Be with you in a minute. Let's just finish this scene." And they continued as if it were the most normal thing in the world for Lyn to have deserted them, to have taken part in an outstanding failure in the West End, and then to return to them once more.

" O.K.," said Nigel. " Let's break." And they jumped down off the stage, which had now been built higher and wider. They chatted happily to her, obviously sincerely pleased at her return. No-one mentioned *Beloved Viper*. The conversation was all about the Blue Door Theatre, and what ideas had she on the production of *Little Women*. Terry, from Tutworth Wells, appeared from nowhere, up to his elbows in paint as usual, and said, " Hullo, you," as if he'd last seen her the day before. He seemed perfectly at home with the rest of the company.

" Come on," said Jeremy. " We'd better get home. Mother is sort of expecting you in time for tea." The five new-comers to the company had found digs in the same road as the others.

" They were a bit doubtful about having me," laughed Ali, showing a mouthful of white teeth in his dark face. " I think they expected me to wear a loin cloth and beat on a tom-tom or something. But when they discovered that I spoke English, and that they'd seen me in films, they decided I *must* be all right."

Lynette's parents welcomed her without fuss.

" Eat up your tea, now," said her mother as if she were ten again and had never left home to be an actress.

"Oh, it's wonderful to have a home to come back to," she thought, remembering how home ties and duties used to irk her in the early Blue Door days, before she had ever been far enough away to appreciate her parents and all they had done for her.

She had been prepared to be quite unhappy for the first few months, but the two rehearsal weeks for *Little Women* were so crammed with work that she literally did not have time. With a long part like Jo, and also the production to contend with, her hands were full. Maddy was playing Amy; Vicky, Beth; Sandra, Meg; Nigel, Laurie; Bulldog, Mr. March; Jeremy, Mr. Lawrence; Myrtle, Mrs. March. They had called a few ex-Academy students down for the small parts left over, and it seemed to be perfect casting. Sandra insisted that they should hire the correct costumes from London.

"We're professionals now, so we must do things in a professional manner," was the phrase on the lips of all of them. There was great excitement in the town over the coming first night of the repertory.

"We've been booked out for weeks," Mr. Chubb told Lyn, "and there's going to be a whale of a queue for the cheap seats."

"Two weeks really is the perfect rehearsal time for rep.," remarked Vicky. "Neither too long nor too short."

By the dress rehearsal they were word perfect and beautifully produced. The costumes were charming, and Terry had surpassed himself with the set.

"And there's nothing in the play to offend anyone," said Nigel. "It's a safe bet."

On the night, the front half of the theatre was filled with their parents, friends, and relations, and they had all chivalrously paid for their seats. The Bishop was there, benign as ever, the Mayor and Corporation, " in mufti " as Maddy put it, and most of the Town Council, Miss Gaunt and all the staff of the girls' school and the grammar school, Mr. Smallgood and Whittlecock, and Mrs. Potter-Smith with her yes-woman, Miss Thropple, both wearing ridiculous hats. Lord Moulcester and a party of friends were there, and a bevy of the Blue Doors' old school friends. Timothy Carew, too, had come down for the occasion. The un-bookable seats could have been filled six times over and some late-comers were standing at the back. Ali and Billy were completely dependable on the stage-management side, so there were no worries for the players, except their own performances. In the new dressing-rooms that were light and spacious and well-equipped they took stock of things.

" Well, we're here, where we always hoped to be. Let's make a go of it," said Nigel. And with wishes for good luck in all directions they went into the tiny wings and said to Ali, " Take it away."

The curtains swished up and the Blue Doors' professional first night had begun. Lyn was horribly, horribly scared. She had not realized how much the first night of *Beloved Viper* had shaken her nerve, but a glance round the stage at the dear old familiar faces of the Blue Doors reassured her. Here she was among friends, among real people, and no-one would let her down.

The audience lapped it up, laughing and crying in the appropriate places. Even Mrs. Potter-Smith had to admit it was good. In the laughter they could each distinguish that of their own parents and particular friends, which added zest to their performances. And then came the final curtain, and with it a burst of applause and cheers that left no doubt that the Fenchester Repertory was to be a success.

" The first of many," said Nigel to Lyn as they beamed

round at each other. Everyone seemed to be smiling as they took the curtain : Lyn, Nigel, Jeremy, Sandra, Maddy, Bulldog, Vicky, Mr. and Mrs. Fayne, Mr. and Mrs. Halford, Mr. and Mrs. Darwin, the Bishop, the Vicar and his wife, Lord Moulcester, Miss Gaunt, Timothy, Terry, Myrtle, Ali, Billy, Mr. Smallgood and Whittlecock, the Mayor, the town councillors, the school children, the whole theatre was one broad smile, and looking round at it all Lynette was glad, so very glad, that she had come home.

THE CURTAIN FALLS

PRINTED IN GREAT BRITAIN AT
THE PRESS OF THE PUBLISHERS